WITH THIS KISS

JANET DAILEY

ZEBRA BOOKS
KENSINGTON PUBLISHING CORP.
http://www.kensingtonbooks.com

ZEBRA BOOKS are published by

Kensington Publishing Corp.
119 West 40th Street
New York, NY 10018

All Kensington titles, imprints, and distributed lines are available
at special quantity discounts for bulk purchases for sales promo-
tion, premiums, fund-raising, educational, or institutional use.

Special book excerpts or customized printings can also be cre-
ated to fit specific needs. For details, write or phone the office of the
Kensington Sales Manager: Attn. Sales Department. Kensington
Publishing Corp., 119 West 40th Street, New York, NY 10018.
Phone: 1-800-221-2647.

Zebra and the Z logo Reg. U.S. Pat. & TM Off.

First Mass-Market Paperback Printing: July 2007
ISBN-13: 978-1-4201-3583-1
ISBN-10: 1-4201-3583-X

10 9 8 7 6 5 4 3

Printed in the United States of America

CONTENTS

WILD AND WONDERFUL   7

BEWARE OF THE STRANGER   169

WILD AND WONDERFUL

CHAPTER ONE

The fire red Porsche convertible hugged the twisting, curving road through the West Virginia mountainscape, a splash of scarlet on the gray ribbon of concrete winding through the spring green country. With the car's top down, the driver was exposed to the lingering sun and the billowing white clouds in the light blue sky.

Rounding a curve, Glenna Reynolds briefly lifted her face to the warmth of the sun. The teasing fingers of a speed-generated breeze tugged at her dark auburn hair, whirling its long curls away from her shoulders. A pair of owl-round sunglasses shielded her gray green eyes from the angling glare of the late-afternoon sun. Contentment born from a day spent pursuing journalistic pleasures was etched in her expressive features.

On the passenger seat of the sports car, a camera was concealed in its leather case, along with a notebook containing scribbled impressions. Together the two contained a collection of springtime images that continued to float in Glenna's mind.

The wildly beautiful mountains and valleys of West Virginia had revealed their May treasures to her. Wildflowers were blooming at their peak, from the delicate lady's slipper to the flame azalea, their multicolored displays of beauty now trapped on film. Jotted notations reaffirmed the camera's record of fox pups playing outside their den, tiny chipmunks darting about the forest floor, and the young fawn camouflaged and hidden at a meadow's edge.

Noted, too, were the sensations of being able to hear the new leaves growing; the fragile spring green rivaled only by the flowering red maple. Another time the hush of the woods had been broken by the drumming of a ruffed grouse. The camera shutter hadn't been quick enough to catch the jeweled flash of a scarlet tanager flitting through the trees, but hastily scribbled phrases had recorded the sighting on the pages of her notebook.

Captivated by the charm of spring, Glenna had taken longer than she had intended. A glance at her watch increased the pressure of her foot on the accelerator pedal. The last thing she wanted was for her father to be concerned. She regretted that she hadn't left him a message warning him that she might be late.

Since his heart attack this last winter, his second one, Orin Reynolds had become more conscious of her absences from him. Her father's attitude came from an awareness of the shortness of his time to spend with her, something Glenna felt, as well. Even though he was as fully recovered as he would ever be, Glenna knew how slim the chance was that he would survive a third major attack.

She no longer took his presence in her life for granted and had adjusted her lifestyle and career to allow her more time with her father. When he had been released from the hospital this last time, Glenna had wanted to give up everything to stay at home and take care of him. Orin Reynolds had rejected this idea, insisting that a temporary nurse and their housekeeper/cook, Hannah Burns, could take good care of him. He wisely informed her that she would need to escape into her writing. His advice had over and over again proved to be correct. If she needed further proof of it, the exhilarating flow of thoughts and ideas from today's outing provided it.

Braking, Glenna slowed the car to make the turn onto the graveled lane leading to the large white house nestled on the mountain slope amid the trees. It was a graceful old building, once the main house of a large estate, but the fertile valley land had been sold off some years ago. All that remained of the former land was the immediate grounds of the house and the few acres surrounding it.

Glenna recognized the car parked in the driveway and smiled wryly. Although the doctor had limited the amount of time Orin Reynolds was allowed to spend at the office of his coal-mining operation to three days a week, her father had insisted on daily reports when he wasn't there. Bruce Hawkins's car was therefore a familiar sight.

The garage was separate from the house, a small stable converted some sixty years ago to hold cars. Its double set of doors beckoned to the red Porsche, but Glenna stopped the car short. There was time enough later to put it away.

Tipping her sunglasses atop her head, she grabbed the camera case and notebook from the passenger seat and left the car keys in the ignition for the time being. Her long legs swiftly climbed the veranda's steps to the front door.

She entered the foyer, pushing the door shut behind her and turning toward the study that had originally been the front parlor of the old house. The solid oak doors slid open at the touch of her hand, bringing the conversation within to an abrupt end.

Her heart was squeezed by the harrowed and worried lines that aged her father's face twenty years. The instant his gaze landed on her face, his expression underwent a transformation; the tension smoothing into a welcoming smile of false unconcern. This sudden masking of his feelings puzzled and frightened Glenna. What was he trying to hide?

Walking toward his chair, Glenna smiled while her eyes searched his face. But her poker-playing father revealed none of his inner thoughts. If she had knocked at the study door she wouldn't have seen that brief glimpse of his inner anxiety.

"Did you start to wonder where I was?" Her voice was cheerful as she placed her camera and notebook on the sturdy oak desk before she reached his chair. Resting a hand on the chair arm, Glenna bent down to kiss his pallid cheeks, a color that had become natural to his complexion.

"I didn't," he insisted with a bright sparkle in his eyes. "I knew you would wander in sooner or later, but I think Bruce was becoming concerned."

Glenna straightened and looked in the direction her father had glanced. Bruce Hawkins was standing beside the fireplace, a shoulder leaning against the marble mantelpiece. His blue gaze was warmly admiring, taking in the wind-tossed curls of her chestnut hair, the loose-fitting velour sweater the color of buttercream that was draping the swelling mounds of her breasts, and the slimness of her hips and long legs in her brushed-denim jeans. The appreciation in his look held a hint of reserve, out of respect for her father's presence.

"Where have you been?" Bruce asked. There was nothing interrogating in it, just casual interest.

"Communing with Mother Nature," Glenna replied. Her gray green eyes swept his straw-colored hair and square-jawed face. Bruce was good-looking, intelligent, and ambitious. Since her father's first attack more than two years ago, he had assumed more and more responsibility for the operation of the coal mine.

It was really only after her father's first heart attack that Glenna had become acquainted with Bruce. The relationship between them had grown slowly until it had reached its present point where they were more than friends but not quite lovers.

Glenna was fully aware that she was the one who wouldn't let their relationship progress any further. On the surface, Bruce was everything she wanted in a man, yet some vital ingredient seemed to be missing. Its lack kept her from making any firm commitment. Sometimes she thought it was loyalty to her father that made her hold back. Maybe she was afraid of leaving him so soon after her mother's death to pursue her own life, her own relationship. Other times, like now, Glenna simply didn't know exactly why she was reluctant.

She knew that one word from her, one indication of acceptance, and Bruce would propose.

"Communing with nature," Bruce repeated her answer. "With your eye on the plan to write a series of articles, I'll bet."

"You guessed right," Glenna agreed. "That's one thing about freelancing; I can slant an article in so many different ways that I can sell the same story line to several different publications."

"And your head is buzzing with all of the ideas," her father mused.

The softness of her throaty laugh was an affirmative answer, although a whole new set of thoughts had subsequently taken the place of her ideas for the nature-oriented articles.

"There's some coffee in the pot. Would you like a cup?" Bruce offered, moving to the china coffee service sitting on the oblong coffee table in front of the sofa.

Glenna briefly resented his hospitality in what was her home, but she suppressed it. Bruce's familiarity was something both she and her father had invited. Besides, he was just being thoughtful. She wondered at her sudden sensitivity to the situation.

"I'd love some, thank you." She took a seat on the sofa while he poured a cup and handed it to her. Black, with no sugar, the way she liked it. Bruce sank his lean frame onto the cushion beside her, his arm automatically seeking the backrest of the sofa behind her head, but he didn't touch her.

"How are things at the mine?" Glenna asked automatically because it was Bruce's province.

She glanced over the rim of her coffee cup in

time to see Bruce dart a sharp look at her father. Then he replied, too blandly, "Fine."

Instantly, she knew there was a problem. A serious one. She sipped at her coffee, while her mind raced back to the anxious expression on her father's face when she had entered the room.

"I invited Bruce to dinner tonight," her father said with a subtle change of subject. "Hannah assured me the main dish would stretch to feed four. I can never decide whether she is trying to fatten us up or feed an army. The woman always cooks enough for ten people."

"Heaven knows you need some fattening up," Glenna observed. Recent weight loss had made his usually brawny frame appear gaunt. She knew he disliked any discussion of his health and turned to Bruce. "Are you are staying?"

"I never turn down an invitation for a home-cooked meal or the company of a lovely woman." There was a flattering intensity of to his look.

"I'll have to warn Hannah that you have designs on her, and her cooking," Glenna teased.

Bruce chuckled and the movement of her father's hand distracted her attention. He was reaching automatically into the breast pocket of his shirt. Orin Reynolds had quit smoking after his first heart attack. Only in moments of severe stress did the habit reassert itself. His shirt pocket no longer held a pack of cigarettes. Glenna noticed the faint tremor of his hand when it was lowered to the armrest. It was not a withdrawal symptom from smoking.

"After two years, you can't still want a cigarette, Dad," she chided to make him aware she'd seen him. Just for a second the facade of well-being slipped to reveal an expression that appeared supremely tired and defeated. A chill raced down Glenna's spine at the sullenness in his gray eyes before he laughed gruffly. Something was very wrong.

"After two years I am still craving the taste of tobacco. There are times when heaven to me is a smoke-filled poker room with whiskey and cigarettes amid a raucous backdrop of fiddle music instead of fluffy clouds, halos, and harps," he joked. "There are times when the quality of life outweighs the quantity."

Glenna forced a smile. "That is a rather morbid observation, Dad." She saw the grain of truth in his words, but her father had always been a fighter, battling the odds stacked against him. His remark, issued in jest, had smacked of surrender. "I suppose it is, but sometimes I . . ." He stopped and sighed. His mouth twitched into a rueful smile, vitality dancing back to glitter in his eyes. "I guess I'm tired."

"Why don't you lie down for a few minutes before dinner?" Glenna suggested. "I'll keep Bruce company."

"Did you hear that, Bruce?" her father mocked. "She sounds so concerned about me, doesn't she? But a father knows when his daughter doesn't want him around."

Her fingers tightened on the curved handle of her coffee cup. It was all she could do to not leap to her feet to help her father out of the chair. He hated any acknowledgment of the weakness of his muscles. It was a slow process, but he rose, unaided, to walk stiffly from the room.

Her throat was hurting by the time she heard the study door slide shut behind him. She stared at the coffee in the china cup she was holding so tightly. There was a stony clarity to her eyes—eyes that had become strangers to tears.

"What is wrong at the mine, Bruce?" she demanded without looking up.

A second of pregnant silence was followed by a hollow laugh. "I don't know what you're talking about. Nothing is wrong at the mine."

"It must be very serious for both you and Dad to lie to me." Glenna set the cup on the table with a briskness that rattled it against its saucer. She rose abruptly and dislodged the sunglasses from their perch on her head. She removed and folded them with a decisive snap before setting them on the table, too.

Her heavy, eyelash-fringed eyes narrowed their gaze on Bruce. "I want to know what it is."

"There isn't anything you can do." He looked grim.

"You don't know that," she retorted. "I haven't heard talk of a strike. And I can't believe the miners would walk out on Dad like that, anyway. If it's a labor problem, surely Dad can iron it out if you can't."

"It isn't labor." He avoided her gaze, his jaw hardening.

Glenna frowned. With that possibility eliminated, she was at a loss. "Then what is it? You're a mining engineer so it can't be anything technical."

"It's the government." That his skill was being questioned forced Bruce into giving the reason.

"What? Taxes?" She couldn't imagine her father being delinquent in employee taxes.

"Nothing so simple," Bruce replied and pushed

to his feet. He shoved his hands into the pockets of his slacks, an action that pushed his shoulders back and stretched the material of his blue shirt across the sinewed width of his chest. "The mine failed its safety inspection."

"How bad is it?" Glenna asked, the feeling of dread sweeping over her.

"They're issuing an injunction to shut the mine down within thirty days if the necessary steps aren't taken immediately to correct the situation," he answered in a voice as leaden as her own.

"You can appeal the ruling and gain more time," she argued.

"That's what I've been doing for the last year and a half," he snapped in a sudden blaze of temper. "We ran out of time. They won't postpone the ruling anymore."

Parallel furrows ran across her forehead. "If you knew it was coming, why did you procrastinate?" Glenna challenged. "Why did you leave it until the last minute? I guess you just dumped this all on Dad this afternoon, when it's practically too late to do anything to stop it. No wonder he acted so defeated. He isn't well. He trusted you to—"

"Orin has known from the start!" Bruce interrupted sharply. "If it was up to me, I would've begun implementing and installing new safety measures. But I didn't have a say in the matter."

"Are you implying that my father knowingly endangered the lives of the miners?" The accusation brought a pronounced silver glitter to her eyes, making them icy and more gray than green.

"For God's sake! He had no more choice in the matter than I did."

He turned away to rest an arm on the mantel of the fireplace, bending his head to rub his hand over his mouth and chin in a gesture of exasperation.

Her anger ebbed. "What do you mean? Why didn't he have a choice?" Glenna frowned. "You said yourself that the solution was to comply."

"That costs money, Glenna." Bruce sighed and straightened to look at her. "That's why the initial ruling was appealed to gain time to raise the capital to make the changes and install the necessary devices."

"He could borrow it. The bank would loan him the—"

"No. Orin took out second and third mortgages on everything he owned almost three years ago to make other needed changes at the mine. There was a time he could've borrowed on his reputation alone, but after these last two heart attacks"—Bruce filled the pause with an expressive shrug of his shoulders—"the banks think of him as an uninsurable risk with overextended credit."

Glenna felt chilled and struggled against the dark despair clouding her mind. Her gaze clung to Bruce's handsome features.

"There has to be someone who will help Dad." She tried to sound calm, and not nearly as desperate as she felt.

Her mind was churning with thoughts. If the mine was closed it would ultimately mean bankruptcy. They would lose the house and everything of value. The effect this would have on her father was something Glenna didn't want to contemplate. She barely succeeded in suppressing a shudder.

"On your father's instructions, I sent out feelers to see if Coulson Mining would be interested in a merger with your father's company—on the chance they might see some tax advantages." Bruce shook his head grimly. "Their reply was a flat 'not interested.'"

"Coulson Mining," Glenna repeated. "Jett Coulson's company? The coal magnate."

"Coal, gas, you name it and he's rolling in it—including gold." Bruce nodded.

With startling clarity Glenna recalled the picture of a grainy newspaper photograph she'd seen of Jett Coulson while reading a trade journal to her father shortly after his first heart attack. The man's hair and eyes had appeared as black as the shining coal that had built his fortune. At the time the photograph had been taken, he'd been in his midthirties, yet his lined features showed toughness beyond his years.

To Glenna, Jett Coulson had seemed all rough, raw manhood. She remembered her father had spoken of him with respect. What she had viewed as ruthlessness, her father had regarded as strength. Jett Coulson's lack of polish and refinement made him a man the miners could relate to, even when they disagreed. It was rumored that Jett Coulson never lied. The standing joke was that a lot of people wished he would.

"Did you talk to Jett Coulson?" she asked, clinging to the one tantalizing straw Bruce had offered.

"Are you kidding?" He laughed harshly. "I'm nothing but a manager—a mining engineer. I talked to one of his underlings."

"There wasn't even a hint of interest?" Glenna persisted.

"Be realistic, Glenna," Bruce sighed. "Why would Coulson agree to a merger when he'll probably be able to pick the mine up for nothing in a few months? Why should he bail your father out of this mess? He's never had a reputation for being a Good Samaritan. It's unlikely he'll have a change of heart now."

"No, I guess not." Her shoulders slumped in defeat. She turned away and walked to a front window to gaze sightlessly at the shadows gathering on the lawn. "What's going to happen to my father? To all those people?" She wasn't aware she had murmured the aching question aloud.

Approaching her from behind, Bruce rubbed his hands over her arms. "Glenna, I'm sorry. I wish there was some way I could help . . . something I could do to prevent this."

She heard the echo of futility in his voice, the forlorn emptiness of his offer. When his arms curved around her and his jaw rested against her hair, there was no comfort in his embrace.

"I don't have much money, but when the mine closes—" he began.

"*If* the mine closes, not *when,* Bruce," Glenna quickly corrected him and moved out of his arms and away from the window. Her back was ramrod straight when she turned to him. "You said it will be thirty days until the injunction takes effect. A lot can happen in thirty days."

"You sound like your father." He eyed her sadly. "Don't be a fool, Glenna."

Those remarks only served to make her more

determined. If her father hadn't given up hope yet, neither would she. Her features took on an air of resolve. The sunlight glinting through the window seemed to set the deep auburn hue of her brown hair afire, as if reinforcing her purpose.

"Dad isn't the type to lie down and let the world step on him. And neither am I."

"I don't think you understand what you're up against." Bruce shook his head. "There's a time for pride . . . and a time to be sensible. I should know, Glenna. I've fought this day for a year and a half. You can think what you like about me, but after a year and a half of butting my head against a stone wall, I know when to quit."

"Is that what you are going to do?" Her lip curled in challenge.

"Not literally. No, I'll see this thing through to the bitter end." There was absolutely no doubt in his expression about what the end would be. Turning, he walked to the desk and picked up the briefcase lying atop it. "I think it would be better if I took a rain check on the dinner tonight. I don't think either of us would be very good company. Make my apologies to Orin, will you?" he murmured quietly.

"Of course." Glenna said with a curt nod and made no attempt to walk with him to the front door.

His glance was faintly mocking when he crossed the room and paused at the sliding oak doors. "I'll show myself out," he said.

"I know you will," she replied coolly.

CHAPTER TWO

The tingling shower spray drummed out some of her tension. The raking wire claws of the hairbrush eliminated more of it while untangling her wind-snarled hair. Makeup and a floral silk shirtwaist bolstered her spirits.

When Glenna met her father in the dining room she felt capable of taking on any obstacle—including the stone wall Bruce had referred to. The minute she entered the room she saw her father's sharp-eyed scrutiny.

"Hannah tells me Bruce decided not to stay for dinner. Did you two have a lover's quarrel?" He sat at the head of the claw-footed dining-room table.

"We aren't lovers so that isn't possible." She pulled out the chair on his right and sat down. Sometimes it irritated her that her father would refer to their relationship as that.

Her father raised an iron gray eyebrow. "You obviously had a difference of opinion about something."

"We did." Glenna agreed said with a quick smile

as she spread the Irish-linen napkin across her lap. "It was over the closing of the mine. He thinks it's inevitable. I don't." She saw the look of anxiety spread across his face and turned her attention to the housekeeper entering the room with a tureen of soup. "Hmm, that smells good, Hannah." The warm aroma of chicken stock wafted from the china serving bowl.

"Homemade, I spent all afternoon fixing the noodles," the plump woman retorted with her usual sassy spirit. "And you'd better do more than pick at my food tonight, Orin Reynolds, or else I'll stick you in a high chair and spoon-feed you. If you think I can't do it, you just try me," she threatened and set the tureen on the table near Glenna with a decisive thump.

Her father barely noticed Hannah, who had practically become a member of the family. Glenna knew that his silence was due to her reference to the trouble at the mine. She took over the task of ladling the homemade chicken soup into the individual bowls.

"Dad loves your homemade egg noodles, Hannah," Glenna assured the woman sternly eyeing Orin Reynolds's bowed head. "Don't you?" she prompted and set a bowl of the steaming soup in front of him.

"How did you find out about the mine?" He lifted his gaze to her face. His expression was a little stunned, a little disbelieving and tinted with relief.

"Did you really think you could keep it from me?" she chided and dished a bowl of soup for herself. "I saw how worried you looked when I first came in. I asked Bruce outright what the problem was at the mine. Bruce isn't as good a poker player as you are. I knew that whatever was bothering you had to do with the mine."

The curving line of Orin's mouth held faint bemusement. "I doubt it was hard to get the answers from him. You have Hawkins wrapped around your little finger. He'd do or say anything to please you, you know that, don't you?"

Glenna flicked him a dry glance, reading between the lines of his comment.

"Don't decide to try any matchmaking, Dad." She filled the last soup bowl and leaned across the table to set it where Hannah would be sitting. "I'll choose my own future husband, thank you." Moving the soup tureen to the center of the table, Glenna returned to the topic of the coal mine and its problems. "Why didn't you tell me about the trouble you were having?"

"I didn't want you to worry." He picked up his soupspoon and dipped it into the bowl, but made no attempt to lift a spoonful to his mouth. "I never thought it would come to this point," her father admitted as Hannah returned to the dining room with a basket of homemade saltine crackers to go with the soup. "I was positive that Bruce and I would come up with a solution that would keep the mine from being shut down. I wasn't really trying to keep it from you. I just didn't want you worrying over something you couldn't do anything about. You have enough on your mind."

"What's this about the mine being shut down?" Hannah demanded. A frown of concern narrowed her eyes. "When did all this come about? And eat your soup. Stop playing with it," she ordered without a pause.

"The mine doesn't meet the safety standards. Unless it complies, the government is shutting it down," Glenna explained. She noticed the faint shock that spread across Hannah's face as the plump woman sank into the chair opposite her. Challenge glinted in the look Glenna cast at her father. "So, what are we going to do about it?"

"We have exhausted just about every avenue of hope," Orin sighed. Leaving the spoon in the bowl, he rested his elbows on the table and clasped his hands together, pressing his fingers to his mouth. There was grim resignation in his features. "I'm at a complete loss to know which way to turn."

The housekeeper glared at him. "Orin Reynolds, I have never known you to give up."

He lifted his head, sending the frazzle-haired woman an irritated look. "Who said I was? I just don't know where to go from here."

Glenna was glad to hear the fighting spirit in that response. It was reassuring, and reinforced her own determination. The future wasn't as dark as Bruce thought. "I want to help."

They exchanged glances. The underlying strain that had tensed his features faded at her supportive remark. There was warmth and affection in his expression.

"You remind me so much of your mother. God bless her soul," he murmured. "She always stood beside me no matter what." After a touching pause he added, "I miss her."

The love her parents shared had been one of

the greatest securities of Glenna's childhood. She was aware how keenly her father had felt the loss of his wife to cancer three years ago. It had been a mercifully swift death, but Glenna suspected her mother's death had precipitated his heart attack a short time later. For a while, she'd feared he had a subconscious death wish to join his beloved Mary, but his will to live was strong.

"What on earth are you going to do?" Hannah questioned, then grimaced. "The soup is getting cold. If you had terrible news like this, why did you wait until I had food on the table before bringing it up? It would have been so much easier, Orin, if you had talked about this before dinner or afterward, but not in the middle of a meal." She sent him a disgruntled look. "You haven't answered my question. What are you going to do?" Hannah ignored the fact that she hadn't given him an opportunity to reply.

"I don't know." He shook his head and reached for the spoon resting in his soup bowl. "We seem to be up against a brick wall."

"If you can't knock it down, there has to be a way to go around it, under it, or over it," Glenna reasoned.

"I thought we had a way around it," he agreed with her logic, his mouth twisting ruefully. "Unfortunately, it turned out to be a dead end."

"You are referring to merging with Coulson Mining?" Glenna guessed.

The spoon he held was poised in midair, halfway to his mouth, the broth dripping off the edge into the bowl as Orin shot her a quick look. "You know about that, too?" he said with faint surprise. "It doesn't sound like Bruce left anything out."

"Not much," she admitted.

He swallowed a spoonful of soup and reached for one of Hannah's crackers to butter.

"Did Bruce tell you that he suggested a meeting with the miners to let them know about the situation and the possibility the mine will be closed in a month?" His gaze slid from the cracker to Glenna.

She attacked her soup, angered again by Bruce's defeatist attitude. "I hope you put him straight on that score," she said.

"I agreed with him." Her father didn't meet her stunned look as he took interest in evenly spreading the butter over his cracker. "He's setting up the meeting between shift changes tomorrow afternoon."

That shocked Glenna. It contradicted his wanting to fight this. She returned the soupspoon to its place beside the rest of the silverware, mindless of the broth stain it made on the tablecloth. "How can you let him do that?"

"It's the fair thing to do, Glenna," he reasoned. "If—," he paused to reemphasize the qualifying word, "if the mine is going to be closed, the miners should know about it before it happens so they have a chance to prepare for the layoff. We should prepare them for the worst that could happen." A heavy sigh brought an air of sadness to his words. "It wouldn't be so tragic if I was the only one who would suffer from the closing of the mine, but so many people's lives are involved. The economy of this whole community revolves around the Reynolds Mine. We'll have our own miniature depression in this valley."

"We are going to try to prevent that," Glenna said.

"I know." He smiled at her encouragement. "I'm fighting just as hard for myself as I am for them. I stand to lose everything, including this house, where our family spent so many wonderful years—" The tightness in his throat cut the sentence short as his gaze made a sweep of the room. It ended its arc to linger on the housekeeper. He reached out to cover the housekeeper's hand with his own, a gesture that revealed the affection he felt toward the irascible woman. "You would be out of a job and a place to live. I had always intended for you to have a tidy pension to retire on, but I doubt if I could afford to give you severance pay."

"Don't you go trying to force your charity on me, Orin Reynolds." Hannah pulled her hand from beneath his, but the gruffness of her voice revealed how deeply moved she was by his remarks. "I can look out for myself. I always have, haven't I?"

"The mine hasn't shut down, and we haven't been turned out of this house, yet," Glenna said. "For now let's concentrate our attention on trying to prevent it, instead of thinking about what we'll do if it happens."

"Any suggestions?" Orin asked, showing he could think of no more avenues to explore.

"Just because Coulson isn't interested doesn't mean another company might not be. Aren't there other mining companies that might be interested in a merger besides Coulson?" she reasoned.

"Considering the mine's indebtedness and the investment capital needed to bring it up to standard, only a large corporation could absorb us—a company that could take advantage of the tax benefits. The only company that fits that bill is Jett Coulson's. And you know what his answer was," he murmured dryly.

"It wasn't his answer," Glenna remembered. "Bruce said it came from one of his underlings."

"But I'm sure it came down directly from him."

"We don't know that."

Her father studied her for a minute, silently following her train of thought. "You think I should get the answer straight from the horse's mouth."

"Why not?" She shrugged. "You haven't personally spoken to him. Neither has Bruce. As competent as Bruce might be as a manager, that doesn't mean he's the right person to present your merger proposition." She watched him mulling over her comment.

"You could be right," he conceded thoughtfully. "Maybe I should arrange a meeting with Jett Coulson."

"Absolutely," Glenna nodded as she watched the hope being reborn in his gray eyes. "You have nothing to lose by doing that."

"You're right." He spooned some homemade soup into his mouth and tasted its flavor for the first time. His bright gaze darted to the housekeeper, a smile of approval curving his mouth. "This is delicious, Hannah."

"Of course it is," the housekeeper sniffed, as if there could be any doubt she would serve less than the best.

* * *

Late the following afternoon, Glenna was in her bedroom. One corner of the room was a miniature study, a small desk cubbyholed amid the bookshelves. A laptop sat in the center of the orderly chaos, and her notes from the previous day's outing scattered around the desktop.

A knock at the door intruded on Glenna's frowning concentration, turning her head from the scribbled handwriting she was trying to decipher. Before she could respond, the door opened and her father popped his head in.

"We're in luck," he announced, entering the room with more buoyancy to his stride than she had seen in a long time.

She pushed all thoughts of the article she was trying to write from her mind and directed her attention to him. A faint smile touched her mouth as she studied his jovial mood.

"What kind of luck are we in?" Glenna joked and tucked the thickness of her auburn hair behind an ear. "Good or bad?"

"Anything would be an improvement over what we've had, so it must be good." He sought out the plump armchair covered in toasted gold corduroy.

"Are you going to tell me what this good luck is, or keep me in suspense?"

"I just found out that Jett Coulson is going to be entertaining some of his lobbyists at The Greenbrier this weekend." Orin's face held a bright smile.

His announcement merely drew a questioning

glance from Glenna. "And that's the good luck?" She didn't quite see what was so wonderful about that.

"It certainly is. Meeting him there will allow a casual approach," he explained. "If I made an appointment to see Coulson at his office there would probably be a hundred and one interruptions, and his time would be limited. At the hotel, I'll have more than one chance to discuss it with him."

It sounded very logical, but Glenna saw a glitch. "But if he's entertaining guests, won't he—"

"It's only an excuse to party. The guests will be entertaining themselves. Coulson will have plenty of free time," her father assured.

"Are you sure?" She wasn't quite convinced. "Wouldn't it be smarter to meet him in an atmosphere more conducive to business?"

Her father chuckled. "More business deals are consummated at social gatherings than are ever accomplished in a corporate office. Once an agreement is reached, it's up to the attorneys to work out the fine details. A handshake from Coulson over the dinner table is as good as cash in the bank."

"Well, you know more about these things than I do. In the meantime, I'll look him on up on the Internet to see if there's anything you could use to our advantage," Glenna said and shifted in her chair to hook a leg beneath her.

"How long do you think it will take to drive from here to White Sulphur Springs? I'd like to get there around noon on Friday."

"It shouldn't take more than two or three hours," she guessed.

"You will be my chauffeur, won't you?" her

father asked, well aware that his doctor would be against him driving that distance alone.

"I'm not going to let you go by yourself." Then she hesitated. "Are you sure you wouldn't rather have Bruce with you?"

He shook his head. "That would be much too obvious. I want it to appear to be a father-daughter outing, all very casual. A weekend vacation will be good for you, anyway. Besides, you can pick up a lot of firsthand material for your writing."

"I'm sure I could, but—," Glenna paused, eyeing her father with concern. "Dad, do you think we can afford this?"

"At this point it isn't going to keep us out of bankruptcy court." His expression became serious. "This is the last roll of the dice. We might as well shoot our whole wad and go out in style."

"You have always been a first-class gambler, Dad," she observed with a faint smile that held warmth but little humor.

"Be sure to pack our best clothes." Her father stood up, the decision made and irrevocable now. "We don't want to look like a pair of beggars when we meet Coulson."

The white magnificence of The Greenbrier was nestled in an upland Allegheny valley. Its forested lawns and mountain backdrop provided the beauty of natural surroundings. The famed spa obtained its initial notoriety from the soothing mineral waters that smelled like a half boiled/half spoiled egg. Still, its guest register over the years included an impressive list of celebrities.

This was not Glenna's first visit to the famous West Virginia resort, but she was still awed by its stately elegance and aura of steeped tradition. The many-storied facade was pristine white with a columned portico entrance.

After they had registered and been shown to their adjoining rooms, she and her father had split up. Glenna had wanted to do some exploring and refamiliarize herself with the hotel complex, while her father wanted to make inquiries and learn the most logical place to "bump into" Jett Coulson.

Her wandering walk brought Glenna into the building housing the indoor tennis courts. She paused to watch a match being played, two couples playing a game of mixed doubles. The good-natured teasing exchanged between the pairs brought a smile to her face.

A shouted reference to the time directed her glance at her watch. It was a few minutes past three o'clock. By the time she returned to her room and changed into her swimsuit, she would have an hour to swim before meeting her father. The fairness of her skin, the complexion of a true redhead, forced Glenna to avoid the sun during the middle of the day when its burning rays did the most damage.

As she started to move away from the tennis court, a hoot of laughter attracted her attention. Turning her head, she glanced over her shoulder. In the split second when she wasn't watching where she was going, she nearly walked into another player. Her forward progress was stopped by a pair of hands that reached out to her before she ran into him.

Her attention was jerked to the front; a hurried apology forming on her lips. It froze there for a full second as Glenna stared at the tall sun-bronzed figure of a man in white tennis shorts and white knit top. A black pair of eyes returned her stunned regard with a shimmer of bemusement as he removed his hands from her shoulders.

Glenna was struck by the irony of the situation. She had accidentally run into the man that her father was contriving to bump into. A smile played with the corners of her mouth, attracting his interest.

"I'm sorry, Mr. Coulson," she apologized smoothly. "I wasn't paying attention to where I was going."

An eyebrow flicked upward at the use of his name. All the toughness was there in his features, just as she had remembered from the photograph she'd seen. But they hadn't captured the perpetual gleam in his dark eyes—the gleam of a rogue wolf.

"Have we met before?" Like his gaze, his voice was direct. Glenna couldn't help but notice the boldness of his sweeping glance. "I can't believe I would have forgotten meeting you."

The line was delivered smoothly, so smoothly that Glenna found it hard to question its sincerity. "We've never been introduced. I recognized you from a newspaper article," she explained and felt warmed by the slow smile that spread across his mouth.

"You have a good memory. They haven't published any articles or pictures of me in some time, Miss—" He paused deliberately.

"Reynolds. Glenna Reynolds." She found herself

becoming intrigued by this man. There was a reckless gambler's charm about him that she hadn't expected. This, plus the unwavering determination etched in his craggy rough and edgy features, made a potent combination. The force of it was affecting her. The last thing she anticipated was being sexually disturbed by Jett Coulson.

"That name sounds familiar to me. Glenna Reynolds." He repeated it as if to jog his memory, his eyes narrowing faintly.

"Perhaps you have—" She started to explain who her father was, but Jett Coulson interrupted her with a snap of his fingers in recollection.

"Glenna Reynolds was the byline on an article that was in the magazine section of the Sunday paper. Was that yours?" His look became thoughtful, a degree of aloofness entering his expression.

"Yes, it was," Glenna admitted with faint astonishment. "I'm flattered that you read it . . . and remembered it."

"I remembered it because of the way you took a boring subject and made it appear interesting," he replied hesitantly.

"Thank you . . . I think." She wasn't sure his remark hadn't been a backhanded compliment. She was slightly irritated that he might be mocking her behind his poker-smooth exterior.

"Is this a business trip or pleasure?" His observing gaze seemed to take note of the turbulence clouding her gray green eyes, and shifted the subject so smoothly that Glenna wondered if she hadn't imagined the tease.

"Both," she admitted.

"You didn't come to write an article about me,

otherwise I would've heard of it. Is it The Green-brier? It's been written about many times."

"The Greenbrier. I guess my challenge will be to do it differently." There was a defensive tilt to her chin, elevating it a degree. She couldn't help but notice again his superior height and unshakable self-assurance.

"I enjoy a challenge myself," he murmured. Then he inclined his head in a slight nod. "Excuse me, but I have a tennis date to keep."

With one last look, he moved past her, his tanned and muscled legs carried him with long strides. Her gaze followed him for several seconds, taking note of the breadth of his ropy shoulders and how his torso tapered to the narrowness of his waist and hips. Jett Coulson was a breed of man she had never seen before—and was unlikely to meet again. He was one of a kind.

CHAPTER THREE

Orin Reynolds was at the poolside when Glenna climbed the ladder out of the swimming pool. She sensed an air of urgency about him as she walked, leaving a trail of water behind her, to the deck chair where she'd left her towel and robe.

"Hi!" Glenna said breathlessly. She'd pushed herself during the swim, but was exhilarated by the activity. Seconds after leaving the pool, the evaporation of water cooled her skin and began raising goose bumps. Glenna shook out the towel and began briskly rubbing herself down. "What's up? I thought we were going to meet in the room."

"I tipped the bellboy. He told me that Coulson usually has a cocktail in the lounge before dinner. I wanted to be sure we got there before he did so we could spot him coming in."

She took off her bathing cap to let her auburn hair tumble free. "I bumped into him—literally— at the tennis court this afternoon."

"Coulson?" her father asked, surprised.

"The one and only." She used the towel to blot

the excess moisture from her swimsuit, a sleek one-piece suit of sea green.

"What did he say?" Her father was keenly alert, studying every nuance of her expression. "Does he know who you are?"

"He doesn't know that I'm your daughter. I didn't get a chance to tell him I was. But he'd read one of my articles and remembered my name from that." This was still something she found surprising and rather impressive. "That was just about the extent of our conversation."

"Mmm." Orin Reynolds seemed to digest that information while Glenna slipped into the loose-fitting floral robe and hooked the wide belt around her slim waistline. "Do you have shoes?"

"Under the chair." She knelt to remove the kitten-heeled slip-ons from beneath the chair. Using his arm for balance, she stepped into first one, then the other.

"Let's go to the lounge." He took her arm and started to lead her away.

Glenna stopped. "I can't go to the lounge like this."

"Nonsense. It's informal. There will be people there in tennis shorts. You are fully clothed." He said trying to convince her.

"Dad! I don't even have any makeup on." Her fingers touched the damp tendrils of curling hair. "And my hair—"

"Nothing you could do would improve on perfection," Orin said while smiling.

"Dad, be serious," she sighed. "At least let me go up to my room for a few minutes. I just wouldn't feel comfortable in the lounge area like this. I was swimming in a chlorinated pool!"

"If you are determined to spoil that fresh, clean look, go ahead," he conceded with an indulging smile. "But don't take long. I don't want to miss him."

After Glenna had freshened up and changed, she met her father at the entrance to the lounge. It was just beginning to fill with the happy-hour crowd. Orin Reynolds guided her to a table strategically located near the entrance so that he could see who came in and out. Their drink order was served—a glass of white wine for Glenna and a Perrier with a lime twist for her father. She had taken her first sip of the wine when Jett Coulson entered the lounge alone. She touched her father's arm to draw his attention to the man inside the doorway, but it was unnecessary. Orin had already spotted him.

Those gleaming dark eyes were making a slow inspection of the room, not in search of anyone as far as Glenna could tell, but simply taking note of who was present. Her father stood up, attracting Jett's attention. His gaze narrowed as it touched Glenna, then returned to her father.

"Mr. Coulson." With a pleasant, informal pitch, her father succeeded in summoning Jett to their table. "I haven't had the pleasure of meeting you formally. My name is Orin Reynolds, of the Reynolds Mine."

There was a firm clasping of hands as Jett murmured a polite, "How do you do, Mr. Reynolds."

If her father's name or that of his coal mine meant anything to Jett, Glenna didn't see any recognition register in his expression. But she understood that those hardened features wouldn't reveal his inner thoughts.

"I believe you met my daughter Glenna earlier this afternoon," her father said, by way of acknowledging her presence.

"Yes, we . . . bumped into each other." The faint pause carried an inflection of dry amusement as Jett nodded to her. "Hello, again, Miss Reynolds."

"Hello, Mr. Coulson." There was a husky pitch to her voice, and Glenna wasn't sure exactly where it had come from. She seemed to be holding her breath, too, without knowing why.

No longer dressed in his tennis clothes, he had changed into a pair of navy slacks and a silk shirt in a subdued blue design against a cream background. The untamed thickness of his hair held a sheen of dampness, and Glenna thought he had probably recently taken a shower. She had been so fully prepared to dislike him; now she found herself wondering why she didn't.

"Sit down," her father invited. "Let me buy you a drink." Then he paused, as if suddenly realizing. "Were you meeting someone?"

"No." He chose the empty chair beside Glenna, across the table from her father.

"What will you have to drink?" Orin signaled to the cocktail waitress.

"Scotch, neat, on the rocks," Jett replied, and her father passed the order to the waitress.

"Who won your tennis match?" Seated this close, Glenna inhaled the tangy scent of his aftershave with each breath she took. It stimulated her senses, awakening them to his rough brand of masculinity.

"I did." He made it sound a simple fact and not a boast or brag.

"Naturally," she murmured dryly, bothered by the sheer confidence of his statement.

He turned his head to regard her with those gleaming, but impassive black eyes. "I always play to win."

"Don't you ever play simply for the fun of it?" Even as she asked the question she remembered his reputation.

"That's the rationale of a loser." A half smile tugged at the corners of his mouth, taunting her. Then he let his gaze slide back to her father. "I would never have guessed she was your daughter, Mr. Reynolds."

"Please, call me Orin," her father insisted and cast a smiling glance at her. "No, there isn't much of a resemblance between us. Thankfully, Glenna takes after her mother, God rest her soul. She was a strikingly beautiful woman."

"Don't mind him. He's prejudiced." She was embarrassed by her father's compliments. Usually when he made such remarks about her looks in front of friends or strangers, she just smiled and let them pass. This time they made her uncomfortable. Or was it the dark and knowing regard of the man sitting beside her?

Jett's Scotch was served. Much to Glenna's relief, the interruption allowed the conversation to drift to another topic. "Tell me, Orin, what brings you here?" Jett questioned with mild interest. "Your daughter mentioned she was here on a combination of business and pleasure. Is that true for you, too?"

Glenna hastened to explain. "I told Mr. Coulson

of my intention to write a travel article about The Greenbrier."

"Glenna has quite a talent with words. She said you had read some of her work." Her father attempted to dodge the initial question.

"Yes, I have," Jett admitted. "Do you help with the research?"

"No," Orin denied with a throaty laugh. "She does everything herself. I don't know which of us is chaperoning the other. I can't say that this is strictly a pleasure trip for me since a businessman never escapes his responsibilities, not even for a weekend. I'm sure you know what I mean."

Jett nodded. "I understand."

"What brings you here?"

Glenna marveled at the bland innocence of her father's expression, as if he didn't have the vaguest idea why Jett was at the hotel. His face held just the right touch of curiosity and interest. She sipped her wine, wondering if Jett Coulson realized he was being bluffed.

"I'm entertaining some lobbyists from Washington." He took a swallow of straight Scotch without flinching.

"I thought I recognized some familiar faces in the lobby. That explains it," her father stated with just the right note of discovery, but Glenna was suspicious of the look Jett gave him. "I wish there were some strings they could pull for me," he sighed heavily. "The government's threatening to shut down my mine at the end of the month."

"That's too bad." The remark did not invite further disclosure of Orin's troubles.

"Sorry, dear." Her father reached over and

patted her hand. It was all Glenna could do to keep from jumping in surprise. "I promised not to bring up that subject this weekend, didn't I?"

It took her a full second to recover, during which she was careful not to look at Jett Coulson. She doubted she was as good as these two men were at concealing their thoughts.

"You did promise," she lied in agreement. "But I don't think I ever expected you to be able to keep it," she added the last so her father could reintroduce the subject.

"Glenna suggested this weekend excursion to distract me from the problems at the mine," her father explained. "But you're here . . . and the coal lobbyists. Which proves, I suppose, that a person can never run away from their problems."

"Not for long, at any rate." Jett rested his arms on the table, his silk-clad elbow brushing her forearm.

The contact swerved his gaze to her. Glenna realized why his look was so deliciously unnerving. He looked at her as if she were the only woman in the entire room. The enigmatic glow in his dark eyes seemed to say that he already knew a lot about her and wanted to know a lot more. His appeal was a devastating combination of virile charm and ruthless determination. Glenna could feel it slowly crumbling her resistance.

"How has your company been affected by the new government regulations?" Her father's inquiry released her from Jett's gaze. "I know you strip-mine the majority of your coal and have the Reclamation Act to contend with, but I'm refer-

ring specifically to the underground coal that
can't be strip-mined."

The two men talked about mining in general for
a while—its politics, new technology, and its future
potential. Glenna became aware that her father
was slowly steering the conversation in the direction he wanted it to take, subtly dropping facts and
figures about his mine. When he nudged her with
his foot, she took the hint.

She pushed her chair back from the table and
smiled under Jett's questioning regard. "You and
Dad will probably talk 'coal' for another hour or
more. In the meantime, I think I'll go to my room
to relax and change for dinner. If you'll excuse
me."

As she rose, so did Jett Coulson. At first she
thought this was prompted by courtesy until she
saw him glance at his watch.

"It is getting late . . . and I have to change before
dinner, too," he announced with casual indifference.

Glenna noticed the absence of frustration and
disappointment on her father's face, two emotions
that he had to be feeling. Instead he was smiling
quite broadly.

"Well, I'm certainly not going to sit here and
drink alone." Placing both hands on the table, he
pushed to his feet. "I'll come with you, Glenna,
and change for dinner, too."

When she noticed his legs appear wobbly from
sitting for such a long time, she absently hooked
an arm through her father's to give him support
without it appearing that it was her purpose. With
measured steps Glenna strolled in the direction of

the lounge exit while she continued to help her father.

"Thank you for the drink, Orin." Jett Coulson kept pace with them. "And for the interesting conversation."

"I enjoyed talking to you," her father returned. "We'd like you to have dinner with us tonight. You are more than welcome to join us, if you're free."

"I'm entertaining guests this weekend." As he paused, his gaze strayed over each of them. "You and your daughter are welcome to sit at my table this evening."

"We wouldn't want to intrude," Orin said. Glenna was surprised to hear her father resist the invitation.

"You won't be intruding. Everyone at the table will probably be talking coal anyway," Jett shrugged.

"In that case"—her father made a pretense of hesitating as he glanced at her—"we'll be glad to accept."

As they left the lounge and walked to the elevator, Jett explained that he had made reservations to dine at eight o'clock in the formal dining room. By the time they reached the elevators, her father was steady enough on his feet that he no longer needed Glenna's support. She released his arm and entered the elevator first. There wasn't any opportunity to talk during the ride up to their floor since other guests had crowded into the elevator, too.

When the elevator stopped at their floor, she was surprised to discover that Jett had disembarked with them. She glanced at her father, who was also frowning in bewildered astonishment.

"Is this your floor?" he asked.

"Yes," Jett nodded with barely a change in his expression.

"Isn't that a coincidence?" her father declared on an incredulous laugh. "It's ours, too."

"Yes, it is." The dry inflection of his voice seemed to doubt it, but Glenna couldn't be sure. "I'll see you in the dining room at eight."

As he moved off down the hall, Glenna walked with her father to their adjoining suites. Suspicion reared its head, but she didn't voice it until Jett Coulson was out of hearing.

"Did you know he had a room on this floor?" she questioned.

"Of course." He unlocked his door and Glenna followed him. "Every gambler knows he has to even the odds if he can."

"Jett Coulson plays poker, too, Dad."

Her remark sent a serious look chasing across his tired face.

"Yes, I noticed. And he's damned good at it, too. I didn't think he would decide to leave when you got up to go." Then he shrugged. "It doesn't matter. I'll have another chance."

At the moment she wasn't concerned about the missed opportunity. "Why don't you rest for an hour? You have plenty of time to get ready for dinner."

"Yes, I think I'll do that." He moved slowly toward the bed and stretched his gaunt frame atop the bed cover.

Glenna studied him for a worried second, then unlocked the connecting door to her separate suite of rooms. She slipped quietly inside and leaned against the closed door. Had she been wrong to suggest this battle to save the mine, their home, everything? For the first time she doubted her father's ability to sway Jett Coulson onto his side.

When she dressed for dinner later that evening, she recalled her father saying that they would go out in style. In a month they would lose their home and business, but tonight she was going to be dressed as elegantly as any woman in the room.

The jade green silk of her dress was an exotic foil to the burnished chestnut of her hair, swept atop her head in a mass of ringlets and secured by jeweled combs that had belonged to her mother. The jade material encircled her throat, leaving her shoulders and arms bare. It was nipped in tightly at the waistline, then flared into a skirt. With it she carried a crocheted shawl of silver threads.

When she knocked on the connecting door, her father was fighting with the knot of his tie. She tied it for him, noting how much good the short rest had been for him. Together they went downstairs, arriving in the dining room precisely at eight o'clock. All but two of Jett's party were already there.

Glenna was aware of the curious glances she received as she was introduced to the men around the table. Their silent speculation increased when Jett seated her in a chair to his right. Her father was given the chair next to her, which put Glenna between the two men. This gave her father virtually no opportunity to talk privately with Jett.

The conversation around the dinner table was lively and focused mainly on coal as Jett had predicted. Her father included himself in the discussion quite easily. Mostly Glenna just listened to the stimulating and intelligent exchanges. She couldn't help noticing how bluntly Jett stated his opinions, never couching his replies in diplomatic terms. In contrast, everyone else appeared to be the epitome of tact, phrasing their remarks so they wouldn't offend anyone.

Suddenly, Jett turned to her. "Are you bored with the conversation?"

The others were busy talking and appeared unaware of the question he had addressed to Glenna. "No, I'm not bored." She lifted her gaze briefly from the prime rib she was cutting to the velvet sheen of his glance. "Dad and Bruce usually sit at the dinner table talking about daily coal production, grades, and tonnage. I'm used to it."

"Bruce?" His voice carried an aloof curiosity.

"Bruce Hawkins," she said. "He manages the mine for Dad." She thought she felt his gaze boring into her, but she looked up as Jett was making a leisurely sweep of the guests.

"Does it bother you being the only woman at the table?" He idly speared a piece of meat on his fork and carried it to his mouth.

Glenna let her own fork rest on the dinner plate, bewildered by his sudden change of topic.

"Why should it bother me?" she asked with a slight frown.

"I didn't say it 'should,'" he corrected smoothly. "I asked if it did."

"No, it doesn't." She answered curtly, wondering where his comment would lead.

"Perhaps you enjoy being the object of so many admiring glances?" Jett suggested.

She wasn't going to deny that she'd noticed. "I'm flattered, but—" Glenna didn't bother to finish the sentence, abandoning the defensive to counter. "Maybe I should ask you that first question. Does it bother you that I'm the only female at a table with all these men?"

"Not as long as you're sitting beside me it doesn't." He didn't hesitate over his answer, issuing it smoothly without as much as a glance in her direction. It was almost as if he'd planned to say this all along.

A question from one of the other guests ended the personal exchange. The vaguely possessive ring that had been in his voice confirmed that he'd singled her out. And that bothered Glenna, creating fluttering butterflies in her stomach. She was coming to see him as a man, rather than just someone her father wished to do business with. She knew this would cause complications in their plans.

She couldn't help but notice more about him. She studied his hard, angular features, taking note of the straight bridge of his nose, the flat planes of his cheeks, his strong chin, and his clean jawline. On either side of his mouth arcing indentations were grooved to soften the harshness of its thin line. Sun creases fanned out from the corners of his eyes, tilting upward to emphasize the enigmatic gleam that was always in his dark eyes.

His hands and fingers were long and strong boned, but there was nothing slender or delicate about them. As Glenna watched their deft and competent movements, her imagination began weaving fantasies about their skill in a lover's caress and the sensations they might arouse on her sensitive skin. That thought was one step away from imagining the persuasive force of his mouth on hers. At that point Glenna brought her wayward thoughts to a screeching halt. Thinking about him in that way would not help their cause and would only serve to heighten her already overstimulated libido.

A much needed distraction was provided when the dinner plates were removed and coffee was served. Someone in Jett's party took out a pack of cigarettes and offered around the table. She shook her head in silent refusal.

"Do you mind if I I smoke?" Jett's eyebrow was quirked in accompaniment to his question.

"I don't mind." Glenna shook her head again.

Jett started to light it, then paused to glance at her father. "Would you like a cigarette, Orin?"

"No." His was a reluctant refusal. "The doctor made me quit smoking three years ago when I had my heart attack." He made no mention of his recent one.

"You seem to have enjoyed a full recovery." Jett exhaled a trail of smoke, studying her father through its grayness.

Glenna was surprised to hear her father admit, "I'm not the man I once was."

When the waiter returned a few minutes later to refill their coffee cups, a debate began among the guests whether to have more coffee or to visit the lounge for after-dinner drinks. The majority decided on the lounge, which started a general exodus from the table.

"Will you be joining us in the lounge?" Jett asked as her father pulled back her chair for Glenna to stand.

The glance she exchanged with her father indicated they were both of the same mind. "No, thank you. It's been a long day and I need my rest."

"Thank you for dinner, Mr. Coulson," Glenna added.

"It was my pleasure."

"We enjoyed the meal . . . and the company." Her father inserted his expression of gratitude. "Good night."

"Good night." His gaze touched each of them, lingering for a pulsing second on Glenna.

Outside the dining room Glenna and her father walked toward the elevators. Glenna was aware that she had too much nervous energy to go to sleep yet. She would simply toss and turn if she went to bed now.

"If you don't mind, Dad, I'm not coming up with you. I think I'll take a walk outside and enjoy a little of the night air before turning in," she explained.

"I certainly don't mind," he assured her. "I'll see you at breakfast in the morning."

"Good night." She brushed a kiss across his cheek, then left him to exit the hotel.

She was nearly to the door when she saw Jett

Coulson approaching. She felt the excited fluttering of her nerve ends, her pulse altering its rhythm to an uneven patter.

"Going for a stroll, Miss Reynolds?" His tone was mild.

Glenna stopped. "I thought I'd walk off some of the dinner before turning in."

He paused beside her, dangerously attractive in his dark evening clothes. "I was going to do the same. Do you want to join me?"

The levelness of his gaze held a silent challenge. Alarm bells rang in her head. Glenna knew exactly what would happen if she took a moonlight stroll with this man. So did he. She'd end up in his arms and if she didn't want that, now was the time to back off. But she knew that if she didn't go, she'd regret it later.

"Why not?" she agreed with a lift of a shoulder and returned the directness of his look.

Chapter Four

Outside the briskness of the night air had Glenna lift the silver shawl to cover the bareness of her shoulders and arms. The touch of coolness seemed to heighten her senses, making her keenly aware of the male figure walking a scant half step behind her.

Jett had allowed her to set the pace and the direction of their stroll. Glenna led him away from the stately white hotel onto the tree-shaded grounds. Once they had escaped the bright lights shining on the building, Glenna slowed her pace to wander beneath the trees.

Overhead the cloudless sky was a patchwork of stars. A misty moon sent its beams to illuminate the lawn wherever the newly leafed trees failed to shade it. Nature's creatures were offering their night songs to the breezeless air.

Glenna paused beneath a tree and leaned carefully against its rough trunk to gaze through the openings of its branches at the sequin-studded sky.

The shawl was hugged tightly around her, in defense of the slight chill.

The opening lines of a song came to her mind. "Almost heaven," she unconsciously murmured them aloud. Straightening from the tree trunk she glanced at Jett. He was watching her, his stance relaxed. "Do you remember the song 'Country Roads'?"

"Mmm." It was an affirmative response.

Glenna wandered to the edge of the shadow the tree cast in the moonlight. The ground beneath her feet was uneven so she moved carefully.

"West Virginia is my idea of 'almost heaven,'" she explained softly while her gaze continued to admire the night sky and the soothing night sounds.

"Is it?" Jett came up behind her, stopping at a point near her right shoulder. "The slogan on the license plate is a better description of West Virginia—'wild and wonderful.' Or is that your idea of 'almost heaven?'"

She sent him a sidelong glance, angled slightly over her shoulder. "Maybe. But I've never attempted to define it."

His head inclined slightly toward her. "What's that perfume you're wearing? It's been driving me crazy all evening."

Glenna marveled at the way he switched topics. Her mind raced to make the transition while her senses erupted with the intimation of his words.

"It's a new scent by Chanel. I've forgotten the name of it." It didn't seem important as she half turned to answer him. Raw warmth spread through her in anticipation of his next move.

His hand found the curve of her neck to tip her head back while his mouth came down to her lips. His kiss was sensually sure and softly exploring, his mouth moving back and forth across her lips with ease. Reaching out, his hand clasped her waist and turned her the rest of the way around to bring her fully into his embrace.

The warmth of his arms enfolded her, languidly heating her body with his. The sensations he was creating within her were much too enjoyable for her to resist. This absence of force was seduction in its purest and most dangerous form.

Her eyes were closed in dreamy contentment as his mouth wandered over her cheek to the lobe of her ear. The sliding caress of his hand along her neck succeeded in pushing her shawl off one shoulder. He bent his head to let his warm lips more intimately explore the rounded bone.

"Your skin reminds me of the smooth petal of a magnolia," Jett murmured against her skin, then slowly straightened.

Glenna raised her lashes to look at him, wishing he hadn't stopped so soon. His unfathomable black gaze wandered over her upturned face in a caressing fashion, yet managed to convey the impression that she was very special.

"Why do I have get the feeling that your father is setting me up for something?" It was a full moment before his casually worded question penetrated her sensually induced state of vulnerability.

Shock ran through her as Glenna realized his timing had been deliberate. Even now, while she was stiffening in his arms, his hand continued to trace the curving arc of her shoulder and neck, a thumb drawing circles on her sensitive skin. Her lips parted in a wordless and angry protest at the accusation, but her voice was temporarily lost to her.

But Jett didn't seem unduly perturbed that she failed to answer him. He continued to regard her with lazy alertness. "Your father is trying to hustle something. I haven't been able to decide whether it's his coal company . . . or if he's hustling you. If it's you, I might find it tempting."

When he lowered his head as if to kiss her again, Glenna lashed out with her hand, slapping his face in a flash of anger. Without pausing, she pivoted out of the loose hold of his arms, her back rigid, and began walking away.

Jett followed her with an amused taunt. "What happened? Did I come too close to the truth?"

"No!" Swinging her head around, she denied it too quickly and too vigorously. She realized that her anger had been born partly because Jett had seen through her father and partly because he could think so clearly while holding her in his arms. She felt somewhat guilty that her father did, in fact, want to discuss a merger with him. She shouldn't have slapped him, but to suggest that her father was hustling her was beyond insulting. Bowing her head she took a calming breath.

She grudgingly offered him an apology. "I'm sorry I slapped you, but don't you ever insult my father or me like that again."

His voice was thick with restrained laughter as his hands reached out to turn her around and span her waist. "Let's kiss and make up."

Glenna flattened her hands against his chest to

brace herself away from him, but he overpowered this resistance with little effort. His hands spread up her spine to shape her to his length, the slickness of her dress offering little protection from the searing impression made by his hard muscled body.

"You are the most—"

His soft, throaty chuckle foretold the futility of that. "I've heard all the adjectives before."

His hand cradled the back of her head to hold it still while his mouth covered her tightly compressed lips. There was no punishment in his kiss, only a devouring kind of passion that ate away at her defenses. It would have been so much easier for her to reject his embrace if he'd been hurting her.

Glenna could no longer remain stiff in his arms and let her body become pliant against his. Jett eased his mouth from her lips. "Should I turn the other cheek so you can slap it?"

She lowered her gaze from his sensually expert mouth to the white collar of his dress shirt, its paleness standing out sharply against the tan of his throat and the dark material of his suit. Her heartbeat was slow to return to its normal rate; so was her breathing.

"If you knew my father, you wouldn't have insinuated something like that. You're a powerful man. Used to getting your way, I'm sure, but," her voice was low, its pitch still disturbed by his kisses, "my my father never 'hustled' anyone in his life."

"Perhaps 'hustle' was a bad choice of verbs," Jett said and loosened the enclosing circle of his arms to permit more breathing room between them. "But I know when I'm being primed."

Glenna knew it was true. "My father is an honest man." She could look him in the eye and say that.

"I don't recall implying that he wasn't," he returned evenly and let his gaze run over her face. "I'm curious what part you play in his plans."

There was no need for her to deny that their weekend was more business than pleasure. "None. I'm just here if he needs me." Glenna shrugged because moral support was the limit of her involvement. She had never taken an active part in his business affairs. It would be a poor time to become involved now when a thorough knowledge of the business and skillful negotiations were required.

Jett didn't appear totally convinced by her reply, but seemed willing to withhold judgment. The corners of his mouth deepened in a dry smile as his arms slid from her to let her stand free.

"Do you think he will need you?" he mused.

Without the warmth of his body heat, Glenna shivered. She was done with his double-edged questions. "It's getting cool. I think I'll go in now."

If she expected a protest from Jett there was none forthcoming. "I'll walk with you."

They retraced their path to the hotel in silence. He stayed at her side until she reached the elevator. He saw her safely inside and punched the button to her floor.

"Good night, Glenna."

In her room, Glenna knocked once on the connecting door to her father's suite. There was only silence on the other side. She hesitated then opened the door to look in. She tiptoed to the bed where her father was sleeping peacefully, so she didn't waken him. It was a while before she fell asleep.

The ringing of the telephone wakened her the next morning. She groped blindly for the receiver as she tried to shake the sleep from her senses.

"Yes?" Her voice sounded as thick as her tongue felt.

"Wake up, sleepyhead," her father's cheerful voice said. "Rise and shine."

Glenna let her head fall back on the pillow while managing to keep the phone to her ear.

"What time is it?" She frowned drowsily.

"Eight A.M."

"Why did you call me? Why didn't you just knock on the door?" She sat up in bed and rubbed her eyes, trying to wipe the sleep out of them.

"I'm downstairs, that's why. I've been up for a couple of hours, took an early morning stroll. I thought I might run into Coulson, but he ordered breakfast in his room." The reference to Jett had Glenna's eyes wide open wide with the memory of last night. "Are you going to join me for breakfast or do I have to eat alone?"

"I'll be down, but Dad . . ." Glenna hesitated. "Don't try to see Jett until I've had a chance to talk to you."

"Why?" There was a puzzled note in his voice.

"I'll explain it all when I come down. Just give me a few minutes to wash my face and get dressed."

It took Glenna a fast twenty minutes to wash,

put on fresh makeup, and don a pair of wheat tan slacks with a matching knit top in narrow stripes of cream and tan. Her father was already seated at a table when she joined him in the restaurant for breakfast.

"What did you mean on the phone? Why do you need to talk to me?" her father queried almost before she had scooted her chair up to the table.

Briefly Glenna explained about Jett accompanying her on the walk last night, leaving out the intimate details of the kiss or his insulting comment. "He suspects that you're setting him up for something," she concluded.

"He said that?" A troubled frown puckered his brow.

"He said he knew he was being primed."

"Mmm." Orin Reynolds thought for a moment. "I don't want him to get the impression that I'm some kind of shyster, so I'll have to be more direct with him. Otherwise he won't believe that I want to make a legitimate business proposition."

"That's what I felt," she agreed.

"I had hoped to get on friendlier terms with him before making my proposal, but that's out." He sighed, then sent her a thin smile. "Thanks for the warning."

The waitress came to take their orders. It was a quiet meal with her father lost in his own thoughts.

There wasn't any sign of Jett around the hotel that morning. They didn't see him until lunchtime when they were seated at a table in the restaurant. Glenna saw him enter the room and managed a whispered "Dad" to draw her father's attention to the tall black-haired man approaching their table.

"Good afternoon." Jett's greeting encompassed both of them, a greeting that they echoed. He rested a hand on the back of Glenna's chair and leaned the other one on the table to face her at right angles. That caressing and intense look was in his eyes. "Would you like to play a game of tennis this afternoon? I have a court reserved for two o'clock."

His closeness had a heady effect on her. She glanced at her father to escape the spell Jett was casting over her. Her father mistook the glance, believing that she was seeking his permission.

"Go ahead and enjoy yourself. I'll find something to keep me amused," he insisted.

"Two o'clock then," Jett said, as if to confirm her attendance.

"I'll be there." Glenna nodded.

As Jett straightened to leave her father spoke up. "There is a business matter I would like to discuss with you when you have time."

Jett eyed her father with a knowing half smile. "I'm available at four thirty, if that suits you."

"It's fine." There was a wealth of confidence in Orin Reynolds's expression, every bit equal to Jett's. "My suite or yours?"

"Yours."

Glenna then remembered, "I didn't bring a tennis racket."

"I'll get one for you," Jett promised and moved away with a waving flick of his hand. He walked over to join two men that Glenna recognized as having attended the dinner the previous night, obviously two of his guests.

"Well, all my cards will be spread on the table by five this afternoon," her father stated with a resigned sigh.

"What do you think he will do?" Glenna picked up her glass of ice water and sipped at it to cool the heat coursing through her veins, all the while keeping track of Jett's movements over the rim of her glass.

"That is one man I wouldn't begin to second-guess," her father declared and crumpled the linen cloth protecting his lap, depositing it on the tabletop. "If you are ready to leave . . ."

Glenna's answer was to push her chair back and stand up. They returned to their suite of rooms so Glenna could change into her tennis clothes. She could hear her father prowling around in his adjoining room, alternately sitting and pacing. His tension became contagious. Everything they had rested on the outcome of his meeting with Jett this afternoon.

Wearing a white headband to keep the hair out of her eyes, she arrived at the tennis courts. Jett was waiting for her. He gestured to a trio of rackets. "Take your pick."

She tried each of them before choosing the second one. Her nerves felt as taut as the racket strings, a combination of apprehension for that afternoon's meeting and the increasing havoc Jett was wreaking on her senses.

They took the court and Glenna agreed with his suggestion to loosen up with a few practice volleys. Usually she was an above-average player, but she was lacking concentration. She started out playing badly.

Halfway through the first set Glenna hadn't scored once. What was more damning to her pride was the knowledge that Jett was not really trying to score. When she managed to get her serve in, he returned it and kept a slow volley going, never trying for a crosscourt or baseline. On her last serve she double-faulted to give him set point.

Angry with herself, and with him for being so condescending, Glenna barely glanced at him when they switched ends. But he goaded her in passing.

"You'd better get your mind on the game. Your problem is you're not concentrating."

The criticism was a stinging prod. Glenna returned his first serve with a blistering crosscourt shot that caught him flat-footed. From that point on her game improved, yet she was never equal to Jett. He would let her draw close, even win a game or two, but each time the match was in jeopardy, he'd slam home a shot that she couldn't return.

The strong competitive streak within Glenna refused to let her quit. Jett was controlling the game, running her legs off, but she kept battling until he won the match point. Perspiration ran in rivulets down her neck as she walked in defeat toward the net. Winded, she was gripping her side while he vaulted the net, barely out of breath.

"Congratulations." The handshake she offered him was limp, as exhausted as her voice.

"Tired?" There was a taunting smile in his tone. Resentment flared wearily in her gray green eyes as she wiped her forehead with the back of her hand. Turning, she walked slowly off the court, aware that Jett fell in step with her.

"You could have annihilated me," she accused. "Wiped me off the court anytime you wanted. You were toying with me, playing cat and mouse."

"I thought it was more of a contest, didn't you?" He handed her a towel.

"I don't think you even worked up a sweat," Glenna complained, her voice partially muffled by the towel she used to wipe her face.

"I did," he assured her on a lazy note. "You're a pretty good player when you concentrate."

"No mouse likes to be patronized." She draped the towel around her neck, letting the ends hang down the front.

"I've never seen a mouse with chestnut hair or such a temper," Jett chided with a wicked glint in his eye.

Her breath had returned to a more even rate. She lifted her head and looked at him. "I'm not really a sore loser, although it might sound like that. It's just that . . . being allowed to come close is almost as bad as being allowed to win," she explained.

"You have a point." His hands caught the ends of her towel, pulling her closer to him. With each breath, she inhaled his earthy male scent, heightened by perspiration and the heat of exertion. It did funny things to her pulse. "But I didn't intend to patronize. You're a fierce competitor. I thought you were entitled to some kind of reward for your efforts. You just wouldn't give up."

"I never quit." It was unthinkable.

Jett wiped her cheek with an end of her towel,

managing to give the impression of a caress. "I realize that."

Then his hand was under her chin, lifting it so his mouth could claim her lips. Glenna tasted the salty flavor of him and swayed against the hard support of his length. She was still thirsting for more of his kisses when he slowly drew away from her clinging lips.

"I suppose you mentioned last night's conversation to your father. Is that why he asked to meet me this afternoon?" Jett murmured.

Dammit! He was doing it again, catching her off guard while her senses were drugged by the potency of his kisses. Glenna straightened from him, and tried to contain her irritation.

"Yes, I told him," she admitted since there wasn't any point in lying. "I think he wants to meet with you to change the impression you were forming about him."

"What does he want to talk to me about?" Jett continued to watch her while he slipped his tennis racket into its protective carrying case.

"Dad could explain it better than I can." Glenna didn't try to convince him that she didn't know. "I told you before I'm not involved with any of his business affairs."

"Then it is about business?" he pressed.

"Yes." she said in a clipped tone. She picked up the tennis racket she had used, holding it in an attitude of indecision. "What am I supposed to do with this?" Glenna made a subconscious attempt to divert the conversation.

Jett motioned to an attendant. "He'll return it." Glenna handed it to the young boy who jogged over. As soon as he'd left Jett asked, "Will you be at the meeting?"

"Probably. Why?" she challenged.

"I just wondered." With a hand resting on the small of her back, he guided her away from the tennis courts.

Glenna was wary of such a noncommittal answer, considering that he was always so direct. "What did you wonder?"

His sidelong glance held her gaze for a moment. "If you were a shill."

"A shill," she repeated in growing indignation.

"A shill is an old-time gambling term. It refers to a partner, a decoy used to dupe the victims into a game—usually a crooked game," he explained.

"I know what it means," Glenna retorted, "and I'm not one."

"It's possible that your presence could be used to divert my attention. You are a very attractive diversion." His glance was swiftly assessing.

Glenna didn't trust herself to look at him, certain she would slap him again. "That isn't why I'm here, but I understand why you'd think so."

"So you said." He nodded.

"You really have a very suspicious mind," she stated in a low, angry breath. "Does everybody have to have an angle, some ulterior motive?"

"They don't have to but they usually do." His delivery was smooth, but there was a wealth of cynicism in his words.

"Maybe it's because you do most of your business with underhanded people instead of honest ones like my father," Glenna suggested dryly.

"Get burned a few times and you'll get leery of fire, too."

Her gaze slid to his face, noting the grimness of his mouth and the forbidding set of his jaw. Glenna realized that his toughness, his hardness, came from harsh experience. It lessened her irritation.

"I don't have to be at the meeting," she pointed out. "If it would make you feel more secure, or less suspicious, I'll go for a swim or something. There isn't anything I can contribute to the discussion, anyway. And I certainly don't want you to think of me as a shill. Neither would Dad."

As they stopped in front of the elevators, Jett studied her for a long second before commenting on her suggestion. "I have no objection to you being at the meeting. If you want to attend, you can."

"I want to be there." She knew her presence would provide moral support for her father, which was of greater importance than Jett's distrust.

The elevator doors slid soundlessly open as a bell chimed overhead. Glenna stepped to one side to let its passengers walk by her before entering the empty elevator ahead of Jett.

CHAPTER FIVE

The meeting was nerve-racking for Glenna. She was curled in a chair off to one side, trying to be as unobtrusive as possible. Her father had begun the meeting by first establishing the profitability of the mine, producing studies and reports for Jett's examination. From there he had gone on to explain the previous years' financial difficulties, then the inspection order for safety improvements, and the long appeals in order to raise the money to comply with the required standards.

All the while Jett had listened, looked over the papers and reports, and studied the man doing the talking. His face had been devoid of expression the entire time. Never once had he glanced at Glenna since greeting her shortly after he had arrived. She shifted in her chair to ease a cramped leg, yet the movement didn't attract his attention.

"I think that gives you a fairly good idea of my present dilemma." Her father leaned back in his chair to study Jett and try to read his reaction. After an instant's pause he laid out his proposal. "And why I am anxious to form an association . . .

a merger with your firm, to obtain the financial strength I need."

Jett glanced over a report in his hand before leaning forward to set it atop others on the table. "You have explained that your credit has been overextended because of recent economic reversals in the industry. While your operation can't be classified as lucrative, it appears to be stable. Lending institutions have made loans on less strength than what you've shown me. Their reason for refusing you can't be based on your indebtedness or lack of collateral. What was it?"

"As you know, a single mine owner is in a precarious position. He virtually has a one-man operation. If something happens to that one man, there is no operation. On the other hand"—her father shrugged—"your company is made up of a team of men. If something happens to one of them, you replace him, but the loss of one man does not jeopardize your company's existence."

"True," Jett agreed and waited for him to continue.

As Glenna studied her father she noticed the tightening of his mouth. She was well aware of the effort it took for her father to finish his explanation.

"In the last three years I've had two heart attacks. A year from now I may not be here. That's why I can't get a loan," he explained. "If I'm gone, who would run the mine? Glenna couldn't. Her skills happen to be in another field. I've always wanted her to concentrate on the work she loves. Without me there's no one to run the operation and make sure the debts are paid."

His statement prompted Glenna to unwittingly ask aloud. "What about Bruce?"

Tired gray eyes sent her a rueful look. "Bruce is

a competent individual when he has someone to give him directions. He's a stopgap, capable of holding things together alone only over a short period of time," he explained to both her and Jett.

Her gaze was magnetically drawn to Jett. He was eyeing her with quiet contemplation, but she was struck by the emotionless set of his features. When his gaze broke contact with hers, it was to slide downward and linger on the soft outline of her lips. This betrayal of interest was the first he'd shown toward her. It was quickly gone as his attention reverted to her father.

"Without this merger I stand to lose a great deal," Orin said, "But I'm not the only one who would suffer. The economy of our small community rests on the mine. I don't know how many could survive if the mine closes for an extended period of time."

"I can appreciate what you are saying and understand the devastating effects this would have," Jett said.

"Naturally I don't have to point out the tax advantages your company would enjoy by absorbing my operation. I wouldn't even make this proposition if there wasn't a way you could benefit from it," her father insisted, then paused as if suddenly realizing he had no more arguments to make. "I don't expect you to give me an answer right away. You need time to consider it."

"If I may, I'd like to take a copy of the reports you've shown me so I can go over them with my partners." He gestured toward the papers on the table.

"You can take those," her father offered.

"Between tonight and tomorrow I'll have a chance to study them." When Jett uncoiled his length to stand, it signaled an end to the meeting.

Whatever followed was merely a formality. "I'll let you know tomorrow afternoon whether I think your proposal is something my company would wish to pursue."

"That sounds fair enough to me." Orin rose with difficulty to shake hands.

Glenna stood, too, as Jett picked up the stack of reports. Her gaze searched his face, but whatever opinion he had was not etched in his features. With a nodded farewell in her direction, he let her father escort him to the door.

When the door was closed behind him, her father turned back to the center of the room, glanced at Glenna, and sighed heavily. "We only have twenty-four more hours to wait before we have an answer. At least we won't be kept dangling for days."

"Excuse me, Dad." She hurried to the door that Jett had just exited. "I'll be right back."

"Where are you going?" he asked.

"I just want to have a word with him." Glenna rushed and disappeared into the hallway. She walked swiftly, and in the corridor ahead of her she saw him opening the door to his suite. "Jett." The firm ring of her voice made him stop to wait for her. He paused on the threshold of his suite, an eyebrow slightly quirked in silent inquiry and speculation.

As soon as she reached him Jett entered his suite, sending an invitation over his shoulder for her, "Come in." From the doorway Glenna noticed a second person in the sitting room of Jett's suite. A conservative suit and tie covered his portly figure and his balding head made him appear considerably older than she suspected he was. When he saw Glenna following Jett into the suite he stood up quickly, self-consciously smoothing his tie down the front of his protruding stomach and trying not to show his surprise.

"This is Don Sullivan," Jett introduced the man in an offhand manner. "He works for our company in an organizational capacity. Don, meet Glenna Reynolds."

"Nice to meet you, Mr. Sullivan," Glenna murmured as the man bobbed his head in her direction with faint embarrassment. She bit at the inside of her lip, wondering if she was going to get a chance to speak to Jett alone.

But he was already arranging it. "Would you mind stepping into the other room for a few minutes, Don?" It was an order, phrased as a question. Before the man could take a step, Jett was handing him the reports her father had let him take. "I want you to look these over, too, so we can discuss them later."

"I will." Again the man bobbed his head at Glenna as he moved his stocky frame toward an inner door.

When it was closed and they were alone Jett turned slowly to meet Glenna's steady look. "You wanted to speak to me?"

"I said that I didn't have anything to add to the conversation, but I wanted to tell you that my father told you the whole truth. He didn't leave anything out," she said evenly. "I wanted to be sure you knew that, considering how suspicious you are."

"I ran a check on your father. The report came back before I met with him this afternoon," he stated. "So I was already familiar with his present situation."

"Then why didn't you let him know?" Glenna frowned.

"If your father is the businessman that I think he

is, he already knows I had him checked out. He would have done the same thing in my place." Jett picked up a sheaf of papers that Don Sullivan had been working on when they had come in, and glanced through them.

The implied compliment for her father eased some of her tension. "I'm glad you know he's an honest businessman."

"Your father mentioned two facts I didn't know . . . and would probably have had difficulty obtaining. So, yes, I believe he gave me a fair picture." He replaced the loose papers on the table where he'd found them and allowed a faint smile to touch his mouth when he looked at Glenna. "Does that reassure you?"

"Yes." There was an inward sigh of relief. A noise in the adjoining room reminded her of the man waiting for him. She took a step toward the hall door. "I won't keep you any longer."

"What? Aren't you going to add more to your father's appeal?" A gentle mockery gleamed in his dark eyes, taunting but not cruelly so.

"Would it do any good?" Glenna countered in light challenge.

"It might prove entertaining," he replied with a raking look that was deliberately suggestive. Then his expression sobered. "Know that I will consider it as seriously as I would any business proposition."

Glenna couldn't expect more than that. "Thank you," she murmured and left the room.

Despite the reassurance, waiting for Jett's decision was difficult both for Glenna and her father. Throughout the evening she wavered between a certainty that Jett would agree and a cold fear that he would not. She knew that whatever was happening between them would have no bearing on his decision. She couldn't expect it to.

She slept restlessly, waking with the first glint of dawn. After lying in bed for nearly an hour trying to go back to sleep, Glenna climbed out of bed and dressed in a pair of dark blue slacks and a cream white velour sweater. It was half-past five when she ventured into the corridor to take the elevator downstairs.

In the hotel lobby Glenna skirted the restaurant with its aroma of fresh-perked coffee in favor of the invigorating crispness of the early morning air, seeking its quiet serenity to soothe her troubled mind. She wandered through the dew-wet grounds with no particular destination in mind.

For a while it seemed she had the grounds all to herself, sharing the yellow morning with only the twittering birds in the trees, until she noticed a man strolling alongside the hotel road. She recognized him immediately, her pulses quickening. She turned to walk toward him, neither hurrying her pace nor slowing it.

As she drew closer, she saw that he was dressed in his evening clothes—or had been. The tie was unknotted and hanging loosely around his neck, the top buttons of his white shirt unfastened. His suit jacket was slung over one shoulder, held by the hook of his finger, and his sharply creased slacks looked wrinkled. There was even a dusty film dulling the polished sheen of his black shoes.

"If you are just coming in, it must have been some party," Glenna remarked when Jett was within hearing. "What happened?"

He ignored her tease and both stopped when only two feet separated them. "You're an early bird this morning."

"I couldn't go back to sleep so I got up." Her gray green eyes inspected the weary lines in his face and the rumpled blackness of his thick hair. "Haven't you been to bed?"

"No. After dinner I went over some business with Don. It was around two A.M. before he left the suite. I went for a walk out in the hills to do some thinking, and stayed around to watch the sun come up." His features took on a faraway look when he partially glanced over his shoulder in the general direction he'd just come from.

Glenna leaned toward him, reading something in his expression that gripped her throat. "Have you decided about the merger?" she asked tightly.

His gaze glided to her face, moving over it for an instant, the line of his mouth slanting. "I'll give your father my answer this afternoon."

"Are you still considering it?" She couldn't help but ask. A breeze came whirling out of the trees to blow across her face, briefly lifting the chestnut hair away from her neck before it danced away.

Jett rested a heavy hand atop her shoulder. "There is a lot to consider, Glenna."

"I'm sure there is," she agreed on a subdued note, lowering her gaze to the front of his shirt. "It's just that the waiting is hard."

"All decisions are hard. Life is hard." His voice was gentle, but the grip of his hand applied pressure to her shoulder bone, drawing her half a step closer. He swung his jacket behind her in order to lock both his hands behind her neck. "It would have been easy if you had been the one to suggest a different kind of merger with me." The seductive pitch of his voice made it plain that he had something much more intimate in mind than a business liaison. "You present a very attractive package."

Glenna was conscious that he had bent his head toward her, but she didn't lift her gaze. If he was trying to divert her thoughts from her father, he was succeeding with his closeness. The flattery wasn't necessary.

"You don't have to say that. I don't need to be sweet-talked out of asking questions about your decision. I can accept the fact that you haven't made up your mind, and I can accept the fact that your decision ultimately has nothing to do with this, us," she told him.

"Glenna, I never say anything I don't mean." The firmness of his tone enforced his statement, compelling her to tip her head up to examine his face.

There were still signs of tiredness and lack of sleep etched in his features, but the smoldering intensity of his eyes made her breathing shallow. Jett eliminated the last few inches to claim her curving mouth while his hands slid down her back to enfold her in his arms.

Her senses erupted with a wonderful raw intensity that needed his embrace to soothe it. Everywhere her body came in contact with his muscled frame a wild current seemed to flow between them; a current that spread its tingling pleasure through the rest of her flesh. The ache of passion knotted her abdomen. It was all she could do to not lose herself in his arms. With effort, she tempered the ardency of her response until she regained control of her senses to end the kiss.

She knew the sexual attraction Jett had aroused in her, but their previous kisses had not led her to expect this flaming leap into desire. It shook her. Glenna felt the weakness in her knees and didn't try to immediately move away from him. Her hands were spread across his shirtfront. Beneath them she could feel the thudding of his heartbeat, its tempo disturbed like hers was.

"Your volatility isn't limited to your temper, is it?" Jett mused.

"I don't know what happened. I—" Glenna half turned, self-conscious and unnerved by how easily he saw through her.

"Hey, I'm not complaining." He chuckled and caught at her hand, clasping it warmly within his fingers. "Why don't we sit down near that tree, rest a little before making the long walk back to the hotel?" He led her toward a large tree on the lawn.

"The grass is wet," she pointed out, the green blades of grass glistening with the sheen of dew. Jett solved that problem by spreading his suit jacket on the grass. "It'll get grass stains on it."

"So? I'll send it to the cleaners." He lowered himself to the ground and pulled Glenna down beside him on the other half of his jacket. The trunk of the tree served as a backrest for him, but it wasn't wide enough for Glenna to lean against it, too. Instead Jett shifted her so she was resting diagonally across his chest, his arms overlapping around her waist. "Mmm." He nuzzled the curve of her neck. "Maybe I couldn't sleep last night because I was missing this."

The stubble of his beard growth was pleasantly rough against her sensitive skin. It conveyed the rasping caress of a cat's tongue as he rubbed his chin and jaw along her neck. The hard support of his chest and arms, and the pressure of his hip bone began to embed themselves on her flesh. Glenna felt herself slipping again into that mindless oblivion of sensation. She changed her position to elude the mouth exploring the sensitive hollow behind her ear, turning sideways in his arms to rest a shoulder against his chest.

"What's wrong?" Jett cupped a hand to her cheek, tipping her head so he could inspect her face.

"Nothing." It seemed impossible that she had only known him for two days. The angled planes of his features seemed so very familiar to her. Glenna wanted to slow down this thing between them before it carried her away.

His hand idly left her face to reach down to lift her left hand. His gaze studied the bareness of her fingers, his thumb running over the tops of them. When he lifted his gaze there was interest, curiosity, and the banked flame of desire gleaming in his look. "No rings," Jett observed. "Have there ever been any?"

"If you mean, have I ever been married? No," she replied with a slight shake of her head.

"Engaged?"

"No." The latent sexiness of his look was having a chaotic effect on her pulse.

"How old are you?" Jett continued with his questions.

"Twenty-four."

"No steady boyfriends?"

"None." At the skeptical lift of his eyebrow, Glenna qualified her answer. "Not unless you count Bruce."

"Bruce Hawkins. The man who manages the mine for your father?"

"Yes. Bruce and I have become close friends since my father had his first attack. Since Dad has to stay home more often, Bruce comes to the house a lot to discuss things with him," she explained.

"He's been like a brother to you then, another member of the family," he deduced.

"Something like that," Glenna said.

His hand continued to massage her fingers, rubbing them in a sensuous manner that aroused all sorts of tremors. "Do you think he regards you as a sister?"

After a pause she admitted, "I don't think so."

"Neither do I."

Jett released her hand to let his fingers seek the mass of hair at the back of her head. By the time Glenna realized his intention she had lost the will to resist. The searing possession of his mouth parted her lips so he could deepen the kiss with the intimacy of his exploring tongue. Hot flames shot through her veins, melting her bones and burning her flesh with a feverish heat.

Her hand slid under his arm to circle the back of his waist, her fingers spreading over the taut muscles of his spine. When he uncombed his fingers from her hair, he cradled her head on the flexed muscle of his upper arm. She let her fingers glide up the front of his shirt to slide inside his collar, discovering the exhilarating feel of his tanned throat beneath her hand and the wild tattoo of the vein in his neck. She was starting to feel too much for this man, who literally held her family's future in his hands.

Glenna shuddered with intense longing. The quiver continued when she felt the touch of his fingers pushing their way under her sweater to the bare skin over her rib cage. The breath she took became lodged somewhere, time standing still as he cupped a ripe breast in the circling cradle of his hand.

Through the spinning recesses of her mind a

voice asked if what she felt was real, or whether it was simply desire that had been suppressed too long and was now being uncovered by an expert. Her conscience rejected becoming sexually involved without the accompaniment of emotion in both partners.

Trembling, but with growing strength, Glenna began to strain away from his drugging kisses. At the first sign of resistance Jett reined in his own passion, not wanting to force her.

When he lifted his head, both were breathing raggedly. Glenna sat up, shakily tucking a strand of auburn hair behind her ear. Silence stretched between them for several seconds. Then Jett rolled to his feet and held out a hand to pull her upright.

"Have you had breakfast?" he asked when she was standing.

"No. I wasn't hungry." She watched him bend to scoop up his suit jacket.

"Are you hungry now?" His fingertips touched her elbow to start her in the direction of the hotel.

"A little."

"For food?" His downward glance noted the very faint blush in her cheeks.

"No."

"Glenna."

Something in his voice made her look at him. He was watching her with an intensity that she found a little frightening.

"What?" she prompted when he didn't speak.

A tiny frown appeared between his eyebrows as his gaze swung to the front. "It wasn't important." He seemed suddenly very remote. Lifting a hand, he rubbed the side of his jaw. "I need a shave . . . and some sleep."

Glena fell into an uneasy silence. Jett made no attempt to break it during the walk back to the hotel. Shortly after they had entered the lobby Glenna spied her father.

"There you are, Glenna." He hurried toward them. "I wondered where you went. Have you had breakfast?" A frown clouded his expression when he recognized Jett and took in his slightly disheveled appearance. "Good morning, Jett."

"Good morning, Orin," he replied and immediately excused himself. "I'll talk with both of you later today."

As Jett walked to the elevators Glenna turned to explain how she had come to meet him.

CHAPTER SIX

Glenna glanced at her watch for what seemed like the fifth time in the last five minutes. Irritated that so little time had passed, she turned and retraced her path to the window overlooking the front grounds of the hotel. It was the same view of trees, grass, and the driveway. She wandered back toward the door of the suite.

"You are going to wear a hole in the carpet if you keep walking back and forth in the same place," her father complained, chiding her good naturedly while he drummed his fingers on the armrest of his chair.

"You aren't exactly a picture of serenity," Glenna retorted dryly.

"No, I suppose I'm not," he admitted, releasing a long breath.

"Maybe I should call him," she suggested. "He might not realize we're waiting for him. There wasn't any specific time mentioned."

"Coulson knows we're waiting to hear from him," he assured her. "He'll be here . . . sooner or later."

Glenna threaded her fingers together, squeezing

them tightly while she tried to ignore the tension churning her stomach. Restlessly, her gaze searched the room for something to distract her attention from the endless waiting.

A sharp knock at the door snapped the fragile thread of her control. She whirled toward the sound then paused to meet her father's glance. He drew in a deep breath and forced a grim smile on his mouth. Taking his lead, Glenna gathered together her composure before forcing herself to walk to the door.

Turning the knob, she stepped to one side as she opened it. She struggled with her nervousness when she met the blandness of his gaze. She even managed a smile of welcome.

"Sorry I kept you waiting. I was delayed or I would have been here sooner," Jett explained smoothly, pausing while Glenna closed the door behind him. "I received a long-distance phone call just as I was about to leave."

Her gaze searched the impenetrable mask of his features. "You look rested. Did you get some sleep?" she asked as they walked the rest of the way into the room where her father was seated.

"A couple of hours," he answered.

Her alert gaze had already noted his smoothly shaven face and the starched crispness of his striped shirt and charcoal slacks. With him, Jett had the reports her father had given him the previous afternoon. Yet, more than the freshness of his appearance, Glenna noticed the coolness of his attitude. The pleasantness was all on the surface. A chill ran up her spine as she darted a look at her father.

When Jett walked over to set the reports on the

table beside his chair, her father said, quite calmly, "It's no, isn't it?"

Her gaze raced to Jett, unwilling to believe her father could be right, but Jett didn't glance at her. He met the pair of gray eyes squarely, without a flicker of regret.

"I'm afraid it is."

Glenna nearly choked on the bitter taste of defeat, but she didn't make a sound. Her personal disappointment was fleeting. If the announcement was a crushing blow to her, it had to be much more severe for her father. It was his life's work that was being lost. Yet the stoic acceptance he was displaying over Jett's decision made her heart swell with pride.

"Very well," he nodded. "It was worth a try."

"May I ask why you turned down his proposal?" Glenna felt her voice sounded quite calm, with only a trace of rawness in its tone.

"It's quite simple." The piercing blackness of his gaze was turned to her. "If my company is interested in acquiring your mine, it would make more economic sense to let him go broke. A merger would mean assuming all of his debts and liabilities as well as his assets. Those debts are more than the mine is worth. This wipes out the tax savings. Therefore, the merger isn't to our advantage."

"I understand." Despite her outward composure, inside she was raging at his coldly logical reasoning. It bothered her that it didn't take any human factor into account.

As if reading her mind, his gaze narrowed and he continued. "Your father would be the only one who would really benefit from the merger. And Coulson Mining is not a charitable institution." He turned back to her father. "This was strictly a busi-

ness matter. We had to make a business decision."
It was a statement that carried no apology for the
outcome.

"I understand perfectly," her father replied. "I
didn't want you to regard it in any other manner."

There was a second's pause before Jett extended
an arm to shake her father's hand. "I wish you luck,
Orin."

"A gambler can always use some of that." A wan
smile pulled at the corners of her father's mouth
in an attempt at humor.

After he had released her father's hand, Jett
rested his gaze for a scant second on Glenna. Then
he crossed the room to the door and left without another word.

His departure released the paralysis that had
gripped her limbs. Glenna moved to her father's
chair, wanting to comfort him and wanting to be
comforted herself. She reached out to tentatively
rest a hand on his shoulder, worried by the lack of
expression in his face. He patted her hand almost
absently.

"We'll figure something out, Daddy." She realized
she hadn't called him that since she was a child.

"No, we've lost it. The mine, the house, everything," he declared on a hollow note, staring off
into space. "If a merger wasn't profitable for
Coulson, there isn't anyone else who can help us.
I'm through. Finished."

"Don't say that." She knelt beside his chair, fighting the tears that were making the huge lump in
her throat. "You're a Reynolds, remember? We
never quit."

He didn't seem to hear her. She searched wildly
through her mind for some alternative, some

other way to save everything, but there was only blankness.

"I'm tired, Glenna," he said after what seemed like several minutes. His eyes appeared empty when he looked at her. "I think I'll lie down for a while. Will you help me up?"

The request frightened her as nothing else had. He had always been too proud to ask for help, or to admit he needed it. His pride was broken. Glenna felt she was picking up the pieces when she slipped an arm around him to help him out of the chair. She walked with him to his bed and spread the light coverlet over him.

"You'll feel better after you rest," she said in an effort to reassure herself. "Later on we'll call room service and order steak and champagne. We're going to go out in style, remember, Dad?"

"I don't think I'll feel like eating tonight." He closed his eyes.

Glenna stared at him, then finally pulled up a chair beside his bed. He appeared to sleep. She remained near him, worried about his heart and wanting to be there if he became ill.

At seven o'clock she had a sandwich sent up for herself and a bowl of soup for her father. She was partially reassured when he wakened and voluntarily sat up to eat the soup. He continued to be withdrawn and unresponsive to her attempts at conversation, but the leadenness of depression had left his eyes. She turned on the television for a while until he announced that he wanted to go to sleep. Leaving the connecting door ajar, Glenna returned to her own suite.

Chapter Seven

Mechanically, Glenna changed out of her clothes into her turquoise green nightgown and matching satin robe. She realized she truly had packed the best of her clothes. So many things were running through her mind, leaving no room to feel like sleeping. She moved restlessly around the room, slipping in to check on her father half a dozen times.

Her head was pounding with the effort to find a solution. Her father insisted that Jett Coulson had been their only possible source of help. And what of their burgeoning relationship? Was it even that? Was he just toying with her because he knew that they needed his help? She didn't want to believe it.

Pressing a hand to her forehead, Glenna tried to rationally think. Jett was attracted to her. He couldn't have faked that. He had made his decision on a purely business basis, she understood that. But what if she appealed to him on a personal level? Could she persuade him to reconsider?

A calmness settled over her. She had to find out. For the sake of her father, she had to try.

With a course of action chosen, Glenna moved to carry it out.

The hotel corridor was empty when she walked out. She walked swiftly to the door of Jett's suite and knocked lightly on it. Only at that second did she consider the possibility that he might not be alone—or that he might not even be there. And then the latch turned. When Jett opened the door a quick glance past him found no one else in the sitting room.

He stood in the opening, one hand holding the door and the other resting on the frame. Under the steadiness of his gaze, Glenna couldn't find her voice. Taking his time, he let his gaze travel over the draping fabric of her robe as it outlined the jutting curves of her breasts and hips. She realized she hadn't changed into something more appropriate. Her hand moved to finger the satin ribbon at the front of her robe to make sure it still secured the front.

Without saying a word, Jett opened the door wider and moved out of the way. She hesitated before gliding past him into the sitting room. She turned around to face him when she heard the click of the door latch. He was wearing the same pale gray striped shirt he'd had on this afternoon, but the sleeves were rolled up to expose his tanned forearms.

"I knew you would come to see me." He went to a table strewn with papers that he'd obviously been working on, and half sat on the edge.

"Then you know why I'm here." Her voice came out a little less controlled and huskier than she'd intended.

There was a pack of cigarettes amid the stacks of papers. Jett removed one from the pack and lit it.

"You came to see if you could persuade me to reconsider your father's proposal." He sounded so distant that Glenna unconsciously moved closer to him.

"Is it so much to ask, Jett?" she questioned. "You have the means. My father has everything at stake. His whole life's work."

"A good gambler always keeps an ace up his sleeve. I wondered if your father was going to play his ace of hearts." He studied her through the smoke screen of his burning cigarette.

"Ace of hearts? Are you referring to me?" Glenna frowned. "I thought we went through this. My father doesn't even know I'm here."

"He doesn't?" An eyebrow was arched in question.

"He's in his room, sleeping. He has no idea that I'm here. If he knew—" When she imagined her father's reaction, she averted her glance from Jett. "He wouldn't approve."

"You're here on your own. I know that. I'm sorry," Jett said.

She watched as he reached across the table for an ashtray. With one hip on the edge of the table and his other leg braced in front of him, he held the ashtray in the palm of his hand, the forearm resting on his thigh. She couldn't help noticing how his relaxed stance stretched the material of his slacks tautly across the hard columns of his legs.

"I don't think you understand how serious this situation is. It isn't just the mine that my father's going to lose, but his home, everything he's worked for all his life. The workers would lose their jobs and the community will suffer through a depression. So many families would be affected.

Not just ours. In his condition my father can't start all over. They depend on him."

"I know, he'll be lucky to end up with the clothes on his back." Jett took a drag of his cigarette, squinting at her through the smoke that swirled up. "That's one of the things I learned when I ran a check on him. I admired the way he underplayed how much he stood to lose, as if he had something tucked away while he was betting his last dollar. He's a proud man with a lot of class."

"You should've seen him after you left this afternoon." Glenna laced her fingers together in front of her, twisting them as she tried not to remember how he'd looked. "You broke him. I've never seen him like that—with no fight left in him—no pride. He's given up. When you left, he laid down as if he hoped he would fall asleep and die. I sat with him, trying to think of a way I could—" Her throat tightened, choking off the last of the sentence.

"That's when you thought to come here." His gruffness drew her glance. An agitated impatience dominated his action as he crushed his cigarette in the ashtray and set it aside.

"You were his last hope, Jett. There isn't anyone else in a position to help him." She took another step toward him, reaching out to touch his arm in a beseeching gesture. "I accept that as a business move a merger with Dad might not be that beneficial to you. But can't you reconsider his proposal on a personal level? Help him because he needs it?"

A muscle flexed in his jaw as his impenetrable gaze locked with hers. With an almost violent abruptness, he straightened from the table, moving so suddenly that one minute her hand was touching his arm and in the next there was only empty air.

"You don't know what you're asking, Glenna."

He shook his head with an angry kind of weariness, his hand on his hip.

"He needs you," Glenna stood quietly in front of him. "Explain to me what I have to say or do to make you listen to me."

"What if I told you to take off your robe?" His glance flicked to the satin bow with raw challenge.

"Is that what you want? Is this what your business decision was about, Jett?" Glenna countered in a tight voice.

"I want you, Glenna. I never lied about that," he answered.

Glenna realized that in her twenty-four years she'd never known a man who could make her feel the way he did. And yet his aloofness and complete disregard for the human level of her father's business proposition angered her. It hurt her that though he couldn't help her father and their community, he could say he still desired her. She knew she'd never see him again, but she wanted to know his touch, if only for tonight. Slowly she raised a hand to untie the front bow. Her fingers trembled slightly as she pulled an end of the ribbon to unfasten it. When it was untied she eased the robe from her shoulders and let the shiny material slide down her arms. Catching it with one hand before it reached the floor, she reached out to lay it on the table atop his papers. Then, boldly, Glenna lifted her gaze to his face.

An inner warmth kept her from feeling the coolness of the air touching her exposed skin. The matching nightgown was styled like a slip. Turquoise green lace, the same shade as the satin material, trimmed the bodice. The clinging fabric revealed the rounded shape of her breasts, her nipples appearing as small buttons beneath the material. After tapering in at the waistline, the nightgown flared gently over her hips, ending just below her knees. The lace-trimmed hemline stopped where the gown was split up the side, almost midthigh.

Jett was making note of each detail before he finally returned her look. The black fires leaping in his eyes ignited an answering spark in the lower half of her body, aroused by the rapacious hunger in his gaze. Glenna swayed toward him. There was a slight tremor in his hands as he reached out to loosely grip the sides of her waist.

"How can I persuade you to change your mind, Jett?" Her voice was one step away from a whisper. At this point, it wasn't about her father anymore. It was about her, what she wanted.

Her fingers were splayed across the front of his shoulders. Beneath the material of his shirt, she could feel the tautness of his muscles, as if he was holding all his instinct in check.

"This is an appeal to the lascivious side of my nature?" he asked as his wandering gaze noted the uneven rise and fall of her breasts beneath the lace bodice of her nightgown. "You came here tonight to convince me to help by tempting me with your body." He said it, but he didn't believe that. He was goading her, pushing her. He couldn't stop himself from doing it.

She gazed straight into those midnight black eyes. "I love my father. I can't stand by while he's being destroyed without trying to save him. I came here to talk to you. To tell you things he may have left out. I also came here because . . ."

"Why did you think you could change my mind?" His breath fanned her temples, warm and tangy, while his hands inched her closer to him.

"I'm a grown woman, Jett. I know that business and pleasure don't mix. But I also know that you have a human side. I thought you felt something for me, but I don't know if what I feel is real or not," Glenna admitted on a breathless note because his mouth was nuzzling her cheek and ear.

Jett murmured unintelligibly, working his way to the curve of her neck. "You're irresistible. You knew exactly what would happen when you knocked on my door."

"I wanted to talk to you, but I knew there would be this." She tipped her head to one side, giving him more access to the sensitive areas he sought and inviting him to continue the stimulating exploration.

From the base of her throat, he nibbled up the other side of her neck. A soft moan escaped her lips as they sought the satisfaction of his kiss. His mouth hardened on hers, spreading a hot and brilliant glow through her body. The pressure of his hands increased, threatening to bruise her ribs as the intensity of his need engulfed him. His tongue probed apart her lips and teeth to unite with hers.

Her hands slid around his neck, her fingers seeking the thickness of his lustrous black hair. A fiery heat seemed to turn her bones to liquid as the crush of his hands fitted her to his length. And still she felt as if she was committing treason. She only wanted to brand the memory of his smell and taste in her mind. The sleek material of her gown was a thin barrier, blocking out none of the sensations of his hard embrace. His caressing hands made restless forays over her shoulders, back, and hips, relentless in their need to touch and possess every possible inch of her.

Slowly, Jett dragged his mouth from hers while raising his head no more than a breath's reach from her lips. "You know I want to make love to you." His low husky voice was a rough caress. "I can feel the way you're vibrating."

"Jett." Her face remained uplifted, her eyes trained on the tantalizing nearness of his mouth, her lips parted in an aching invitation for his possession. His mouth brushed her lips as she spoke his name, claiming them.

The tidal wave of passion that flooded through her made it impossible for Glenna to argue with his statement. His arms shifted to scoop her off the floor and hold her cradled against his chest.

The door to the bedroom was open. Jett kicked it the rest of the way open and carried her into the dark room. Slowly lowering her feet to the floor, he stood her up beside the bed. His hands glided up her sides, pulling her gown with them and lifting it off over her head. The room was all in shadows with only a glimmer of light shining in from the sitting room as he began unbuttoning his shirt. Glenna could barely see what he was doing. A wild anticipation licked along her veins, sending tremors over her skin.

His arms clasped her shoulders to draw her naked body to the hair-roughened bareness of his chest. Despite the dimness, his mouth found her lips and locked sensually over them. While kissing her, he removed the rest of his clothing. Her arms opened to Jett, now undressed, gathering his muscled torso into her embrace. Her breast swelled as his hand took its weight in his palm. A muffled groan escaped his throat before his mouth claimed her yielding lips. She couldn't believe that it felt so right with him, while her father was lying in bed in their adjoining suite thinking that life, their life, as he'd known it, was over. The effect was like a bucket of cold water. He dragged his mouth from hers and stiffening, lifted his head.

"Glenna?" His puzzled question indicated that he'd noticed. It was almost as if he could read her mind. She needed to feel him and her hands glided over the steel smoothness of his shoulders. "I can't. I'm sorry."

There was a long silence during which Jett remained perfectly still, looking at her in the darkness. Then, with a heavy sigh, he turned away from her. "I can't help your father, Glenna." An iron thread ran through his low statement.

She knew this, but the icy tone still gripped her by the throat, numbing her. "I want to know why." It was barely a whisper.

"I can't help him," Jett repeated his statement more forcefully.

All she could see was the dark silhouette of his back. "I know that you care for me. I can feel it."

"Yes, I do," he muttered tersely. "And I wish to hell that I didn't!"

Glenna could barely hold back a choke as she began to find her discarded gown. Jett bent to pick up his pants. She covered herself and heard the rustle of the material as he stepped into them and zipped them up.

She walked past him to the doorway and into sitting room.

Chapter Eight

Her fingers curled into the material of the gown, its silken texture contrasting with the rawness of her nerves. She knew that he'd come out of the bedroom and she would have to face him.

He walked in seething with unspent energy. "Why did you do it?" His voice shook on the hoarse demand. His dark gaze sliced to her, slashing over the provocative nightgown that covered her shapely form. He walked over and picked up her robe. "You'd better put that on, too," he snapped.

Jett half turned away, tense muscles rippling and flexing along the back of his shoulders as he ran a hand over his rumpled black hair. Glenna slipped her arms into the sleeves of the robe.

"Why?" He repeated his question with the insistence of hardness.

"I came here to talk with you. To make you change your mind about helping my father. I did not come here to make love to you, Jett. Yes, I want you. I wish I didn't, but I do. And not because of what you can do for my father. I wanted *you*. But not like this."

Jett retorted with a fury that was barely contained. "What do you expect from me, Glenna? A sexy red-head knocks on my door in the middle of the night, dressed in a clinging negligee. When I let her in, she asks for my help. I want to go to bed with her, so I take advantage of the situation; the same as any man with a normal sex drive would do."

The anger of shame scalded her. "I trusted you, Jett. I thought you cared for me. Am I just another redhead?" Glenna choked on a bitter laugh.

"If that was true, we wouldn't be talking right now." With long impatient strides, Jett crossed the width of the room to a credenza and opened a door to take out a decanter of Scotch and a glass.

At the moment, Glenna found no consolation in the fact that she'd driven him to drink as she watched him splash a jigger of Scotch in the glass and bolt it down.

"Whatever gave me the ridiculous idea that you even had a human side? That once I appealed to it you would agree to help my father? I should have realized what kind of man you were when you said you knew he would be financially ruined if you turned him down. You weren't interested in help-ing him—only yourself."

"I *can't* help him!" Jett angrily stressed the verb, slamming the glass down on the credenza.

"You *won't* help him because it doesn't suit you to do so. You can't get any bigger than Coulson Mining. I'm not an expert, but even I know that!"

"Do you think your father is the only one in the industry who has suffered financial problems?" he challenged. "Multiply his problems a hundredfold and that's what I had during our long strike. My company lost money then, too, because the overhead and management went on. My stock of coal supplies was exhausted because I had contracts to deliver coal. When that ran out I had to buy coal to make the shipments, which meant paying a higher price. My firm is recovering just as your father's would have if he hadn't ran afoul of the safety regulations. I can't absorb his losses without risking my company. I can't do that. It's his life versus hundreds. Can you understand that?"

His harshness, his roughness made Glenna see how impossible it had been from the outset—how hopeless. She burned over the way he had dangled them on a string, letting them think he might help them when he knew all along he couldn't.

"You let us think you were considering the proposal," she accused.

"I did consider it . . . very seriously," Jett said while gritting his teeth as if suppressing the anger.

"Do you expect me to believe that?" she taunted. "You've already made it clear that it was impossible from the beginning. And yet, you knew I'd come here to try and make you change your mind. . . ."

He began taking ominous steps in her direction, his dark eyes blazing. "I can answer that in one word—you. It has to be obvious that I'm attracted to you, that I was from the moment I met you. When I found out how much trouble your father was in, I wanted to believe there was a way I could help because I cared about you. Why the hell do you think I stayed up all night, walking and thinking and scheming?"

"You knew this morning what the answer would be." Glenna's eyes were luminous with the gray green color of storm-tossed seas. "Why did you drag it out?"

"If I told you this morning, what would you have done?" he challenged coldly, coming to a stop in front of her. The intimidating breadth of his naked shoulders and chest towered before her eyes. "You'd have hated me, the way you do now. The name Coulson Mining means dollar signs to you. Even now, after I've explained it to you, you still believe I could have helped your father. *I* would end up getting blamed for your father's failure. So I stole this morning. And I would have taken tonight with you."

He raked her with a look that reminded Glenna just how willing she had been.

"It's business, right? The way you feel about me or the way I feel about you doesn't factor into it. You don't have to remind me of that," she said.

"You aren't going to give me credit for telling you the truth, are you?" he declared with disgust.

Sarcasm crept into Glenna's voice as she blindly turned away. "Good night, Jett."

"I can't prevent your father from losing what he has, but if you need anything, Glenna—" Jett began.

"I'll never come to you," she flared. "I never want to hear your name again." She knew his name would always remind her of the way she had opened herself to humiliation. She wanted to appeal to his heart, but instead she found calculating stone. She might be inexperienced and not well versed in corporate tactics, but she wasn't a fool. If Jett wanted to do something to help, he could. It might not have been merging with the mine, but there were other ways, other avenues he could've offered. She was a Reynolds. She'd do anything she could to help her family. She might care for this man, but she didn't need him.

She hurried toward the her door, which she'd left propped open since she wasn't carrying her keycard. Jett called her name, but she didn't pause. Afraid he would come after her, she rushed down the hallway to her suite, slipped inside the room, and closed the door.

"Glenna? Glenna, is that you?" Her father's voice called to her from the open door to the adjoining suite.

Quickly, she swallowed the sobs in her throat and wiped hurriedly at hot moisture on her cheeks.

"Yes." Footsteps approached the doorway. She sniffed back some tears and tried to sound calm. "Did you want me, Dad?"

"Where have you been?" The forlorn question was echoed by his expression when he appeared in the opening. "I called you a few times but you weren't here."

Glenna was careful not to face him directly as she turned down the covers of her bed and took her time plumping the pillows. "I'm sorry. Did you need something?" Although she tried hard to conceal it, there was a definite waver in her voice.

"Where were you?" His attention sharpened at the way she avoided his question.

Hesitating, she realized she couldn't hide the truth from him. "I went to talk to Jett," she admitted thinly. "I thought I might persuade him to change his mind."

There was an awkward silence. "At this time of night?"

His words struck a raw nerve and lifted her hurt gaze to his paling face. The tiredness and defeat became mixed with dismay. She'd hoped that her father wouldn't think that more than talking had taken place, but she knew her father had always been a perceptive man.

"Yes," Glenna whispered as she began to shake with the sobs she could no longer hold back. "I'm sorry, Dad, but I just couldn't stand by while you lost everything." It seemed to take him a long time to cross the room to where she stood. Intense sadness gleamed in his eyes. Quietly he studied her wretched expression.

"What happened, baby?" he asked with grim concern.

"Nothing." She shook her head in a mute kind of pain and shuddered when his arms went around her to comfort her. "He said that he insists that he isn't in a position to help you."

"Jett is an honest man, Glenna. The decision was not up to him alone, although I suspect that if it had been . . ." Her father paused, not needing to finish the sentence.

"No." It was a rasped answer as Glenna began to cry softly. "I don't want to hear that. I wanted to help you, Dad."

He gathered her into his arms and hugged her close. "I truly appreciate it, Glenna," he murmured.

"I just couldn't take no for an answer. I was so

desperate that I didn't stop to think how embarrassing it might be to you."

"I'm afraid I let you down," he sighed heavily. "I put up a fight because I thought I would lose everything in life that mattered. But I still have you, Glenna. I should have remembered that."

She closed her eyes. "Can we leave first thing in the morning?"

He patted her gently. "You climb into bed. Maybe tomorrow morning things won't look as bleak as they do now." With an arm around her shoulder, he urged her toward the bed.

"Are you all right?" Self-consciously she wiped at the tears on her cheeks and lifted her head to study him.

"I will be," he promised, but he looked exceptionally tired when he smiled to reassure her.

After she was in bed he tucked the covers around her and bent stiffly to brush a kiss on her forehead. Before he left the room he turned off the light. Lying beneath the covers in the dark, Glenna thought about the episode with Jett and how much worse it could have been. Had she made love to him, it would have been worse. Knowing that she had stopped gave her a sense of pride. She didn't know where her family would be come tomorrow, but at least she had that.

A hand shook her awake. She groaned a protest, but the hand on her shoulder was insistent that she should wake up. Finally she rolled onto her back and opened her eyes. Memory rushed back with the sunlight flooding the room. First, Jett announcing that there would be no merger, then her father's despondency, followed by her disastrous attempt to talk Jett into changing his mind. Pain sawed on her nerve ends.

"Good morning." Her father was standing beside her bed, smiling down at her.

Glenna blinked and tried to refocus. Her father looked so different from the man she had seen last night. He was dressed in a bright sport shirt and blue slacks. There was color in his freshly shaved cheeks and a twinkle in his eye.

"Come on. Get up," he coaxed. "It's a new day outside and I'm hungry for breakfast."

Confused, she pushed herself into a sitting position and stared at this cheerful replica of her father. Her expression drew a hearty chuckle from him. That only deepened her frown.

"Why are you so happy?" She shook her head in total bewilderment.

"Why are you so glum?" He grinned.

Her mouth opened, but all she was capable of doing was releasing a short incredulous breath. Helplessly she searched for some explanation for his attitude.

"How can you say that?" she said finally.

"Because I've just spent a night counting my blessings," he informed her.

"I know we have some, but . . ." It wasn't that she wanted him to become depressed again, but the change in his attitude was so drastic that Glenna was worried. "But we're losing the business and our way of life."

"Well, that's blessing number one," he stated with a brisk nod of his head.

"A blessing?" she echoed.

"Yes, because now we know it's a fact, so we can stop wondering and worrying whether we're going to find some way or someone to bail us out of our mess," Orin Reynolds explained as if his reasoning was perfectly logical.

"Dad, are you feeling all right?" Glenna eyed him warily.

"I'm fine. A good dose of optimism will cure what's ailing you, too. Hop out of bed and I'll give you your first injection over breakfast." He glanced at his watch. "I'll give you twenty minutes to get dressed and meet me downstairs at the restaurant."

As he moved toward the door, Glenna protested. "But Dad, I don't want to see Jett. He might be there—"

"That's blessing number two." He winked. "He's already checked out of the hotel and gone."

The vision of his beaming smile stayed with her after he had disappeared into the outer hallway. Driven by curiosity Glenna climbed out of bed. His sunny disposition was forcing her to venture out of her somber mood whether she wanted to or not.

Exactly twenty minutes later she joined him in the restaurant. He'd already taken the liberty of ordering for her. She stared at his choices. First, a glass of orange juice—liquid sunshine—two eggs sunny-side up, a rasher of snapping-crisp bacon, and golden brown toast with orange marmalade.

"Dad, I'm not hungry enough to eat all this." Actually she wasn't hungry at all.

"You'd better eat it." He shrugged good-naturedly. "After all, we can't be sure where our next meal is coming from."

"And you're smiling about that," Glenna accused, quickly swallowing the sip of orange juice she'd taken. "I don't understand because last night—"

"Last night I was selfishly looking at all I was losing instead of what I was gaining," her father interrupted.

"What are you gaining?" She couldn't see where there was anything. "We are going to lose our home."

"We're going to lose a *house*," he corrected with gentle patience. "It's just walls, ceilings, and windows. It's too big for us and costs too much to heat. What do we need all those rooms for? And look at how many things we've accumulated over the years. We can sell two-thirds of the furniture and still have enough left over to furnish a small house. What we do sell, we can call them antiques and make a handy sum."

"But—"

"I know what you're going to say," her father interrupted again with a knowing smile. "What about all the memories? Happy memories are stored in your heart, not in a house. They are something you can never lose."

"And what about the mine?" Unconsciously Glenna found herself heartily eating the breakfast her father had ordered.

"Ah, yes, the mine. What a responsibility—what a burden that has been lifted from my shoulders." Orin Reynolds sighed in contentment. "No more worrying about payrolls, insurance, unions, contracts, taxes, regulations, deliveries, and the hundred and one other things that are part of running a business."

"But what will you do?" She frowned.

"Do you know what I remembered last night?" he asked rhetorically. "Do you know I never wanted to run the mine? But it was the family business, so when it came my time I took over for my father."

Glenna never knew that. She had never even suspected it. "What did you want to do?"

He paused for a minute, considering her question. A sudden gleam sparkled in his gray eyes, dancing and mischievous. Chuckling laughter flowed, its contagious amusement making Glenna smile.

"I remember when I was a teenager I always wanted to make moonshine." He laughed louder. "Maybe that's what I should do, take what little money we get from selling the furniture and buy a patch of ground back in the hills to brew up some moonshine."

"Dad, you can't be serious!" She was amused, astonished, prepared to believe almost anything after the revelations of the last few minutes.

"Why not?" His expression continued to be split by a wide grin. "I've heard that there's still money to be made in it. If any revenuers come around, we can try a little of your friendly persuasion on them."

She looked at him in amazement, and felt her cheeks warm at the reminder of her attempt at persuading Jett the previous night and where it almost led.

"There are so many things I've missed out on, Glenna. This was why your mother and I always insisted you do exactly what you love." His voice was softly insistent, gentle in its tone. "I'm proud that you wouldn't take no for an answer. You're a Reynolds and we don't quit," he continued, "but sometimes you have to know when to let something go, especially when there are so many things to look forward to. But I don't think that the fate of our family is all that's bothering you, darling. Do you want to know what I think it is?"

Glenna couldn't help shaking her head and letting out a slightly exasperated, "Daaad . . ."

"I think you were beginning to like Jett Coulson. When he didn't accept my proposal, you felt that it was somehow a rejection of you and our way of life, too. Well, Glenna, it's kind of hard to explain, but business and pleasure really aren't a good mix." His accuracy strangled her voice, forcing her to nod in admission. There was a fine mist of tears in her gray green eyes, enhancing their greenish cast. Her father reached over to crook a finger under her chin and lift it.

"You hold your head up," he ordered with a smiling wink. "I've been around for a while and if I know anything, I know that he feels the same way about you. If he's so dumb that he doesn't see what you're made of, then he isn't worth your tears."

She smiled, a little tightly, but the warmth and adoration shining in her eyes wasn't forced. "How do you do it?" There was a thread of amazement in her emotionally trembling voice. "I was feeling so terrible this morning. I still hurt, but—" There was an expressive shake of her head as she paused.

"That's what fathers are for." He leaned back in his chair, a touch of smugness in his look. "To bandage up their children's wounded hearts and make them feel better. Clean up your plate," he admonished with paternal insistence. "We have to get packed and make the drive back. There's a lot of things that needs to be done, plans to be made. Instead of sitting back waiting for things to happen it's time we started making them happen."

"You make it all sound like an adventure," Glenna murmured wryly.

"It's going to be."

It was difficult not to believe him. Glenna hadn't seen her father this carefree and lighthearted since her mother was alive. Perhaps the mine and all its problems had been too much of a burden for him over the years. She knew it had taken its toll on his health. Now, without the pressure and stress of saving the business, he was like a new man. His mood was infectious.

CHAPTER NINE

It was late in the afternoon before they finally arrived home. Hannah had evidently been watching for their return, because she was out of the front door before Glenna turned off the car motor. She came puffing down the steps to help with the luggage.

"It's about time you got here," Hannah said the minute they were out of the car. "Don't keep me in suspense. What happened? Did you see that man, Coulson?"

Her father glanced across the top of the car at Glenna. "Whatever happened to 'welcome home'? I'd even settle for a plain 'hello.'"

"Hello and welcome home. Now tell me what happened," she demanded. "Was he there? Did you talk to him?"

"Yes, he was there, and yes, we talked to him." He nodded his head with each answer. "But he turned us down flat."

Hannah stared at him. Glenna could appreciate the housekeeper's confusion. How could a man look so cheerful when he had just announced—for all intents and purposes—that he was going broke?

"You're pulling my leg," she accused.

Her father assumed an expression of shocked innocence. "I haven't even laid a hand on you, Hannah. How can you say that?"

"Orin Reynolds, you know precisely what I mean," the housekeeper scolded him impatiently and turned to Glenna. She was having trouble hiding a smile as she popped the trunk to remove their luggage. "You tell me what happened, Glenna."

"Dad told you the truth, Hannah." There was an instant's hesitation before she added, "Mr. Coulson wasn't interested in Dad's proposal."

"Would I lie about something like that, Hannah?" her father chided.

"Well, I certainly didn't expect you to be smiling about it," she retorted. "Don't you realize that you're going to be losing the roof over your head? Where are you going to get the money to put food on the table? Providing, of course, that you still have a table. And—"

Picking up one of the lighter suitcases, her father clamped a hand on Hannah's shoulder and said, "You wouldn't happen to have a recipe for a good sour mash?"

The plump woman had taken one step toward the house. She stopped abruptly at his question, her mouth opening in silent shock. Glenna wouldn't have been surprised if she had dropped one of the suitcases in her hands.

"What's the matter with this man?" She turned on Glenna for an explanation. "Has he taken leave of his senses?"

"It's a long story, Hannah," Glenna laughed. "I'm sure Dad will tell you all about it."

The housekeeper eyed him sternly before starting again for the house. "It'd better be good. Otherwise I'm calling a doctor. You could be having some side effects from that medicine you're taking," she grumbled.

As they reached the front door a car turned into the driveway. "It's Bruce." Glenna recognized his reliable four-door.

She and her father waited on the stoop while Hannah went inside.

Bruce stopped the car beside the red Porsche and smiled a greeting as he climbed out.

"It looks like I timed it just right," he remarked, noting the luggage they were carrying and moving to help them. "How did it go?"

"It didn't." Her father held the door open for Glenna to precede him into the house.

"I was afraid of that," Bruce replied with an I-told-you-so look and followed them into the house. "What are you going to do now?"

Setting the luggage inside the door, her father took the question seriously and didn't tease him the way he had Hannah. "Since we can no longer postpone the inevitable, we might as well start planning for it and make it as painless as possible." He led the way into the study.

"How?" Bruce raised an eyebrow and glanced at Glenna as if expecting a protest from her, but she had been over all this with her father during the drive home.

"We can begin the necessary legal proceedings to turn the company assets over to its mortgage holders and debtors. Tomorrow I'm going to contact a real-estate company and put the house on the market. We'll go ahead and have that meeting with the workers." His gaze swept the room in a mental assessment of its contents. "We have a lot of furniture, household goods, and miscellaneous items. We need to decide what we're going to keep so we can start selling the rest and get the best price that we can."

"But where will you go?" Bruce appeared a little dumbfounded by Orin's calmness.

"That's another thing." Her father stopped beside his desk and absently picked up a wood-carved decoy that served as a paperweight.

"We need to look for a smaller place to live, maybe closer to town, although we might find a cheaper place if we stay in the country."

"What will you do without the income from the mine?" Bruce was well aware that a man of Orin's age with a history of heart trouble would have a difficult, if not impossible, time finding work.

Glenna offered her solution to that. "We'll be fine. Tomorrow I'm going to start filling out full-time job applications. I should still be able to keep submitting freelance articles and supplement my income with writing."

"I used to be pretty good at woodworking." Her father studied the handmade decoy in his hand. "When you were younger, Glenna, I used to mess around in the workshop a lot. Remember the doll-house I made for you and all the doll furniture?"

"There were lights in the room that you could turn on and off, operated by batteries," she recalled.

"That was enjoyable, building that." He smiled as

he reminisced. "It would be good therapy, too. Maybe I could set up a little shop. I have all the tools."

"Why'd you ever stop doing that?" Glenna wondered aloud.

"I don't know." He considered the question. "The business began taking more of my time, more paperwork, more problems. Then your mother died and . . . you know the rest."

"I think the workshop is an excellent idea," she concluded. "What about you, Bruce?"

"Sure," he agreed with a trace of vagueness. "It sounds good."

"What's bothering you?" her father questioned at the bewildered look on Bruce's face.

"I was just wondering how you came up with all these plans when you only talked to Coulson this weekend."

That drew a smile from her father. "Once you stop concentrating on keeping your head above water, it's easy to decide to swim to shore."

"I guess that's true," Bruce conceded.

"How were things at the mine while we've been gone? Did anything happen that I should know about?" It was an inquiry that was almost reluctantly made.

There was definitely relief in his face when Bruce shook his head.

"No, it's just been routine."

"Good." He nodded and began turning the decoy in his hand, inspecting it absently. Coming to a decision, he set the wooden duck down. "I think I'll walk out to the garage and see what kind of shape my tools are in." He was halfway across the room before it occurred to him that he was being a little rude. "You will be staying for dinner, won't you, Bruce?"

"I'd like that, thank you, if you think there's enough to go around," Bruce accepted.

"With Hannah cooking there always is." Her father continued to the foyer. "I won't be long."

Alone in the parlor-turned-study with Bruce, Glenna wandered to the fireplace. In the last few minutes she had caught herself making comparisons between Bruce and the more dynamic Jett. One puzzle had been solved. At last she understood why she hadn't let her the relationship with Bruce develop into a more serious one. Despite all his good qualities, and Bruce had his share, there was a vital ingredient missing—chemistry. Without it there was no volatile combustion.

Glenna knew now that her relationship with Bruce would always be a casual one, but she still cared about him, and was concerned about his future. She turned to look at him.

"What are you going to do, Bruce, when the mine shuts down?" He had become such a part of her life in the past three years it was difficult for Glenna to picture a time when he wouldn't be around.

"I've managed to put a little money aside. I thought I might take a couple of months off, enjoy a long vacation for a change." He smiled lazily. "I can give you and your father a hand settling into a new place, and help him set up his workshop if that's what he finally decides to do. That way I can take my time and look for a really good job instead of taking the first one that comes along."

"Will you continue your work at other mining

companies?" If he accepted a position away from this immediate area, Glenna knew they would inevitably drift apart. Sooner or later, she supposed, that had to happen.

"Of course." He moved to stand beside her and lean a hand on the fireplace mantel. "That's where my expertise and experience are."

"But is it what you want?" It had been something her father had been forced into doing. "Do you like it?"

"Like it?" Bruce repeated with a shake of his head, an ardent glow firing his eyes. "I love it."

"Doesn't it ever bother you to go down that shaft?" Glenna was curious.

"I feel at home there. In a strange way I feel safe, as if I was in the womb of the earth. It's something I can't really explain," he shrugged finally. "I wouldn't want to do anything else. What made you ask that?"

"I guess because I never knew until this morning that Dad never wanted to run the mine. He's been in the business all these years, but it's never been what he wanted. And still he's struggled and fought all this time to keep it running." She knew it spoke of his dedication and sense of responsibility to his family and community. "It's crazy, isn't it, that out of something bad there is good. Dad is finally free of the mine."

"It's hard to believe he's the same person I saw last week. He's a changed man," Bruce commented. "I was afraid of what this would do to him. But you're right, he seems relieved and happier than I've seen him."

"I know. It's wonderful."

"You've changed, too, Glenna." His gaze narrowed slightly, as if puzzling over the difference.

"Me?" She stiffened a little, sensitive to his scrutiny, afraid of what that probing gaze might discover.

"I don't know quite what it is, but you don't seem the same. It's as if you've grown up overnight. Which is crazy," he mocked at his own statement, "because you were an adult before. You just . . . seem more like a woman now."

She moved away from the fireplace to escape his gaze. "Maybe you've just forgotten what I look like in the four days since you've seen me," Glenna said, trying to joke her way out of the conversation. "You just don't want to admit it."

Bruce laughed. "I'm not likely to forget what you look like." Pushing away from the fireplace, he followed her. "I know what it is." The difference dawned on him slowly. "You look somehow more at ease now. You still seem as confident and self-assured as always, capable of tackling anything, but the nervous energy is just not there anymore."

"That's silly." Her laugh sounded faked, even to her.

"No, it isn't. All of this has hit you just as hard as your father, and you look a little afraid, but . . . still content somehow."

She hugged her arms around her waist in an unconscious gesture of self-protection. "It's hit me hard and I'm feeling a little lost, but I learned a lot in the past few days," she said, uncomfortable with this rather intimate line of talk.

His hands gripped her shoulders to turn her

around. "You know I'll help in any way I can. You don't have to face this thing alone. I'll be with you."

When he bent to kiss her, Glenna turned her head aside and his mouth encountered the coolness of her cheek instead. "Don't, Bruce." There was no need to experiment to see how his kiss would compare with Jett's. It couldn't. Glenna stood rigid within his hold, not fighting him as she stared to the side.

"What have I done, Glenna?" He was irritated and bewildered by her rejection. "Anytime I get close to you anymore you pull away from me."

"It isn't you. It's me," she replied aware of how true that cliché was in this case, because he really was a great guy, but just not great for her. It wasn't fair to let him think he'd done anything wrong.

Sighing heavily he let his arms drop to his side. "Do you want me to leave? I don't have to stay for dinner."

Glenna lifted her head to look at him. "I want you to stay for dinner, Bruce. I like your company." She wanted to make him understand her view of their relationship.

"My company but not my kisses." He read between the lines.

"I'm sorry, but yes," she admitted. Her expression remained composed, gentle but firm.

"Well, I guess we've got that clear." His mouth tightened grimly as he turned away and walked to an armchair. "Why don't you tell me about your weekend, then?"

"There isn't much to tell." Glenna wished he'd chosen a less disturbing topic. "The Greenbrier is a fabulous place, but it wasn't exactly a pleasure trip."

"What was Coulson like?" His choice of subject went from bad to worse.

"Just about what you would expect—although he's difficult to describe." Which he wasn't. Black hair and eyes; hard, compelling features; with a latent and yet all pervasive sexuality about him that awakened hers. "He's intelligent and self-assured." She remembered that he had walked in the woods and watched the sunrise. "He's a hard-edged businessman but seems to have an appreciation for the serenity and beauty of nature." She probably shouldn't have said that.

"How was he to deal with?"

A wry smile broke around the edges of her mouth as she remembered his afternoon meeting with her father. "Jett is . . ." Glenna paused, realizing how easily his first name had slipped from her, "probably a better poker player than my father."

"Jett. You were on a first-name basis with him?" Bruce raised an eyebrow.

"We saw him on a social basis first. I called him Jett. He called Dad Orin." Glenna shrugged and tried to make it appear an insignificant item. "There's nothing special about that."

"He's a bachelor, right? Good-looking, too." His gaze searched her face.

"Yes." She was trying hard to look and sound indifferent, but just thinking of Jett made her remember things that made her blood run warm.

"He flirted with you," he accused, jealousy simmering in his eyes.

"What does it matter?" Glenna had had enough of his questions. "It really isn't any of your business, Bruce."

Taking a deep breath, he released it in a long sigh. "Things are changing too fast for me to keep up. I know we never had anything, but still I . . ."

The awkward moment following his comment was filled by the sound of footsteps in the foyer. Glenna recognized her father's tread and glanced toward the study door.

"Hannah sent me to tell you dinner is ready," he said from the doorway. "The condemned are going to eat a hearty meal tonight. I hope you brought your appetite with you, Bruce."

The sandy-haired man was slow to respond. Glenna was relieved when she saw him fix a smile on his face. "When Hannah's cooking I always bring my appetite, Orin." Standing, he waited politely for Glenna to pass and followed her to the dining room where the table was set.

"What kind of shape were your tools in, Dad?" She sat in her customary chair on her father's right while Bruce took the one opposite her.

"They are dirty and need oiling, but they're in good shape considering how long it's been since they were used last," he said. "I'm going to enjoy puttering around out there again."

"Make sure you don't get too tired," she cautioned.

"I won't," he said as Hannah entered the dining room carrying a green salad and four wooden bowls on a tray. Her father shifted closer to Glenna so he wouldn't be in Hannah's way as she lowered it to the table. "Glenna, do you remember where we stored your dollhouse? Was it in the attic or that back bedroom?"

Hannah dropped the tray on the table and whirled away. "I'm calling the doctor."

"Why?" Glenna was the first to recover. "Hannah, what's wrong?"

She paused near the kitchen door to impatiently explain. "First he comes with a lot of crazy talk about making moonshine. Now he's asking about dollhouses. He's going through his second childhood. That's what it is."

Laughter began slowly then gathered force. Orin managed to catch his breath and finally explain his plans to Hannah.

CHAPTER TEN

The radio was turned on full blast, which was the only way Hannah could hear it above the vacuum cleaner. The racket was getting on Glenna's nerves, but she knew Hannah was almost finished cleaning the living room.

Stretching, Glenna ran the long-handled dust mop around the top of the walls where the cobwebs invariably gathered. A faded blue bandanna was tied around her head to protect her auburn hair from the dust. A plaid shirt and brushed-denim jeans made up the rest of her work clothes.

It seemed strange to see the study empty of furniture and the fireplace mantel bare. The last load of their belongings was stacked in the foyer, waiting for her father to return with Bruce and one of his friends to take it to their new home.

Everything else was already gone. The larger items had been sold individually through advertisements in the paper. Others had been included in a garage sale. The items that were left had been taken to an auction and sold.

She and Hannah were busy cleaning so the new owners of the house could move in that coming weekend. And Hannah liked to listen to the radio while she cleaned. Between the radio and vacuum cleaner, Glenna could barely hear herself think.

"Glory be! Glenna!" Hannah shouted from the living room. "Come in here!"

Glenna raced to the living room, certain that it had to be some disaster. From the doorway everything appeared fine. Hannah was by the window with the vacuum cleaner and the portable radio blaring on the floor near Glenna's feet.

"What is it?" Glenna shouted. Hannah answered her. At least Glenna saw her mouth moving and heard pieces of words above the din of the radio and the vacuum cleaner, but not enough for it to make sense.

She reached down to switch the radio off, and Hannah turned off the vacuum cleaner. The sudden silence was heavenly to Glenna. She could even hear herself sigh.

"There's a helicopter out there in that cleared patch of field by the driveway," Hannah announced and motioned for Glenna to come to the window and see.

"A helicopter?" She took a step toward the window.

"It's mine." A man's voice spoke behind her. Not any man's voice, but Jett's.

Glenna turned to find him standing inside the opened front door. A pair of mirror-dark sunglasses hid his eyes from her, but there was no mistaking him. The sleeves of his white shirt were rolled up the length of the cuffs and he was wearing dark slacks. His coal black hair was windblown.

After the initial shock was over, the blood rushed through her veins. Two months had not dimmed her memory of him nor lessened the impact he made on her. The longing to erase that one night when she had almost made love to him had gnawed at her like a cancer.

"I knocked, but with all the noise no one heard me," he explained.

"I'm sorry." Glenna found her voice, thin though it was. "We were busy cleaning." She loosened her grip on the dust mop. It moved slightly as if to illustrate her explanation.

Hannah came forward and stopped beside Glenna to study the man the helicopter had brought.

"Hannah, this is Jett Coulson . . . of Coulson Mining." She added the last bit in case the housekeeper didn't immediately make the connection.

"Hannah Burns is . . . has been . . . our housekeeper and part of the family for years."

After today it would be the past tense. Hannah was starting a new job as a restaurant cook, which Glenna's father thought was perfect since she loved to cook and would always make enough for large numbers.

The introduction was acknowledged by twin nods. Hannah was plainly curious, eyeing him warily while she tried to decide what he wanted. The mirrored sunglasses made Jett's reaction even more unreadable.

"Was your helicopter forced down?" What a twist fate had made if he had reentered her life by accident.

"No. We landed quite safely," he replied in lazy assurance.

"Why are you here?" Glenna felt crazy little quivers running over her skin.

"I came to see you." It was a simple statement.

"My father should be back shortly."

"I said"—Jett paused to take off his sunglasses and slide them in the pocket of his shirt, turning his dark eyes fully on her—"that I came to see you."

She caught her breath. Her poise was holding, but it was becoming brittle. She lifted her chin a little higher.

"What is it you want?" she asked smoothly.

"I want to talk to *you.*" The emphasis reminded her that Hannah was beside her.

Glenna darted a glance at her. No one but her father knew of what had happened between her and Jett.

"Why don't you finish packing up those boxes in the kitchen, Hannah?" she asked, knowing full well there was nothing in the kitchen to be packed. Before Hannah could remind her of that, she silenced her with a look.

With a sniff of disapproval, Hannah turned on her heel and stalked to the kitchen. Glenna's gaze wavered when she tried to meet Jett's again. His was moving over her, making her conscious of her appearance. Her hand reached up to remove the bandanna from her head. She combed her fingers through the weight of her hair, raking the rich chestnut curls as she turned aside.

"You said you wanted to talk to me," she reminded him.

"Coulson Mining has negotiated a contract to

operate the Reynolds Mine. I wanted to tell you before you heard it from some other source."

"Congratulations. You got the mine after all!" Glenna hadn't said it with bitterness, but the connotation was there just the same.

"I hoped you wouldn't resent it." The grimness of resignation laced his voice, drawing her glance to the quiet study of his eyes.

"I can't see why it matters how I feel about it." She lifted her shoulders in an uncaring shrug.

"It matters," Jett said with calm insistence. "This contract is business, Glenna."

"You told me that it would make more financial sense for your company to obtain the mine after Dad lost it. This management agreement certainly proves it," Glenna replied.

His hand caught her arm, holding her. "After all this time, don't you understand?" he said in an urgent voice. Heat spread from his hand through her system, scorching nerves that had not fully healed from the last time. "I did what I had to do, Glenna."

Without making it look too obvious that she needed to escape his touch, she moved away.

"Yes, I do, Jett. The best thing that happened to us was when you turned down my father's proposal for a merger. We don't hold your decision against you."

"Don't you?" His tone was skeptical.

"That's difficult to believe, isn't it?" She faced him, summoning all her composure. "I'm happy that the mine won't be shut down completely and all those workers won't be out of a job. You should see my father now that he's free from the burden of the mine. He'll be here soon. We've sold this house to move into a smaller place," she said, while offering a faint smile. Their way of life had changed, but in the grand scheme of things, everything was really going to turn out for the better.

He glanced around the room, emptied of furniture and all signs of habitation. There was a rigid line to his jaw. "You said you would lose your home."

"It's too big, and the upkeep was too high, anyway."

"What are you going to do?" His intense gaze bore into her.

"I have a great job at a printing company. I'll keep on writing in my spare time." The last thing Glenna wanted was his pity. "Dad is going to have a workshop where he can make toys, dollhouses, rocking horses, and the like. He's always wanted that."

"You don't appear to have a problem in the world," Jett observed dryly.

"Everyone has problems, but we're managing ours very well," Glenna replied. "The situation didn't turn out to be the disaster we thought it would be."

"Well, I guess you didn't really need my help after all." As much as she didn't want to admit it, she needed and wanted a lot of things from him, but his help wasn't one of them. After they returned from that weekend trip, Glenna couldn't stop thinking about him and would go online every so often to read articles about his appearances and accomplishments. Occasionally, there'd be a picture accompanying an article and it'd set her right back to the night they'd almost made love.

"We're doing better than just fine." She had been, at least, when it came to him. She still had feelings for him, but there were many things that occupied her time these days, such as her new job and her writing. And then he'd walked into her home and it was almost as if time had stood still.

"What if I said your father could have his same position at the mine again, with fewer responsibilities?" He leaned a hand against the inner door frame, his dark head tipped to one side.

"I thought you came to talk to me, Jett. And no, I don't think he'd be interested, but you'd have to ask him yourself." Her tension was building under the strain of his nearness. She could feel the threads of control threatening to snap. "I'm sure he would appreciate the gesture, though."

"It isn't a gesture. It's a serious offer." His face held that impassive poker expression. "It wasn't his lack of skill or competence as a manager that shut down the mine, but a series of outside influences that were beyond his control. He knows the miners, the working conditions, and the potential of the mine. We can both benefit from his experience and knowledge."

"Like I said, I don't know why you're telling me this or why now. You'll have to speak to my father." Irritation crept into her reply.

"Glenna, I . . ." The mask dropped from his features, and in its place was the smoldering intensity of his gaze. Glenna started to turn away from its desire-filled heat. His hands snaked out to stop her and forced her to face him.

"Have you forgotten? Don't you remember that night? What happened between us?" Jett demanded. His voice had dropped to a hoarse whisper. "I couldn't help your father at the time. Was I wrong to let you go?"

"You're mixing business with pleasure, Jett." With her head turned away from him she stared sightlessly at a bare corner of the room. The blood was thundering in her ears, and her hands rested lightly against his middle, ready to stiffen if he tried to pull her closer. "I don't want to talk about that night. I want to forget it."

"I haven't been able to forget it any more than you have." His hand tunneled under her hair and lifted aside its weight to expose the curve of her neck. He bent his head to run his mouth along it, reexploring old territory with familiar ease. "I have dreams about it at night," Jett murmured with his lips moving against her skin and his breath caressing sensitive areas.

Glenna closed her eyes to try to shut out the wild sensations licking through her veins, but it only made her head spin. She tried to stop his nuzzling by turning her head into him and lifting a shoulder to deny him access to her neck. Jett just began kissing the edge of her cheekbone near her temple.

"In my dreams my mind became filled with the perfume of your body." Jett continued talking against her skin, leaving male-rough kisses to punctuate his sentences. "I could feel the roundness of your breasts in my hands and hear the sweet seduction of your voice whispering in my ear. I'd wake up hungry for the taste of your lips."

"Don't." Her breath was coming in tiny gasps of tormented pleasure.

His hands were sliding down her shoulders and spine, applying pressure to bring her closer. Her forearms remained stiff, but her elbows started bending, forcing her hands up the muscled flatness of his stomach to the rock-ribbed wall of his chest.

"Why did you have to come here?" Glenna asked.

"I stayed away as long as I could." Jett dragged his mouth over her lips, his warm breath mingling intimately with hers. "I wanted to give you time to get over the hurt. You don't know how I dreaded telling you and Orin that I was powerless to help. I didn't want to be the one to put that forsaken look in your eyes."

His strong teeth took gentle love bites of her lips, separating them. She felt defenseless. Her fingers curled into the material of his shirt, clinging to it to avoid clinging to him.

"When we turned the merger down, I still had hope that I could keep you, us, out of it. I thought that I could make it clear that it was strictly business and that I could persuade you to keep on seeing me," he continued while his hands pulled her hips to rest against the powerful columns of his thighs, turning her bones to water. "Then you came to my room late that night, I didn't want to talk anymore. I just wanted you."

She tried to elude his mouth, but it followed her.

"I knew that as soon as you realized your attempt to change my mind was hopeless, you probably would never want to see me again. I haven't stopped wanting you, Glenna."

Drawing her head back, she tried to wade through her dazed senses to study him. "I didn't know if what I felt was real or if you felt the same way. If we hadn't met under these circumstances . . ."

"It wouldn't have mattered. I know that now. I couldn't stop thinking about you, but I wanted to make it right," Jett explained, letting the short distance remain between them while the compelling possession of his gaze roamed over her face. "The little I learned about you that weekend is seared in my mind. I feel like I know you, Glenna."

She knew exactly what he meant. There was no need for more words. She met him halfway and gave over to his demanding kiss. She couldn't believe that he was here, in her arms. That he was telling her that the power of her reaction to him wasn't one-sided.

"I want to keep on seeing you." His voice was muffled against her throat.

"I want to see you, too," she whispered, because she didn't ever want to stop seeing him. That, she was certain of.

Jett lifted his head and ran a hand over her cheek before tangling his fingers in the thick mane of her hair. "Where are you moving? How far is it from here?"

The trembling roughness of his voice and the implied possession of his touch went straight to her heart while also giving her a sensation of power.

"The new house is only a few miles away," she told him.

The velvet blackness of his gaze became shadowed by regret. "Do you know how impossible it is for me to commute back and forth between here and Huntington even with a helicopter at my disposal? My schedule fills a sixteen-hour day. I would barely arrive here before it was time to leave."

"I know. I guess we better make the most of the time we do have," Glenna said and winked.

"Move to the city," he urged. "At least there we

can spend more time together and I won't be wasting so much time traveling to and from. You don't need to worry about work. I have some connections at one of the newspapers. I can arrange for you to be hired as a reporter."

"It isn't that easy, Jett." She shook her head. "This is my life you're talking about. I can't just uproot. We've signed a year's lease on the house. Besides, Dad wants to live in the country. I had been planning on moving out on my own some time ago, but I can't walk off and leave him, not in his condition. Don't ask me to do something like that, Jett."

"I can't only see you a couple of times a month, Glenna," he said in what sounded like a desperate plea.

"We'll find a way. It's been such an agonizing two months," she admitted and traced the outline of his cheek with her fingertips. "If it hadn't been for Dad and Bruce, I think I would have crawled in a hole and buried myself."

A muscle flexed along his jaw, tightening its line with grimness. His attention shifted to a lock of curling auburn hair, the hardness of regret darkening his eyes. Glenna swayed toward him.

The slamming of the front door stopped her while the sound of her father's voice took her out of Jett's arms. "Fred is backing the pickup truck to the door so we can load these boxes, Bruce. Did you ask Glenna about that helicopter outside?"

As she turned toward the doorway to the foyer, she saw Bruce frozen within its frame. His very stillness indicated that he had been standing there for several seconds, if not several minutes. Glenna could tell by the numbed look of disbelief on his face that he had seen and heard enough to know what had been going on. The atmosphere in the room became electric when his gaze met Jett's in silent confrontation.

Her father's appearance on the scene kept it steady. Glenna was standing freely beside Jett when her father paused in the doorway. The instant he saw Jett a broad smile spread across his face.

"Jett!" He greeted him with obvious delight and came striding across the room, a picture of health. "What brings you here? I saw the helicopter outside, but I didn't get a good look at the insignia."

"You're definitely looking better, Orin." Jett shook hands with him.

"Thank you, Jett. I'm feeling better, too," her father said with a decisive nod, then turned to invite the third man to participate in the conversation. "Bruce, come here. I want you to meet Jett Coulson. Bruce Hawkins was my engineer and manager at the mine," he explained to Jett.

Bruce walked stiff legged across the room like a challenger about to do battle. "I've heard a great deal about you, Mr. Coulson." He measured him with a firm handshake.

"Orin has mentioned to me what an asset you were," Jett returned as he sized the sandy-haired man up with a sweeping look. Neither made a reference to Glenna, but when the introduction was over, Bruce assumed a protective position at her side.

In the interim her father ran a quick eye over Glenna. He noted the glowing flush in her cheeks and the slightly uncomfortable atmosphere that prevailed.

"What brings you here, Jett?" her father questioned with a smile of benign interest. "Is this a social call or business?"

"A little of both," Jett admitted, sending a glance at Glenna to indicate the social side of his visit. "I stopped by to let you know we've negotiated a contract to manage your mine."

"My ex-mine," her father corrected without bitterness. "Congratulations. I'm glad to hear it's going to be in competent hands. When will this take effect?"

"Soon. We'll have to make the necessary changes to pass the safety inspection before we can go into production. But first I want to find myself a good man to put in charge. You immediately came to mind. Would you be interested?" Jett casually said.

"Oh, no, you don't!" Her father laughed. "I just got that elephant off my back."

"I would like you to seriously consider it," Jett persisted. "The responsibilities would be considerably fewer this time around. You have all the qualifications and experience I'm looking for, plus a knowledge of this particular mine's characteristics."

"I'm flattered that you thought of me, but I'm not interested," her father refused as Glenna had guessed he would. "But if that's what you're looking for, Bruce fits the description. He may be a little shy on the experience side, but I'd recommend him. I happen to know he's looking for a position that would keep him in this same general area. Isn't that right, Bruce?"

Before he answered Bruce slid a look at Glenna. The glance confirmed she was the reason he didn't want to move away. It was a message no one in the group missed, including Jett. Glenna felt the penetrating study of his gaze.

"That's true, sir," Bruce replied to her father's question.

"Would you be interested in the job?" Jett inquired in that brisk yet smooth tone Glenna knew so well.

"I might be." Bruce didn't reject it. "It would depend on the terms of employment."

"Come by the mine office tomorrow morning at ten and ask for Dan Stockard. I'll tell him to expect you," Jett said.

"I'll be there," Bruce nodded, committing himself to no more than a job interview.

A knock at the front door interrupted the conversation. "I'll answer it," her father volunteered. "It's probably Fred checking to see if we're ready to load the boxes."

But it was the copter pilot instead. "Sorry, Mr. Coulson, but we're already going to be ten minutes late for your next meeting. I thought I should remind you."

Regret rippled through Jett's expression before he moved toward the foyer. "I'm ready." He paused to let his gaze encompass the three of them. "Goodbye." But he looked directly at Glenna when he said, "I'll see you soon."

"Take care," she murmured, and was warmed by the silent promise of his words and the brief flash of his smile.

Glenna was only half-aware that Bruce was standing by her elbow and looking directly at her. Self-consciously she turned her head to meet his look.

"It was more than just a mild flirtation that weekend, wasn't it?" His question didn't expect an answer, and the faint rise of color in her cheeks was the only one he needed. He moved past Glenna to the door. "I'll see if Fred is ready to load this stuff," he mumbled.

When the door closed behind him, her father raised an eyebrow and gave her a wry smile. "It sounds like Bruce walked in on a private moment."

"You could say that," Glenna said and listened to the sound of the helicopter taking off.

"Would it be fair to assume that you and Jett have straightened out your problems? That he wasn't a fool after all?" The knowing glint in his eyes twinkled at her.

"I think we have and . . . I don't think he's a fool at all, Dad." She then eyed him suspiciously. "Why did you recommend Bruce to Jett?"

"Because what I said was true. He's the better man for the job," he shrugged.

"Yes, but I'm sure you know that Bruce has feelings for me that I can't reciprocate. By saying that he wanted to stay in the same area, it just kind of implied that it was because of me," she reminded him.

"I can't help the conclusion Jett reached," her father said with a beaming smile. "Besides, it won't hurt Jett to wonder whether he might have a little competition. And Bruce is a wonderful man who'll make the right woman very happy sometime soon."

"Dad." She sighed and shook her head.

A voice echoed through the empty rooms of the house. "Can I come out of the kitchen now?" Hannah called with terse impatience.

"Hannah. I forgot her!" Glenna realized with a

laughing gasp. Her father found it all very amusing, but Hannah's sense of humor didn't match his when she came out.

By the end of the week Glenna still hadn't completely settled into their new house. Except for the day they had actually moved, she had worked the rest of the week, which left the bulk of the unpacking to be done in the evenings.

After the Friday evening meal she was in the kitchen unpacking the boxes containing the good china and crystal that had been their family's possessions for generations. They had been among the few things she and her father had not sold.

Glenna was on her knees unwrapping the tissue from the dinner plates when someone knocked at the back screen door. A lingering sunset silhouetted the figure outside, but she recognized him at a glance.

"Come in, Bruce," she called without getting up.

"I saw Orin out at the workshop. He's like a kid with a new toy," he remarked as he entered the kitchen.

"He spends nearly all his time out there."

"Do you want some help with this?" Bruce knelt down beside her.

"Sure." Glenna handed him a plate with its tissue-paper covering.

Bruce unwrapped it and added it to the stack on the counter, announcing almost casually, "I start work Monday morning at the mine." Outside of that one remark he'd made when Jett had left, Bruce hadn't referred to him since.

Glenna sat back on her heels to look at him. "They offered you the manager's position?"

"Yes."

"And you accepted it?"

"Yes."

"Why?" That question was too blunt. She quickly tempered it. "I thought you were going to take a couple months off before starting another job."

"I discovered I had too much idle time on my hands with no way to pass it. Plus, the offer was a good one." He concentrated on his task, not looking up as he listed his reasons. "And I liked the idea of going back to your father's mine. I feel as though I left a job half-done and I need to finish it. Are you sorry I accepted it?"

"No." Glenna shook her head, auburn hair swaying. "As long as you didn't take it for the wrong reason."

"I don't think I did."

With the last of the dinner plates out of the box, Glenna stood up and positioned the step stool in front of the cupboard. Climbing it, she opened the door to the top shelf where the china was being stored.

"Would you hand me the plates, Bruce?" She half turned to take the plates he passed up to her a few at a time. The phone rang when he gave her the last. "Will you get it? It's probably for Dad."

"Sure." Bruce walked to the phone. "Reynolds's residence," there was a pause, and then, "yeah, she's here." As she climbed down the step stool, he gave her the phone. "It's Jett."

Her heart flipped over and her hand was unsteady as she reached for the phone. "Hello?" Glenna had been half expecting to hear from him before the weekend, but now she was slightly surprised by it.

"Hello. Guess you have company." There was a thin thread of grimness in his tone.

She didn't need to explain anything to him and discussing why Bruce was in her home while he was there was rude. Bruce continued kneeling beside the box on the kitchen floor, unpacking the china sauce dishes.

"Did I interrupt anything?" His question was slightly challenging.

"No. I was unpacking the last of the boxes, trying to get the last of our things put away," Glenna explained. The suspicion of jealousy in his voice was a little gratifying even if it was unjustified.

"Did Hawkins tell you he's going to work for my company?"

"Yes, he did." She turned and spoke to Bruce. "I'll be right back." Glenna then walked into the living room and sat down on the couch. "Did you call to talk to me or to talk business, Mr. Coulson?" Glenna said saucily. "How are you?"

Jett laughed. "I'm all right, but missing you. I was hoping to come down this weekend, but some things happened at the mine that needed my immediate attention. I was thinking that maybe you could come up."

"I'm really busy settling in and I have a new job, so it's kind of difficult for me right now." Her words were filled with disappointment. Still, Jett had to learn. Maybe everything revolved around him in his world, but she didn't.

"I'm sure that Bruce will do his best to entertain you and help out," he responded a little dryly.

"So, when do you think we could see each other?" Glenna said.

"Hopefully, I'll get everything squared away and I can come see you early in the week. I'll call you before then."

"Or you can just e-mail me. Whatever's easiest," she said.

"I'll see you soon, beautiful."

"Bye, Jett." She waited until she heard the disconnecting click on his end of the line before she hung up. When she turned, Bruce was quietly studying her.

His sudden presence startled her.

"Are you in love with him, Glenna?" he asked.

She hesitated then rubbed her arms, remembering how it felt when Jett touched her. "I don't know, Bruce. It's complicated. I hardly know him, but still . . ." She didn't know what to say that would lay out the way she felt for Jett without hurting Bruce anymore.

"Is he in love with you?" was Bruce's next question.

That required a more cautious answer. "We haven't really talked about that, Bruce. But he feels as strongly about me as I feel about him."

Bruce straightened and walked to the step stool. "Where do you want these sauce dishes? On the same shelf with the plates?" And just like that, the subject was changed.

CHAPTER ELEVEN

On Monday, Glenna left the printing office early to run some errands for the company on her way home. Although she knew most of the customers, she didn't stay to chat. She'd been thinking about Jett all day, and though they kept in contact via e-mail, she knew she'd talk to him today.

That was the reason for the gleam in her gray green eyes and the smile that hovered on her lips. Even the mountain air seemed electric with anticipation as she turned into the driveway. She wasn't quite used to the small house where she lived, but it was the last thought in her mind when she stopped the car.

As she slammed her car door and walked through the front door, she heard the phone ringing. Jett would've tried her cell first, but just in case, she raced to it only to hear the ringing cut off as her father answered it. She was breathless and yet radiant by the time she got near.

"Is that—" She never completed the question,

silenced by the sharply raised hand of her father and the stern white look in his expression.

Glenna only heard him say, "I'll be there immediately." His tone was clipped.

"What is it? What's wrong?" She read all sorts of dire things in his expression. "What happened?"

He moved into action, taking her arm and steering her back toward the front door. "There's been a cave-in at the mine. That was Bidwell on the phone." He opened the door and ushered her outside.

"Bidwell." Glenna remembered he had been one of the foremen on the shifts. A single line creased her forehead as she dug the car keys out of her purse again. "Was anybody hurt?"

"They think there are six men trapped." He left her and walked around to the passenger's side of the car while Glenna slid behind the wheel.

"Oh, no." His statement had stopped the hand that started to insert the key in the ignition. On the heels of her alarm came another more frightening thought. "Bruce?"

"He's one of the men believed trapped."

The statement caught at her breath, squeezing her lungs until she wanted to cry out. Her rounded eyes sought her father. Neither had to say the things that were silently understood. Bruce could be trapped or buried under a rubble of rock, he could have escaped harm or be seriously injured. He could be with the others or isolated from them. Still her father's calm strength reached out to invisibly steady her and prevent any panic from letting her imagination run riot.

"Was there an explosion?" Her hand trembled as

she succeeded in inserting the key in the ignition. "Fire?"

"No fire." He relieved one of her fears. "Bidwell was outside the entrance and said he felt the ground vibrate, then heard the rumbling inside the mine and saw the coal dust belch from the opening."

Glenna started the car and reversed out of the driveway, picturing the scene in her mind and thinking of the terrible dread that must have swept through the workers. She blocked it out because she knew it would give rise to panic. She concentrated on her driving, suddenly impatient with the twisting mountain roads that denied speed.

"When did it happen?" she broke the chilling silence that had descended on the car.

"About twenty minutes or so before Bidwell called me," her father answered. "He notified the main office first, then called me."

Even though her father had no more to do with the mine, Glenna understood the reasoning. This was a close-knit community. In a time of crisis everybody helped. When miners were trapped, every mining man in the area volunteered his services. With her father's experience and intimate knowledge of the mine, he would be notified in the event of an emergency.

Time was the enemy. It ticked away as Glenna drove as fast as she dared. She wondered if the word had reached Jett. She wanted to call his cell phone, but didn't trust doing that and driving. Besides, she was sure it had by now. Bruce and the men trapped with him had to know that every available resource was being gathered to rescue them. If they were still alive. A chill went through her bones, making her shudder.

On the last mile to the mine Glenna encountered traffic headed for the same destination. News of the cave-in had traveled fast through the West Virginia hills. Many had already arrived on the scene when she turned the car into the parking lot.

Leaving the car parked alongside others, Glenna hurried with her father toward the fence gate. There was already a hubbub of miners, families, and townspeople milling outside the buildings and entrance.

A small wiry man separated himself from the group to meet her father. Glenna recognized him as Carl Bidwell, the foreman who had called with news of the accident.

"Am I ever glad to see you, Mr. Reynolds," he declared.

The man's face was pale and etched with lines of stress and worry. Glenna knew her face showed the same brittle tension and fear as the faces of all those around her. Her gaze sought the mine entrance, but the steadily growing crowd of people blocked it from her view. Bruce was somewhere inside that mountain. Glenna clung to the belief that he was still alive. He had to be. He'd been like a brother to her, a constant source of support for her father. The way she'd hurt him knifed through her.

"Has anything developed since you called me?" her father questioned. "Have you made contact with any of those inside?"

The negative shake of Bidwell's head was in answer to both questions. As others in crowd recognized Orin Reynolds they pressed forward, besieging him with questions he hadn't had a chance to ask for himself.

The chopping whir of a helicopter interrupted the conversation, drowning out the voices as it approached. All eyes turned to it. Glenna recognized the Coulson Mining insignia on its side. Coming in low over the heads of the crowd, it whipped up a wind that swirled dust clouds through the air. Turning her head aside, Glenna shielded her eyes from the blowing particles of dirt with her hand and tried to keep the dark copper length of her hair from blowing in her face.

It landed on a helicopter pad within the fenced area around the mine, kicking up more dust to obscure the vision of those on the ground. Three men in business suits emerged from the chopper and crouched low to avoid the whirling blades as they hurried toward the crowd. The minute they were clear, the helicopter lifted off.

With a profound sense of relief, Glenna recognized Jett as one of the three men. Just the sight of his sun-bronzed features gave her strength. Once free of the overhead threat of the chopper blades, he straightened his tall frame and let long strides carry him to the knotted group of onlookers. His hand reached up to absently restore some order to the untamed thickness of his black hair.

The concentration of concern had darkened his features. Glenna felt the penetration of his gaze the instant he singled her out from the crowd. He immediately began walking in her direction. He spoke to her father first.

"I'm glad you're here, Orin." He grasped her

father's hand, the edges of his mouth lifting in a grim semblance of a smile.

"Bidwell phoned me," her father replied.

"We can use your help," Jett said.

"I'll help any way I can. Even if you hadn't asked, I would have been here. Like the others"—her father's glance encompassed the crowd of people gathered at the site—"waiting to lend a hand if needed."

"What's the status?" Jett made a search of the encircling ring of people. "Where is Hawkins?'"

Someone on the outer edge answered, "He was in the mine when it collapsed."

Jett's gaze swerved sharply to Glenna, revealing that he didn't know until that moment that Bruce was one of the missing men. His piercing look seemed to reach out to comfort. Tears sprang into her eyes and her chin began quivering. He reached out and hugged her. She clung desperately to him and the chill of uncertainty seemed to lessen a bit with his warmth.

Quickly, she composed herself. This was the time for clarity. Not emotions. She pulled back and looked into his eyes. Something flickered across his expression, a raw frustration mixed with a savage kind of anger. Then a poker mask covered his features.

"Let's go to the office." At that statement the crowd separated to form a corridor through which Jett walked toward the mine buildings. Bidwell, the two men from the helicopter, Glenna, and her father followed him. Jett continued issuing directives as he walked. "I want to see a diagram of the mine. I want to know the location of the collapse and the approximate location of the men inside when it happened."

Glenna swallowed the lump in her throat. Her father's arm was around her shoulders as they followed Jett and the others into the building.

"How many men were inside? Eight?" Jett shot the question at Bidwell.

"We thought it was eight when we first called you, but we accounted for two men. It looks like there are only six inside, sir," the wiry man replied.

Jett paused in an outer office. "Do you have their names?"

"Yes, sir."

"Have all their families been notified?"

"All except two, sir. We haven't been able to reach them, yet."

Jett swung around to face Glenna, "Are you all right?" he asked.

"Yes," she assured him.

"Would you get the names of the two men from Bidwell and see if you can make sure their families are notified?" It was an unpleasant task, but he needed her help and he believed she could handle it.

"I will." Glenna wanted to help in any way she could.

While Jett, her father, and the other two men went to the inner office, Bidwell remained behind to give her the names before joining them. Both families knew Glenna through her father. It took her the better part of an hour before she was able to locate them.

With that done, Glenna decided to empty out the morning black dregs from the large coffee urn and make fresh coffee. Anything, however small, would help at this point. Coffee and more would be needed before all this was over.

All the while there was a hum of activity around her. Directives came from the private office where Jett had set up his headquarters, and reports flowed back in. The crowd outside grew larger with friends and relatives of the trapped men as well as the multitude of volunteers. The press arrived, first newspaper reporters and later on television crews.

Cleve Ross, one of the men who had arrived with Jett, emerged to issue a statement to the news media. It dealt in specifics, pinpointing the location of the cave-in on a diagram and the possible location of the men inside when it happened. Although the extent of the collapse wasn't known, the statement held out hope that the men were behind the wall of rock and dirt. The report contained little that Glenna hadn't already known.

Afterward, she and two office workers volunteered to answer the incessantly ringing telephones and respond to the endless inquiries regarding the fate of the trapped miners. It kept Glenna busy, even if it didn't allow her thoughts to stray from the worry over Bruce and his companions.

As she hung up with the latest caller she heard a familiar voice behind her and turned in the swivel chair to see the plump figure of Hannah.

"I can't stand here holding this forever," she was complaining, a large foil-mounded baking sheet in her hands. "Someone will have to clear a table to set this on."

Directly behind her there were two high-school-aged girls carrying similar pans, and a boy holding a large commercial coffee urn. A man came hurrying to clear space on a long worktable.

"Hannah." Glenna ignored the ring of the phones and rose quickly to cross the room. "What are you doing here?"

"I knew you and your father would be here," she replied with a brief glance. "I figured nobody would be thinking about their stomachs at a time like this. So I took it upon myself to do it for them. I brought some cold sandwiches, salads, and chips. A couple of the grocers donated the food, and these young people volunteered to help fix it."

She set the baking sheet down and folded back the aluminum foil to reveal the stacks of sandwiches, then motioned the two girls to set their trays beside hers. The boy found a place for the coffee urn beside the one Glenna had fixed.

"Go get the rest of the things from the car," Hannah ordered, and her trio of helpers set off to obey.

"Thank you so much. These people haven't eaten in hours," Glenna said.

Hannah's practicality had a steadying influence on Glenna. Her mere presence offered support and the comfort of someone who had weathered many a crisis with Glenna before.

"We certainly aren't going to feed the entire mob of gawkers out there, but the men's families and the workers are going to need some nourishment before this is over. People always have more hope when hunger isn't gnawing at them," Hannah philosophized.

The remark made Glenna aware that she was starving. The three teenagers returned with sacks of chips, paper plates and cups, and huge bowls of potato salad. Glenna helped them arrange the assortment of food into a buffet. When word spread there was food in the building, there was a flow of hungry people with the alternating shifts of rescue workers having priority at the table.

A security man who had worked for her father and had been rehired by Coulson approached Glenna. She knew the man only as Red, although his hair had long ago thinned and turned gray.

"Miss Reynolds," he addressed her removing his cap. A deeply etched worry shadowed his pale eyes. "There's a Mrs. Cummins out there with two small children. Her husband is one of the men in the mine. I tried to get her to come in and eat, but she refused. She just sits out there with the little ones huddled around her, starin' at the entrance to the mine. Maybe if you spoke to her, she'd listen."

"I'll see," she promised.

Leaving the security guard, she stopped to tell Hannah where she would be in case she was needed and went outside in search of the woman. Local sheriff's deputies had joined the company's security force to cordon off the area around the mine entrance and separate the sightseers from those directly associated with the situation.

Glenna had no difficulty spotting the woman the guard had described. She was standing away from the others, a four-year-old pressing close to her legs, a two-year-old in her arms, and her rounded belly indicated a baby on the way. Twilight was pulling a dark curtain over the mountainscape, but floodlights made the fenced yard around the mine and its buildings bright as day. Glenna crossed the lighted space to the woman and her children.

As she drew closer she heard the four-year-old boy whimpering, "I want to go home, Mommy. I'm hungry."

"No. We can't go 'til Daddy comes," the woman replied as if repeating it by rote, her attention not straying from the mine.

"Mrs. Cummins." Glenna saw the ashen strain on the woman's face as she half turned in answer to her name, reluctantly letting her gaze waver. "I'm Glenna Reynolds."

The surname immediately drew a response. "Have you heard something?" the woman rushed. Glenna was shocked to see the woman was probably her same age, but worry had aged her with haggard lines. "Tom? Is he—"

"There hasn't been any news. I'm sorry," Glenna explained. "It might be a while before we know anything. We have sandwiches and hot coffee inside. Why don't you come in and have something to eat? You'll feel better.'"

"No." The woman had already lost interest in her. "I'm not hungry."

"Maybe you aren't, but you have to think of the children and the baby you're carrying," Glenna insisted, but the woman indifferently shook her head.

The little boy tugged at his mother's skirts and repeated, "I'm hungry." He didn't understand what was going on amid the silence of all the others in the crowd, broken only by the murmur of hushed voices.

"If you won't come in," Glenna persisted, " is it all right if I bring out some sandwiches for your kids?"

The woman hesitated, then nodded an absent agreement. But Glenna wasn't satisfied. She hated leaving the woman alone like this. "Is there someone I could call to wait with you? Family or friends?"

"No." The woman shook her head and protectively hugged the little girl tighter in her arms, a hand reaching out to touch the little boy at her side in silent reassurance. "All our kin is in Kentucky. Tom . . ." Her voice broke slightly. "Tom just got enough money saved to send for us last week."

The woman's voice broke Glenna's heart. "I'll bring some food for the children, and a hot cup of coffee for you."

The woman didn't respond and Glenna turned away. As she started to cross the yard, another woman called to her. It was the wife of one of the miners who had escaped the collapse.

"Is she all right?" she questioned anxiously. "The poor thing doesn't know a soul here."

"She's frightened. I'm going to bring out something for them to eat. Why don't you stay with her until I come back? I don't think she should be alone."

"Of course, I will," the older woman agreed quickly.

When Glenna reentered the building she went straight to the buffet table of food and fixed two plates for the children. She added more than they could eat so their mother would eat what was left.

Walking to the coffee urn she noticed Jett standing not far from it, deep in conversation with two other men. His suit jacket and tie were gone and his sleeves were rolled short of his elbows. Lines of sober concern were cut into his features, his dark eyes narrowed with concentration. Glenna wished she could go to him, touch him, and ease some of the burden he carried, but now was not the time.

She filled a paper cup with hot coffee, unaware that Jett's gaze was reaching out for her. She adjusted the plates until so she could carry them and the cup comfortably, and then returned outside.

When she got back outside, Mrs. Cummins and her small children all sat cross-legged on the ground. The poor kids acted starved, hardly waiting to be given the plates before snatching the sandwich halves to begin eating. Glenna offered the cup of coffee to Mrs. Cummins.

"No. I don't want anything," she refused irritably.

Mrs. Digby, the miner's wife who had been standing by silently, pursed her lips in temper. "She was thoughtful enough to bring you the coffee and your kids something to eat. The least you can do is thank her."

"I'm sorry. All I can think about is Tom," the woman began while her gaze remained fixed on the mine's entrance.

"All you can think about is yourself," Mrs. Digby criticized.

"Please, she's scared," Glenna said. She had no idea what it was like to be married with two children, plus one on the way, and not know if your husband was dead or alive or suffering. People reacted to tragedy in different ways, and just knowing Bruce was trapped had almost sent her to her knees.

But Mrs. Digby paid no attention to her. "Do you think you're the only one whose man is in there? Miss Reynolds has a man in there—Bruce Hawkins—and you don't see her standing around feeling sorry for herself. She's trying to help. You have two little hungry babies here and look who is making sure they have something to eat."

When Glenna saw that the woman's words had shocked Mrs. Cummins into an awareness of her children, she understood her tactics. When soft words failed, a figurative slap in the face usually worked.

"Is it true?" Mrs. Cummins searched Glenna's face, seeing someone else's plight other than just her own. "Is your man really in there, too?"

"Yes." It was a small deceit. This woman needed someone to commiserate with. Bruce wasn't exactly her man, but she cared deeply for him. "He is," she said softly.

"I'm sorry. I didn't know." She reached for the coffee Glenna had brought. "Thank you . . . for everything."

"It's all right." When she handed her the cup, she noticed a fourth long shadow intruding on the ones they cast. She turned to see Jett standing to one side, and she turned to take a step toward him. A question leaped into her eyes as she scanned the impenetrable mask of his features, but a brief shake of his head told her there was no news.

"I came out for some fresh air and to find you," he said.

Glenna took the last few steps to be closer to him. She found it difficult to talk; all her thoughts were overshadowed by the knowledge that men were trapped in the mine beneath them. It seemed wrong that her pulse should quicken because she was near him.

"The accident happened when they were installing an air duct to make it safer to work in the mine," he said.

Mrs. Cummins, within hearing distance, started to cry. Jett regretted saying anything, but knew that she'd want to know. Glenna stood there trying to stop herself from falling apart. How ironic. They'd gone in to make the mine safer and ended up trapped. She looked at Jett and saw something else she couldn't quite place in his features. She found it hard to have a conversation under the circumstances. She turned away instead, saying, "I'd better go in. Hannah may need me." He said nothing when she walked away.

Chapter Twelve

Twenty minutes later Glenna saw Jett enter the building and go directly to the private office, never glancing her way. She squared her shoulders and helped Hannah rearrange the buffet table into a snack counter. A few stragglers came in to eat some of the remaining sandwiches.

At half-past ten her father came out of the private office and stopped to talk to her, "If you're not too busy, could you bring Jett some coffee? If there's anything left, would you bring him some food? He hasn't eaten anything." His face looked strained, but there was a solid confidence and strength about him. It instantly warmed her.

"I will," she said as he continued on his way to the washrooms.

Holding the coffee and food, she knocked on the inner office door. She walked in when she heard him answer. Jett barely glanced up when she entered, seated at his desk and bent over an array of papers and diagrams.

"I brought you some coffee and something to

eat," Glenna said and set it down on a small cleared space on the desktop. There was no one else in the room as he reached for the coffee, but showed no interest in the sandwich. "You need something. Dad said you haven't eaten."

Her voice seemed to make no impression on him, his concentration not wavering from the papers he was studying. Jett took a sip of the coffee and set it back down to lean an elbow on the desk and rub a hand across his mouth and chin.

"That's where they have to be if they are alive," he declared aloud, his jaw hardening. A wave of grim exasperation broke over him. "Dammit, right in the bowels of the mountain!"

"Bruce called it a womb," Glenna remembered, and that got Jett's attention. She was drawn to the window that overlooked the mine yard, its dusty panes creating a haze. "He said he felt safe inside it, safe and protected. I know he isn't afraid, and that helps me."

The squeak of the swivel chair told her Jett had gotten up. "I promise you it won't be his tomb, Glenna." He came to stand beside her by the window. "I'll get him out of there."

She lifted her gaze to him, a smile touching her mouth. "I know you will." She knew it as surely as she knew her own name. Some powerful force seemed to flow between them in that moment. She glanced at his desk and the untouched sandwich. "Is there anything I can get you? Anything you want, Jett?"

"I want you, Glenna." He reached out to possessively take her hand and draw her toward him. His gaze ran roughly over her face. "I missed you."

She was surprised by the raw emotion in his words and face. When his mouth moved hungrily onto hers, she tried to make him understand with her kiss that she loved him. She realized she loved this strong, confident man who was capable of facing the world with a poker face but who was overflowing with emotion. Her heart beat wildly, a searing rapture that knew no end.

But there was something desperate in his need, something raw and aching that a single kiss couldn't satisfy. His hands were all over her—stroking, feeling, caressing—yet never able to get their fill of her. Through it all, her senses clamored with the desires he aroused. They quivered through her every nerve end like concentric circles in a pond, each ripple as perfect and delightful as the first.

A knock on the door she had left ajar brought the embrace to an abrupt end. Before the shutters fell to block out his expression, Glenna saw the glitter of wildness in his eyes and was shaken by the force of it.

His broad shoulders and back blocked her from the view as Jett turned his head to the side, but didn't turn around to see who it was.

"What is it?" he said over his shoulder.

"There's a phone call on line two—about that equipment—you wanted to know whether it was available or not," was the answer.

Glenna heard the sigh rip through him, heavy and long. The grip of his fingers loosened on her arms, gradually letting her go altogether, "All right. I'll take it." He left her to walk to the desk and pick up the phone, punching the second button for the incoming call. "Yes."

Their moment of privacy was gone. The present situation had reclaimed its priority. Glenna slipped quietly out of the room, inwardly radiant with the emotions Jett had aroused, yet confused by his attitude.

Walking back to her station, she passed her father on his way back into Jett's office and immediately noticed the tiredness in his face, something that had escaped her notice only moments before.

"Are you all right, Dad?" Her concern was instant.

"I'm fine," he insisted, but on a weary note.

"Don't overdo it," Glenna warned. "Get some rest. Isn't it enough that I have to keep wondering about Bruce? Don't make me start worrying about you, too."

"Glenna is right." Jett's voice came from a few feet behind her. He had the coffee cup she had brought him in his hand. "Sack out on the couch, Orin, and get some rest. I'll wake you if anything develops. I want that ambulance outside used for the men in the mine, not you."

Her father glanced at the couch in the outer office. "Maybe I'll lie down for a little while," he conceded to his tiredness.

"The equipment?" Glenna referred to the phone call he'd taken before she left.

"It's on its way." He left the office, walking past her. "The coffee is cold," he said by way of explanation as he poured a fresh cup from the urn. Someone came in and immediately sought out Jett to make a report. Within a few minutes he was surrounded by people. Glenna walked to the desk to take up her post answering the telephones.

Around midnight the activity slackened. The

strain and the late hour began to take their toll on Glenna. She found a straight-backed chair in a quiet corner and settled onto it, resting her head against the wall. It wasn't long before she dozed off and dreamed of the workers being rescued and Jett's arms around her.

The first gray light of dawn wakened her, but her senses were slow to leave behind the dreams. The first thing she noticed was Jett's unique smell. With her eyes closed she could feel the rich fabric of his suit jacket against her cheek, the texture of it and the scent of him surrounding her. It was several seconds before she realized she was lying down, not seated in the chair propped against the wall.

Glenna slowly opened her eyes. She was on the couch in the private office. His suit jacket was folded to make a pillow for her head. Jett had carried her in here and laid her down, slipping off her shoes and leaving the sensation of a soft kiss to linger on her lips.

"Good morning." Jett was standing beside his desk, leaning on it while several others, her father among them, studied papers spread in front of them. Jett was half turned to watch her, but the others only glanced her way. His face was haggard and drawn from no sleep; a dark stubble of beard shadowing the lean hollows of his cheeks, but a slow smile spread across his mouth. A warm reckless gleam was in his ebony eyes, catching at her heart.

"Better have some coffee," he advised.

"Yes," she murmured and sat up, wiping the sleep from her face. At the same time, she sent him a warm half smile. She sobered quickly as she remembered the reason they were all gathered in this place. "Is there any news?"

The special look was erased from his expression, replaced with a cool aloofness. "No. Nothing." Jett turned his back on her, focusing his attention on the quiet discussion of the other men.

Sighing over the loss of that brief intimacy, Glenna rose and went to the washroom in the outer area to freshen up. No one had made fresh coffee since late last night, so she put on a fresh pot. By the time it had finished, Glenna had called her job to tell them she wouldn't be coming in, and Hannah had arrived. This time she brought pans of homemade sweet rolls, still warm from the oven.

With the aroma of hot rolls and freshly perked coffee, a crowd of people invaded the building. Workers, families, and members of the news media arrived to learn the progress that had been made during the night, if any.

Before the rolls and coffee were gone, Glenna fixed a large tray to carry to the men closeted in the inner office. Her appearance broke up the discussion under way, especially when they saw what she brought.

While she was passing out the coffee and rolls, one of Jett's advisers said, "The reporters are going to want a press conference, an update on our progress. We won't be able to put them off for long."

"Schedule it for seven o'clock." Jett rubbed a hand over his beard and glanced around the room. "Does anybody have a razor?"

A razor was found as well as a clean shirt. The outer office was transformed into a makeshift conference room, complete with television lights and microphone stands. Glenna sat back in a corner of the large room where she was out of the way of the proceedings.

At exactly seven, Jett came out of the office accompanied by three other men. The first was in work-stained clothes, the man physically superintending the rescue efforts. The other two were the key advisers Jett had brought with him. These three read the prepared statements and fielded the questions from the reporters while Jett remained in the background.

At the very last second, a reporter directly addressed him. "Mr. Coulson, would you explain why you are personally directing this rescue? Don't you have any qualified people working for you who could handle the operation?"

Jett moved to the microphones, but before he responded to the question, Glenna saw his gaze seek her out in the far corner of the room. "The three men with me are very highly qualified and extremely capable. They have answered your technical and, sometimes, very pointed questions for the past twenty minutes. I believe that proves their ability."

"But you didn't answer my question," the reporter reminded him.

"No, I didn't answer it," Jett agreed with a taunting half-smile. "Because if I was in Huntington, you would ask why I was there when six men are trapped in one of Coulson mines. It's incredible that at a time like this you would question why the head of the company was present." His barbed retort brought a moment of silence to the room. He glanced around it and announced, "That's all the questions for now."

Jett and the other three men shouldered their way through the crush of reporters trying to get one last question answered, and disappeared into the private office. It took almost half an hour before the bulk of the news media gathered their gear and left.

An hour later things had returned to normal—at least as normal as it had been the night before—with telephones endlessly ringing and people forever coming in and out of the building. Glenna wasn't sure the exact minute the atmosphere changed, but it started as a thin thread of excitement flowing in from outside.

It was a collective emotion that everyone seemed to notice at the same time. The voices of the waiting people seemed louder, somewhat cheerful. The building buzzed with questions. From a window someone saw the rescue operation's superintendent crossing the yard to the building. The word instantly flashed that he was smiling. It brought everyone to their feet and the men out of the inner office.

Glenna gravitated to Jett's side, afraid to anticipate the good news yet full of hope. When the door opened to the man, a white smile was showing in his coal-dusted face.

"They're alive," he announced. "The second unit punched into an unblocked air shaft and made contact."

Cheers went up around her, but Glenna dug her fingers into Jett's forearm, "How many?" she asked.

"Six. All six of them!" he confirmed. "Hawkins

said there was one broken leg, but the only other injuries were minor bruises."

She went weak with relief and turned into Jett, hugging her arms around his waist and burying her head against his chest. "Thank God. Thank God," was all she could whisper. She felt the answering tightness of his arms around her and the pressure of his cheek against her hair. Then his hands slid to her shoulders. She pushed away from him and looked up, beaming with the good news. "They're alive," Glenna repeated under his probing gaze.

His hands moved to pull her arms from around him and hold her hands in front of him, but when Jett spoke it was to quiet everyone. "Let's save the celebration until we have them out of there." A sobered chorus of agreement followed his suggestion. "When will that be, Frank?" he asked the man.

"Hell, we'll make it by noon!" the man declared on a decisive note of optimism.

"Don't take any chances," Jett cautioned. "Do it safely."

"Yes, sir."

"There's still work to do." Jett broke up the party, sending them back to their individual duties. Glenna received a brief glance before he let her go to return to his office with his select group.

With the uncertainty removed, the atmosphere in the building was much lighter. People talked louder, joked, and found more reasons to laugh. The high spirits were infectious.

The four hours passed quickly, then time dragged when it started to stretch into five. As the moment of final success drew closer, everyone was outside waiting for the rescued miners to emerge. Jett was one of the last to come out, but he didn't join Glenna standing with her father on the fringe of the anxious families.

Two ambulance attendants waited close to the mine entrance with a stretcher for the one injured miner with the broken leg. It was the attendant with the closest view who raised the shout, "They're coming!"

As expected, the injured man was first, carried in the saddle of two men's arms. Glenna stretched on tiptoe for a glimpse of Bruce, wanting to see that he was safe and unharmed. He was one of the last to come out.

Glenna hurried forward with all the other families to greet them. A wide but tired smile spread across Bruce's face when he saw her approach. He dragged off the hard miner's hat and narrowed his eyes against the bright sunlight.

Laughing and crying at the same time, Glenna hugged him, not caring about his coal-blackened clothes and face. There were so many voices, she couldn't hear hers or his above the others. When Bruce kissed her, she kissed him back. But when his tongue tried to enter her mouth, she was a little taken aback and drew away from his arms, her smile of joy slipping a little. A troubled light entered her eyes, making them more gray than green. Bruce probed her expression, his smile fading.

"I'm glad you're safe, Bruce. I—"

"You don't have to say anything." He shook his head to check her explanation and loosened the arms that held her. "It's all right." His gaze drifted beyond her to scan the crowd, stopping once on a target. Then he took her hand, turning her around. "Come on."

He laced his fingers with hers so she was walking beside him. It was several steps before she realized he had a specific destination, and that destination was Jett. He seemed relieved but she felt the piercing stab of Jett's gaze knife into her. Of course he'd seen what had just happened.

When they got to him, Jett's face seemed even more troubled.

"I got him out for you, Glenna." His voice was a low. "Please don't ask for more than that."

She was shaken by the suppressed emotion that rumbled through his voice. His features were set in rock-hard lines, but there was no mask to conceal the bitterness under the expressionless surface.

Jett's reaction only made Bruce smile with a wry twist of his mouth. He took Glenna's hand and extended it to Jett. "I believe this lady is with you," Bruce said calmly.

There was a puzzled flash in Jett's expression. After a second's hesitation, he reached out to claim her hand. His gaze sharply locked sharply with hers and seemed to probe deeply into the recesses of her soul. Neither seemed to notice when Bruce moved away to take the cell phone where his family was no doubt anxiously waiting.

"Glenna, I thought . . ." There was an uncertain quality in his voice. "Are you with me?"

The smile that broke on her face was one of vague disbelief. "Since the night I came to your room . . . probably even before that," she admitted.

His fingers tightened on her hand, squeezing the

delicate bones. "Last night I heard you tell those women that Hawkins was your man."

"I only said that because it made Mrs. Cummins feel less alone in her fears," Glenna explained earnestly. "And I do care about Bruce, but as a good friend. I already told you that."

"It happens," Jett said, towering closer, "when a woman has seen a man as a friend for a long time, she can suddenly realize how much he means to her when he's in danger."

"That didn't happen in this case," she assured him.

"It could have. Bruce was there when you needed him. I wasn't. He helped you through the rough times when I couldn't." His fingertips stroked her cheek in a caress that bordered on reverence. "When I saw how worried you were about him, I was determined to get him out of that mine. I couldn't let you down again, even if it meant you wanted him instead of me."

"It's you I love, Jett." Glenna swayed toward him.

He gathered her into the crush of his arms and began smothering her face with rough kisses. In that moment she was convinced of the depth of his feelings for her, and a wild joy raced through her blood.

"I love you, too, Glenna. I don't want any misunderstandings between us about that. Marry me, Glenna." The words came in a raw whisper from his throat.

"I'll marry you," Glenna answered with a smile before his mouth came down on hers.

BEWARE OF THE STRANGER

Chapter One

Samantha's fingers punched relentlessly at the keyboard. A furrow of concentration formed between her dark eyebrows and the line of her mouth was grim with determination. Regardless of her efforts, she couldn't make the computer go any faster. It dated from the days of the dinosaurs, in computer terms—it was at least seven years old and it had seen a lot of use. The software programs on it materialized with maddening slowness, and e-mail took forever to open. She might as well have been pecking the keys of a manual typewriter.

Peering into the flickering, slightly curved monitor screen was giving her a headache. Her little finger missed the "a" in "Yale" and the typed word became "Yle." The spellchecker didn't even pick it up.

Sighing impatiently, Samantha backspaced and corrected the error, noticing again that the letters on the keys were nearly worn off. The image of the sleek ergonomic keyboard and big flat-screen monitor she used at home flitted through her mind. Her new computer was about a hundred times faster than this old thing. If only she could bring the whole shebang to work, she thought, and immediately shelved the idea. An expensive model like that would raise too many eyebrows and too many questions.

She looked at the document she working on, aghast. For mysterious reasons known only to itself, the computer had erased everything she'd done in the last five minutes.

"Damn!" Samantha muttered in exasperation.

"Problems?" The question was loaded with good-natured ribbing.

Samantha shot the dark-haired girl a quelling look. "This isn't the kind of computer that can make an idiot look good. You actually have to know how to spell and type to get anything done on it."

"Tsk tsk."

"I just don't have your know-how, Beth. Care to share it?"

Her snappish reply carried a trace of envy. There wasn't a computer in the place that Beth couldn't operate with lightning speed and efficiency. It didn't matter how old it was either. And she understood the ins and outs of all the news editing software as well.

"Poor Sammi," Beth laughed. "You have to think like a computer."

"Meaning?"

"Meaning that computers are linear. One thing at a time is all they can handle. Makes Mr. Lindsey lose his temper, too. She was referring to their mutual boss and the owner-editor of the newspaper. "He's been pounding with both fists on his keyboard for years."

"Well, the angry ape method isn't my style. But maybe I should try it. I'm well on my way to a mental breakdown as it is." Samantha made a face. Her sense of humor had returned, however wryly.

"What are you working on?" Beth ignored the comment except for a faintly sympathetic smile that touched her lips. "I'm not busy. Forward me the file. Maybe I can straighten it out."

"No, thanks." Samantha shook her head firmly. Her thick, luxurious, seal-brown hair tumbled about her shoulders. "It's the Around & About column. It's so dull you'd fall asleep before you were half-done. I wish Har—Mr. Lindsey would let me spice it up a bit." She quickly corrected her near reference to their boss by his first name.

Beth wrinkled her nose. "You should. Just telling the truth would do it." Her tone was irreverent. "'Mrs. Carmichael's daughter, Susan, came home from college. Lock up the liquor.' Or how about 'Mr. Donald Bradshaw and the fifth Mrs. Bradshaw entertained guests from out of state. The soon-to-be-sixth Mrs. Bradshaw was nowhere in sight.'"

Samantha snickered. "It would be easy," she asserted, "if I were allowed to do a little snooping. Take this item about Frank Howard, our esteemed attorney and Yale graduate, who had one of his former classmates spend the weekend. Apparently this former classmate applied for the position of District School Superintendent, and Frank Howard just happens to be chairman of the school board. Now if that doesn't smack of political maneuvering and collusion, nothing does."

"Really?" Beth breathed, her eyes widening. "A

school superintendent scandal? We could win a Pulitzer!"

"Not yet," Samantha said dryly. "Anyway, no one's been offered the position. But I doubt if anyone else will get it other than our chairman's friend and fellow alumnus."

"Does the boss know?"

"Yes." Samantha opened up a new document and stared at the white rectangle on the screen in front of her, then shot a disgruntled look at her handwritten notes. "And he reminded me that he doesn't want anything like that in the column."

Harry Lindsey had said a bit more than that. Samantha had listened to his twenty-minute lecture concerning the diplomacy needed to operate a small-town newspaper. He had pointed out that the tamest items in the column could be turned, through conjecture and supposition, into juicy gossip, a fact Samantha was well aware of.

He had also forcefully pointed out that the people who liked to see their names in print in Around & About owned community businesses, ran ads in his newspapers, and provided a lot of the income to keep the newspaper going—no small thing in the era of eBay and Craigslist.

A good editor didn't offend his clients just to sell copies unless there was ample justification. A little political back-scratching did not fall into that category unless there was fraud or criminal intent involved. And such matters, he'd said pompously, steepling his fingers, were best left to the courts.

It was a statement Samantha couldn't argue with. Her father did plenty of back-scratching. In fact, it was his considerable influence that had gotten her this job with Harry Lindsey for the summer. She'd wanted to learn the basics of reporting, and what better place to do it than on the staff of a small-town newspaper? With this experience and a diploma in journalism that she would have at the end of her next college year, Samantha was confident that she could get a job with a national paper. Her ambition was to become one of the best investigative reporters around.

But realistically, she had to concede the wisdom of Harry's attitude. Samantha sighed. For the time being, she would simply have to curb the instinctive urge to dig below the surface of a given situation. The big bad world would give her plenty of opportunities to make the most of her natural curiosity and intelligence.

Getting her name on a byline would be a huge thrill, as opposed to mere reporting. It wasn't a goal she talked about too much. To her surprise, a lot of her female classmates and even some of her colleagues on the paper, like Beth, spent more time obsessing about whom they would ultimately marry.

It didn't even seem to have much to do with finding happiness. No, the talk was about shoes and gowns and the holy of holies: hair. The few who actually sported a diamond on their third finger, left hand, did a *lot* of talking about hair—and veils— and bridal-gown trains—and rice versus confetti.

There were three or four others who were as dedicated as Samantha was to the pursuit of their careers, and she was glad she wasn't the only one. At twenty-two, Samantha had few illusions left about men, at least as far as she was concerned. She didn't hate them or even dislike them. Samantha had simply faced the fact that there could never be "one" man in her life.

OK, she hadn't been asked. But she knew she was attractive. According to the last magazine quiz she'd subjected herself to, her freshly scrubbed, wholesome features fell into the category of All-American Beauty. There was even a suggestion of sensuality to the curve of her lips. If someone else were writing a matchmaking profile for her online, they could say that the brown of her eyes, the same richly dark shade as her hair, sparkled with animation and a zest for life.

She smirked at her faint reflection in the monitor and mentally added more to her imaginary write-up. There was a frankness in her expression that was decidedly fresh and appealing. She really didn't know how to be coy and flirt. Of course, someone truly intelligent might discern a glimmer of shrewdness in the warm brown depths, an inheritance from her father and a trait that Samantha intended to put to use in her chosen career.

The truth was that she was every man's ideal of a perfect sister. She'd received that backhanded compliment so often it had lost its sting. That could have been overcome with the right man. But Samantha wasn't sure she knew a way around that obstacle.

This summer's charade had made it all too clear once more. Being a new female face in a small town had gotten Samantha a lot of male attention—until her wholesome looks made them think she might be as good for them as nonfat yogurt and sugar-free candy. Or so she'd surmised. No one had actually ever said that in so many words. But the mere thought was depressing.

At a local dance, she'd overheard her date being teased that it must be like kissing his sister when he took her home. It was the last time the man had asked her out.

The few, very few, who had remained attentive would run for the hills the minute they found out she was Reuben Gentry's daughter, Samantha knew. She had discovered very early in life that the male ego was fragile. Men weren't willing to marry a woman whose father would overshadow them their entire lives. Unless they were hoping that the wealth and power he commanded would somehow rub off on them.

Samantha wanted nothing to do with a man like that. Good thing that her knack for reading people was as good as her father's. She usually identified that kind the instant she met them and steered clear.

For a while Samantha had thought if she could find a man as powerful and wealthy as her father, she wouldn't have to worry about the problem of being Reuben Gentry's daughter. She'd even been engaged to one when she was eighteen—way too young to get married, which was just one reason it had lasted only a month. She'd found out two things. First was that money always wants more money, and her fiancé considered their engagement more of a business alliance with her father. And secondly, she didn't love him.

The broken engagement had made her wary of getting serious about a man again. Affairs . . . well, why not? But all in good time. Physical needs were important. It was even possible that she would fall in love with someone, but it wouldn't last—Samantha knew that.

She preferred to think of herself as a bachelorette, an adorable if somewhat retro term. If anything, she was proud not to be consumed with the idea of marrying a perfect man she was never going to meet anyway.

Reuben Gentry had always silently understood the burden she carried as his daughter. Only once had he said anything about it, and that had been after her engagement was broken and Samantha had explained why she'd done it. He had suggested that she might prefer some anonymity, hinting that he wouldn't object if she changed her name.

Samantha had refused outright, declaring, "I'm not ashamed of who I am!"

Her cheeks dimpled slightly as Samantha suppressed a smile. Only for this summer had she concealed her identity, wanting to work for the small newspaper without the usual notoriety that followed her.

Her smile wouldn't go away and the corners of her mouth turned up. Only minutes ago she had been wanting to add spice to the column with someone's else gossip, when she was the biggest story in the entire town. Imagine how everyone would be set back on their heels if they found out that Samantha Jones, the nobody from nowhere, was really *the* Samantha Gentry.

"What are you smiling about?" Beth wanted to know.

Samantha let her mouth curve into a full smile.

"Just imagining the readers' reactions if I actually printed the truth," she replied.

Beth shrugged, not finding the idea all that humorous any more. She started flipping through the magazine lying on her desk and stopped turning pages when a brightly illustrated column caught her interest.

"Ooh, here's my horoscope for the month," Beth said aloud and began reading it. "'June will be calm with plenty of warmth and laughter. Weekends will mean pleasant jaunts but not too far from home. Your closest friends will be a source of joy.' Nothing about weddings," she sighed. She glanced over the rest of the page. "Here's yours, Sammi. Do you want to hear it?"

Samantha shrugged. "I don't care." She didn't put any stock into horoscopes. To her they always seemed to be couched in words that could be interpreted any way the reader wanted.

Her lack of enthusiasm didn't deter Beth. "'June will be an uncertain month. Beware of strangers entering your life. They may not be what they represent. Check the facts before trusting your intuition. Travel is not recommended.'"

"Wait until I tell the boss that," Samantha laughed. "I've finally gotten him to agree to let me do a feature on that lady celebrating her hundredth birthday in the next town, and now I'll have to tell him I can't do it because my horoscope says travel isn't recommended."

"He'll be furious," Beth agreed seriously.

"Oh, honestly, you don't really believe all that hogwash, do you?" Samantha declared with an incredulous shake of her head. She had been kidding, but Beth seemed to have taken her joke literally.

There was a defensive tilt to Beth's chin. "These forecasts are quite accurate."

"It depends on how you read between the lines," Samantha muttered, a little surprised that someone as efficient and practical as Beth could be superstitious about astrology forecasts, which she considered about as significant as the advice in a fortune cookie.

But she wasn't about to become embroiled in any discussion about the facts or fantasies of astrology. With a dismissive shake of her head, Samantha turned back to her computer paper and began punching away at the keys. Beth said no more, slightly offended by Samantha's openly skeptical attitude toward something she half, if not completely, believed in.

When the column was typed, Samantha clicked print and looked over the hard copy that the equally ancient printer coughed up, double-checking the spelling of the names with her notes. The street door opened and Samantha glanced up automatically. The tall, dark-haired stranger who walked in caught and held her attention.

Although Samantha had been living in the small town less than a month, intuition told her positively that the man wasn't from around here. He was dressed casually in a forest green suede jacket and jeans whose wear revealed a lot of nice leg muscle, nothing flashy or overly affluent. His easygoing air wouldn't attract attention, yet Samantha couldn't shake the feeling that word would have reached her if there was such a man around. He wasn't the kind anyone ignored.

He walked directly to Beth's desk, which, besides being a reception desk, doubled as the classified ads section. Behind his relaxed attitude, Samantha sensed an uncanny alertness. The smooth suppleness of his stride suggested superb physical condition. Beneath the jacket, she guessed that the breadth of his shoulders tapering to a lean waist would confirm it.

The stranger stopped at the desk. "I'm looking for Samantha—"

A warning bell rang in her mind. "I'm Samantha Jones," she interrupted swiftly.

The man turned toward her at the sound of her clear voice. Instinct insisted that he had been aware of her watching him from the instant he walked through the door. She rose from her chair, the frankness of her gaze not wavering under the steady regard of his. Again, with deceptive laziness, he smiled and walked toward her desk.

"The photo on your father's desk doesn't do you justice, Ms. Jones." She picked up his very slight emphasis on her assumed name. The man spoke quietly yet firmly, as if he was unaccustomed to raising his voice. The iron thread of command was there without the need to shout.

Perhaps that was what had first tipped off Samantha to the fact that he had come to see Samantha Gentry and not Samantha Jones, the reporter. It was a trait her father looked for in his executives and associates. The reference to her picture on Reuben Gentry's desk confirmed the stranger's unknown connection with her father.

Samantha didn't recognize him, but that wasn't so strange. She knew very few of the people who worked with and for Reuben Gentry. Mostly they were faceless names.

"Your father?" Beth's voice echoed blankly from her desk. "Sammi, I thought you said your father died two years ago."

For a fraction of a second, Samantha felt trapped by her own charade. "Yes, he did," she continued the white lie, calmly meeting the faint narrowing of the stranger's gaze. "But this man evidently knew my father."

"That's right." The well-shaped masculine mouth, an underlying hardness in its line, twisted briefly as the man went along with her story.

Obviously, he was bringing a message from her father, one he couldn't deliver in front of Beth, who believed Samantha's father was dead. Samantha reached for her handbag sitting beside her chair.

"Beth, we're going to the back room for some coffee," Samantha stated without satisfying the curiosity gleaming in the girl's eyes.

A table and folding chairs occupied the corner of a back room. A large coffee urn sat at one end of the table cluttered with clean and dirty paper cups and plastic spoons. It hardly resembled the plush boardrooms where Reuben Gentry held his meetings, but Samantha didn't even attempt to apologize for the ink- and coffee-stained tabletop. She walked to the urn and began filling one of the clean paper cups.

"I'm sorry, but I don't know you." Her gaze flicked briefly to the stranger. His veiled alertness was almost a tangible thing. "I assume Reuben sent you." It had been years since she had referred to her father as such.

"Owen Bradley, your fa—"

Samantha straightened. "You're Owen Bradley?" The statement came out smothered in an incredulous laugh. A dark eyebrow flicked upward in silent inquiry. Immediately she pressed her lips together and tried to stop smiling. "I'm sorry, I didn't mean to laugh. It's just that, well, you're not at all like I pictured Reuben's go-to guy for everything important."

She looked again at the man now identified as Owen Bradley, her father's chief assistant. Her image of Owen Bradley had been really different—never having seen him, she thought of him as a short, thin man, with pale skin and thick glasses, highly efficient—basically, a walking computer.

But this Owen Bradley, the real Owen Bradley, seemed to belong to the outdoors. His features were roughly hewn out of hardwood. Male virility was chiseled from the solid angle of his jaw through the faint broken bend of his nose to the smooth slant of his forehead.

Close up, Samantha realized that his eyes were not dark brown as she had first thought. They were deep charcoal gray, like thick smoke, with the same obscuring ability to conceal his thoughts. There was nothing handsome about him, yet she felt some invisible force stealing her breath away.

Turning back to the coffee urn, she set another white cup beneath its spigot. "Do you take cream or sugar?" The husky quality always present in her voice was more pronounced.

"Black."

"It's liable to be very black," Samantha warned. She handed the cup to him, noticing his large hands. The roughness of his fingers suggested hard physical labor. "That's the way Harry likes it. Since he's the first one here in the mornings, that's the way he makes it, regardless of anyone else's preference." She added two spoonfuls of powdered cream to her own cup of the almost syrupy black liquid.

"I don't mind." He sipped the potent liquid without the slightest grimace.

Samantha suppressed a shudder at the undiluted strength of the coffee he had just swallowed. Normally she preferred black coffee, too, but this wasn't really her idea of coffee.

"Have a seat." She gestured toward the dilapidated folding chairs.

The man named Owen Bradley chose one that put his back to the wall. His gaze scanned the room and corridor with lazy interest. Samantha doubted if he had missed any detail in that brief look.

"I was told you'd changed your name, Miss Jones, but I hadn't realized you'd killed your father off in the process." On the surface it sounded like an apology for his inadvertent reference to her father in front of Beth, but Samantha didn't think it really was.

"Only for the summer." Sitting in a chair opposite him, she absently smoothed her short denim skirt. "It seemed easier than coming up with a fictitious background and activities for him as well as myself."

Samantha wasn't entirely sure why she was explaining except that she didn't want her father's assistant thinking she had permanently disposed of her father even in her mind. "Why did Reuben send

you instead of relaying a message through Harry?"
Harry Lindsey, the editor, had been Samantha's
communication link with her father.

"He tried, but Harry went out of town yesterday
without his BlackBerry or his cell phone, apparently. Or he isn't answering either one. Anyway,
your father sent me up from New York."

"I'd forgotten about that." Belatedly Samantha
remembered Harry's sudden departure from the
office yesterday and his expected return at any
moment. The newspaper underlings, of course,
were not allowed to bother him. Then she tipped
her head to one side, curiosity gleaming in her
candid brown eyes. She wasn't surprised that her
father hadn't attempted to contact her directly, but
she did wonder why he had thought it necessary to
send Owen Bradley to see her. "Is it something
urgent?"

"Your father arranged to have a couple of weeks
free. He wants you to spend them with him," the
quietly spoken voice informed her, not a flicker of
expression chasing across his raw-boned features.
"As Reuben put it, he wants you to spend one last
vacation with him before you spread your wings
and permanently leave the nest."

Aww. That sounded like Reuben, Samantha thought
with a sigh. Her fingers raked the thickness of
the hair near her ears as she hesitated before
responding.

Owen Bradley must have sensed the reason for
her hesitation. "You can ask for a leave of absence,"
he began. "Not a problem. Harry never needed another full-time reporter on his staff anyway."

Her temper flared for an indignant second. Initially Samantha had thought he was accusing her of being a spoiled and indulged rich girl whose daddy had created a job for her. But the dark smoke of his gaze was without censure. She checked her rising anger, giving Owen Bradley the benefit of the doubt. He was possibly only reassuring her that she wouldn't be leaving Harry in the lurch.

"I could take a week off," she conceded, wanting to be with her father yet knowing the summer was short and wanting to gain all the experience working on the newspaper she could. "Where's he going to be? Bermuda? St. Croix? Hawaii?" she asked, naming his favorite vacation haunts.

"Thousand Islands," was the calm reply.

The chain of islands in the St. Lawrence Seaway in upstate New York had once been a playground for very wealthy people and, as such, it was no great favorite of her father's. But it wasn't like that now. She wondered why he hadn't mentioned the plan to her. "Oh," was all Samantha said.

"He's rented a summer place on one of the islands," he explained patiently. "Not too far from Clayton."

"I've heard of it." It would have been nearly impossible not to, because she had lived the majority of her twenty-two years in the state of New York.

Samantha knew perfectly well that Reuben Gentry liked to be ahead of the crowd. Now that the Thousand Islands had become a simple vacation spot, she supposed he had decided to investigate it.

"Is there anything wrong?" Owen Bradley had been watching her turn over the information in her mind and now questioned the result.

"With his choice?" Samantha thought it over and

shook her head. "None. It just surprised me, but I should have learned to expect that from Reuben by now. When am I supposed to leave to meet him?"

"Today."

"What?" Her mouth opened. "Why didn't you e-mail me or something?"

"It is short notice," he agreed with a faint smile, not really answering her question. "A couple of important meetings were postponed and Reuben took advantage of it to take time off. I'm supposed to drive you there today."

Samantha sighed. Once her father made a decision, he never wasted any time carrying it out, and this spur-of-the-moment vacation was no exception. She thought of the clothes she had to pack and the laundry she had been putting off until the weekend, plus all of her sportswear hanging in her bedroom closet at her father's apartment.

"You don't have to bother with packing," Owen Bradley said, reading her thoughts. "Your father doubted if you would have what you'd need, so he sent some clothes up this morning. Any personal items can be bought when we get there."

"He's thought of everything," Samantha mused, lifting her shoulders in a helpless shrug of compliance. "I suppose he's already there waiting for me."

"He'll meet us there the day after tomorrow, Saturday."

She had just lifted the paper cup to her lips when he answered. "Us?" she questioned, taking a quick sip. The powdered cream hadn't improved the bitter flavor. "Is this going to be one of those half-business, half-pleasure vacations?"

"Something like that," he agreed and finished his coffee.

Samantha did the same and frowned at the taste it left in her mouth. His charcoal gray eyes crinkled at the corners in smiling sympathy, but he didn't comment. As he straightened from the chair, she couldn't help noticing the bulky fit of his dark green jacket across his chest. Too bad that a man with his muscular physique couldn't afford her father's tailor, but Samantha would have been the first to admit that there were more important things in life than clothes.

"It's about a six-hour drive to Clayton. If we leave now, we can make it before dark," Owen Bradley stated.

"Can't we wait until Harry comes back?" She threw him a worried look. "I'd like to explain . . ."

"I have a letter here for him." He removed a plain white envelope from the inner pocket of his jacket. "I'll leave it in his office if you'd like to, uh, freshen up before we go."

A letter. How old-fashioned. Maybe it was sealed with wax and the impressive insignia from her almighty father's ring.

There were no more objections left to make. With a quiet nod, Samantha rose. As they entered the corridor leading to the front, she pointed out Harry Lindsey's private office and continued to her own desk as Owen Bradley stopped to leave the letter. Beth was instantly at her side.

"Who is he?" she whispered eagerly.

"A friend of the family." Samantha shut down her computer and quickly began straightening her desk.

"Did you know him?"

"Not exactly. I knew *of* him." She handed the other girl the printed-out column she had completed just before Owen Bradley arrived. "I saved it in the Around & About file if Mr. Lindsey wants any changes made when he comes back. There's been a family emergency and I have to leave."

"With him?" Beth's eyes rounded. "Are you sure it's safe? He looks kind of dangerous to me."

"He looks like a man to me," Samantha smiled. In her mind she put "man" in capital letters.

"Are you positive you know who he is?" Beth persisted in a low whisper. "Did you ask for any identification? Remember what your horoscope said . . . *beware of strangers.*"

"Oh, honestly!" Samantha laughed aloud this time. How could Beth take that nonsense seriously?

"It's just coincidence, I suppose, that your horoscope warned you about strangers this month and now a stranger that you think you've heard of walks in today," Beth declared in a wounded voice.

"That's all it is." Shaking her head at the disbelieving look in her co-worker's eyes, Samantha turned and gazed squarely at Owen Bradley standing silently in the hall opening.

There was a flash of white as he smiled. "Ready?"

"Yes," Samantha picked up her handbag, catching a reassuring glimpse of her cell phone. Just why it reassured her, she couldn't say. It was about three inches long and two inches wide, and not the kind of thing she could use for self-defense. But she'd decided that the only thing dangerous about him was the havoc he could wreak with her senses. That smile had increased her pulse rate and its charm had been directed at her only for a few seconds. It was a shame he worked for her father. Nothing would ever come of the attraction she could feel growing.

Enjoy it while it lasts, Samantha told herself. A series of pleasant interludes was as good a way to have a love life as any. There was no sense shying away from the first potentially exciting male to come her way simply because the attraction was doomed to die.

Why not take advantage of the fact that it would be difficult for him to say no to the boss's daughter, especially when the boss was Reuben Gentry? But Samantha smiled at herself, knowing she would never take advantage of that fact, no matter how attractive she found a man.

CHAPTER TWO

The telephone poles were whizzing by so fast that they looked as close together as fence posts. Samantha's hand tightened instinctively on the car door's armrest as they approached a curve in the highway. Centrifugal force pressed her against the door, but the car hugged the road all the way around the curve into another stretch of straight highway.

"Is someone chasing us, or do you just always drive this fast?" she murmured, half-joking and half-serious.

"Sorry." Owen Bradley's gaze flicked to her absently, almost as if he had forgotten she was sitting in the passenger seat. For the past two hours, Samantha was nearly positive he had. His foot eased its pressure on the accelerator and the powerful car slowed to a speed closer to the posted limit.

"I didn't mean to frighten you by driving so fast," he apologized.

"Normally it doesn't bother me when it's on the divided highway of an interstate, but on these secondary highways with their curves and intersections . . ." Samantha left the rest unfinished.

It wasn't that she questioned his driving skill. He

seemed to be in total control of the sports car every minute. It was some of the other idiots with licenses that she worried about meeting.

"True, but the back roads are a lot more scenic," he replied.

Staring out the window at the rolling hills dotted with groves of trees and pastoral farms, Samantha silently agreed it was beautiful, especially now that it wasn't so much of a blur. She shifted to a more comfortable position in the seat and the dark gray eyes slid briefly to her again.

"Getting tired?" he inquired.

"Stiff from sitting," she acknowledged with a smile that said it was to be expected after more than four hours on the road. They had stopped once for gas and she'd stretched her legs then, but that had been two hours ago.

"There's a good restaurant in this next town. We'll stop there to eat," he told her.

More silence followed, but it wasn't really so bad, Samantha conceded. In fact, it was rather nice. Not that she wouldn't have liked to find out more about the real Owen Bradley now that she had met him. He had answered her polite questions readily enough at the start of their journey, but he hadn't volunteered any information she hadn't already heard from her father.

He'd seemed disinclined to talk about himself and the conversation had drifted into generalities and finally into silence. Although she knew a lot of facts about Owen Bradley, the man remained an enigma in many ways.

His latent animal grace suggested a man who was highly physical as well as intelligent. It was hard for Samantha to visualize him spending as many hours in boardrooms and offices as his position with her

father demanded. He was in his middle to late thir-
ties and unmarried—that fact had been relayed by
her father at some point, because he had wanted
someone at his beck and call and not tied down
with family.

It seemed unlikely that Owen had never been
married. His blatant masculinity would attract a lot
of women; Samantha could feel its pull on her. Was
he divorced or widowed? Or single and happy, like
her? She would find out the answers eventually. She
wasn't training to be a reporter for nothing. As a
matter of fact, she could find out the details from
her father when she saw him on Saturday.

Three-quarters of an hour later, they were sitting
in the restaurant, their meal eaten, and lingering
over their coffee. Owen had asked her a couple of
questions about her job with the newspaper, which
she had answered.

"This coffee is a definite improvement on
Harry's," she added after answering his questions.

With a smile, she glanced from her cup to his
face. He wasn't looking at her but watching the activities of the various people in the restaurant. Their
corner table gave him an unlimited view and he had
been taking advantage of it ever since they had sat
down, only occasionally glancing at Samantha.

His lack of attention irritated her. She was the
boss's daughter and he could at least pretend to be
interested in entertaining her. Samantha tipped her
head to one side, seal brown hair falling around her
shoulders.

"Am I boring you?" she asked bluntly.

The unreadable smoke screen of his gaze turned to
her, and she admired the nearly black hair growing
thickly away from his wide forehead. His sexy mouth

was slightly curved, a suggestion of hardness in the otherwise sensual line of his masculine lips.

"Not at all," Owen Bradley assured her. His low voice never seemed to vary in volume.

Now that Samantha had begun, she wasn't going to turn back. "I wasn't sure you were paying attention to what I said." Might as well be honest.

"That's not true. You were telling me about a feature article you were going to do on an elderly lady named Jane Bates who's celebrating her hundredth birthday, and your angle about having her discuss how women's attitudes have changed over the years and how it's affected her, if at all."

Exactly right. "I stand corrected," Samantha apologized wryly. "I thought you were thinking about something else."

"I never forgot for a minute that you were sitting beside me." He regarded her steadily for several disturbing seconds.

Samantha wasn't certain how she should take that—whether he meant that he wished he could have forgotten about her or that she had made too much of an impression for him to do so. She had the uncomfortable feeling he was indulging her.

"Do you have a sister?" she asked finally, bracing herself for the words that would sting. She had lost her immunity with him.

"No." Amusement gleamed briefly in his eyes. "But if I did, she'd probably look like me and not like you." Samantha blinked. He pushed his chair away from the table and rose. "The sun's going down. We'd better get back on the road."

Inside the car once more, Samantha didn't attempt to check her curiosity. Half turning in her seat, she studied the roughly carved profile for a thoughtful second.

"Why did you say that?" she asked.

"What?" The headlight beams were slicing through semidarkness of twilight. His gaze didn't flicker from the road.

"That I wouldn't look like your sister if you had one," Samantha answered evenly.

"It's true. But that isn't what you're really asking, is it?" He glanced into his rearview mirror before pulling into the other lane to pass the car ahead. "No one who's worked closely with Reuben would miss the comments made about him and his daughter."

"So you've heard me described as attractive in a sisterly kind of way," she concluded.

"I've met a lot of men and none of them had a sister that looked like you." The mocking glitter of his charcoal eyes lit on her for an instant. The quiet voice was teasing her and Samantha laughed softly. A pleasant warmth invaded her body. The contentment she felt had nothing to do with a full stomach or the refreshing outside air from the vent. She relaxed in the bucket seat and gazed out the window at the first evening star twinkling in the purple sky.

The stars were out in force when they finally drove through the quiet streets of Clayton, New York. With a sure hand on the wheel, Owen Bradley drove through the town, not stopping until he reached a docking area on the riverfront.

No boats were moored there, so Samantha assumed it was a place where boats simply took on or let off passengers. When Owen reached behind the seat for his briefcase and stepped out of the car, she followed suit.

The night's darkness had colored the river black, and the rippling current reflected the silvery beams of a crescent moon, creating an effect of silvery lace against black satin. The horizon was an indistinguishable mound of lumpy shapes.

A strange voice broke the gentle silence, causing Samantha to nearly jump out of her skin. "The boat will be here shortly."

Spinning to face it, she saw a man, as tall as Owen Bradley, standing beside him. The shadows of a building concealed his features from her gaze.

"Thanks, Bert," Owen said, and then handed the man something.

Evidently it was the car keys, since the man opened the driver's door and slid behind the wheel. He reversed the car and started back the way they had come. Almost instantly the sound of the car's motor was joined by that of a boat, its navigational lights approaching the dock.

Samantha felt a hand on her elbow and was taken and turned to Owen, who led her to the side of the street within the shadows of a building. "Wait here," he ordered firmly, and walked in long easy strides toward the river's edge.

A sailboat came into view, its canvas furled, an empty mast jutting into the darkness. At almost the same instant that the boat cut its power to come into the dock, Samantha heard the car stop at the corner. She glanced at it, seeing a woman step from the sidewalk and climb into the passenger side before it drove off. Bert whoever-he-was obviously had a girlfriend, she thought, smiling to herself, and turned back to the dock.

A line was being tossed to Owen from the boat. With quick expert twists, he had it looped around a mooring pin and signaled to Samantha to join him. An older, burly-looking man was on deck to offer her a steadying hand aboard. He was built like a football player, muscle-necked and barrel-chested.

"Thanks," she murmured, but the man was already disappearing to another part of the boat.

The line was freed and Owen stepped on deck. "You'd better go below while we get under way."

The night air was cool on the water. If Samantha had had a sweater to cover the bareness of her arms below the short sleeves of her blouse, she might have argued that she would rather stay on deck. Instead she went below without protest.

The boat's engines throbbed with power as they moved away from the dock. The lights of the town began to recede. Samantha doubted if two minutes had elapsed between the time the car had stopped at the dock and the boat had left.

There was a brief shake of her head as a bemused smile touched her mouth. Only Reuben Gentry could have organized an operation as efficient as this, with someone waiting to take the car and the boat probably waiting just beyond the dock.

Settling onto a cushioned seat in the cabin, Samantha rubbed her shivering skin to erase the chilling goosebumps. On deck, footsteps approached the stairwell to the cabin. A few seconds later Owen's tall frame appeared above.

"Comfortable?" he inquired with that lazy movement of his mouth into a smile. His briefcase was set on a nearby cushion.

"Fine," Samantha nodded, "although I wish I'd brought a sweater."

He glanced sharply at her crossed arms and her huddled pose. "I think there's a spare windbreaker around here you can wear."

He walked past the galley area and disappeared from her view. She could hear him opening and closing doors in what was probably the sleeping quarters. For an instant, Samantha had thought he might offer her his jacket. She smiled wryly. He did seem protective, and probably would do it—but he also seemed familiar with the boat and its contents, and most likely there was a jacket on board that would fit her better than his.

"Here you go." He reappeared, offering her a light blue windbreaker. Samantha quickly slipped it on, losing her hands in the long sleeves. It didn't fit her at all—in fact, it was several sizes too large, but it offered protection, and that was what mattered. "Sorry, but there wasn't anything smaller."

"That's all right." She rolled the sleeves back to her wrists and spared a glance out through the narrowed windows. But the glass only reflected a dark picture of the interior of the cabin. "How much longer before we arrive at the island?"

"An hour, more or less," he said blandly. He moved toward the steps leading to the deck and paused. "There's some coffee in the thermos. Help yourself." He gestured toward the galley to indicate its location. Warmth was briefly visible in his smoky gaze. "I can't guarantee it's better than Harry's, but it is hot."

"Thanks," Samantha smiled, and he disappeared up the steps.

The coffee turned out to be delicious. She curled both hands around the cup to let her cold fingers take advantage of its heat. Relaxing against the cushion, she leaned her head back and listened to the throb of the boat's engines. It seemed to be the only sound in the entire world, except for the occasional murmur of conversation between Owen and the burly boatman above.

Almost inevitably, or so it seemed, her thoughts focused on him. In so many ways, he was a contradiction—for instance, his buff body and obvious intelligence. Not that the two couldn't go together, but Samantha had difficulty visualizing him as her father's assistant. He was definitely the take-charge type, not the assisting type.

Following a CEO around wasn't exactly hard physical labor. She was amused by the way he tried to disguise being on alert—his air of idle distraction bordered on aloofness, yet he was aware every second of what was happening around him.

The quiet, low-pitched voice was always firm with purpose and authority. Something in its tone suggested that whoever decided to cross him should beware of the consequences. Behind the composed features and slow smiles lay an intriguing quality that she would have to call hard. There was a hint of ruthlessness in his gaze that she found very attractive.

It would be an interesting challenge to find out what made him tick, Samantha decided. Swallowing the last of the coffee, she leaned back again and closed her eyes. His subtle compliment that Samantha didn't look like the sister of anyone he had known returned. She realized Owen was adept at handling women, too.

One minute she'd been irritated because he didn't seem to be paying any attention to her, and then, within the space of a few words, he had made her feel important and beautiful without uttering any extravagant compliments she wouldn't have believed anyway. He had to be aware of the impact his virility had on the opposite sex.

Yet it wasn't the direct assault that a strikingly handsome man would make. It was a slow undermining that removed the ground from under a girl's feet and sent her toppling before she realized what was happening. That was the danger Beth had instinctively sensed, Samantha decided. Admittedly, he was a devastatingly potent combination.

The long drive had tired Samantha more than she had realized. She drifted into a state of half sleep, lulled by the hypnotic throb of the engines. Her head bobbed to one side, waking her. She sat up straight, rubbing the side of her neck and chiding herself for dropping off.

The steady rhythm of the engines altered its tempo. Stifling a yawn, Samantha glanced at her watch, but she couldn't remember what time they had arrived at the boat. She had the feeling that she had been dozing for much longer than it seemed. As she started to peer out of the narrow windows, footsteps again approached the stairs to the cabin.

"We're coming into the island now," announced Owen, coming halfway down the stairs.

"I'll be right there," Samantha answered. Picking up her cup, she carried it to the galley sink and rinsed it out. As she started toward the steps, she noticed the briefcase sitting in the cushion and picked it up, glancing briefly at the initials. She ascended to the deck just in time to catch a shadowy glimpse of rocks, trees, and shrubs. Then the island was obscured by a solid wall of black that suddenly surrounded three sides of the boat and blocked out the night sky. It took her a full second to realize that they had glided silently into a boathouse. The engines were cut. In the dimness, Samantha could just barely make out the shapes of the two men making the boat fast as it rubbed against the side of the inner dock. A solitary light bulb was switched on when the boathouse doors to the river were shut. It cast more shadows than the darkness it illuminated.

After the incessant hum of the engines, the silence seemed eerie. Water lapped against the hull and the men's footsteps echoed hollowly on the boards of the dock. The boathouse seemed like an enormous cavern with its high walls and a ceiling lofty enough to accomodate the tall-masted sailboat with ease.

"Ready?" Owen's voice prompted from the dock.

Samantha moved toward him, accepting the steadying hand on her arm as she stepped from the boat deck onto the dock. The boat rocked slightly as she pushed off and she stumbled against him, the briefcase making her balance awkward. Immediately, his large hands spanned her waist to hold her upright. The hard length of him was imprinted on her hips and thighs.

Tipping her head back, Samantha started to make a self-mocking comment about her clumsiness, but the words never left her parted lips. The mesmerizing quality in his gaze stole her voice and breath, and her pulse tripped over itself. When his attention slid to her mouth, she was sure he was going to kiss her, and she held her breath in anticipation.

The grip on her waist lingered for several more seconds, then he firmly held her steady as he stepped back. Disappointment surged through Samantha. She tried to hide it with a shaky laugh and a change of subject.

"You should ask Reuben for a raise when he gets here on Saturday," she joked, needing to feel like that moment of intimacy had not been about to happen.

His expression was immediately shuttered, yet there was a noticeable alertness behind his smile. "Why do you say that?"

"Because it doesn't suit his corporate image to have his assistant running around carrying a secondhand briefcase with someone else's initials," she answered as she offered it to him.

It was an expensive briefcase all the same. But it showed the telltale marks of much use. Near the handle were two gold letters: C.S. Samantha had noticed them briefly when she had picked the case up from the cabin seat.

"I think Reuben can afford to buy you a briefcase with your own initials, Owen," she declared.

She assumed he'd bought it used because it was sturdy and durable, capable of taking the beating of travel and use that his position would demand, not because of the status of its designer.

He took the briefcase, glancing at the initials thoughtfully before meeting her smiling and unwary look. "I'd forgotten that as a reporter it's your job to notice things," he mused aloud. His thoughts were unreadable as he paused. "I'm not Owen Bradley."

Samantha's brown eyes widened. "You said—"

"No, you said I was Owen Bradley," he corrected her lazily. "I simply didn't bother to deny it. Actually what I had been going to say was that Owen Bradley had told me where I could find you."

"Then who are you?" she demanded with an accusing frown.

"Chris Andrews. The 'S' is for Steven, my middle name." His finger tapped the initials on the briefcase. "The 'A' was knocked off sometime or another."

"Chris Andrews?" Samantha repeated in disbelief. "*The* Chris Andrews?"

"I don't know how many you know." A mocking smile played at the corners of his firm mouth.

As far as Samantha was concerned, there was only one Chris Andrews. He wasn't exactly a rival of her father's, but their competitive interests often clashed. Still, Reuben Gentry admired his business and financial skills even when he cursed him. And like her father, he shunned publicity. Samantha had only seen his picture in the paper once, and that had been a while ago. He was a whole lot more rugged now. She could have kicked herself for not recognizing him. But at least she knew she hadn't been kidnapped by a crazy stranger. If she called her father right now, he'd vouch for the guy.

Maybe.

"Does Reuben know you've brought me here?" she demanded, still trying to sort through the astounding revelation and find its true significance.

"Of course," Owen-Bradley-who-turned-out-to-be-really-Chris-Andrews replied, nodding without hesitation. "I told you, he'll be here Saturday."

"Why?" She tipped her head to the side.

"Because I invited him," he said blandly.

"This is your home?" asked Samantha. "Your boat?"

"Yes."

"Why am I here? And why is Reuben coming?" All of her reporter instincts rushed to the fore, and she ran through a mental list of sharp questions for his motives that she decided to save for later. Samantha drew herself up to her full height of five feet six inches and still had to look up to see his face, raw-boned and impassive.

"Reuben owns stock in some companies I've been trying to buy and he has been unwilling to sell. It's an amicable disagreement. I invited him here for two weeks in hopes of negotiating a compromise. He accepted, but I wouldn't attempt to guess at his reasons," Chris Andrews replied.

"That still doesn't tell me what I have to do with it or why I'm here," Samantha reminded him smoothly.

"You're here for the same reason I gave you at the newspaper. Reuben wants to spend some time with you before you fly away into the world. He asked if you could come and I agreed."

"Why would you agree? Wouldn't my presence distract you and my father?" Her tone was accusing. She wasn't exactly sure what she could accuse him of, besides getting her up here under false pretenses.

He only shrugged. "Possibly, but I'm willing to take the risk," he said diffidently. "Besides, if having you here will put your father in a good mood, it might make the negotiations easier. You're as cute as a bug."

She put her hands on her hips and glared at him. "I don't believe you said that. And I don't think my father thinks I'm that cute—he had to raise me, after all. Besides, what you mean is that having his daughter around might make him act less tough. I'm here to soften him up, is that it?"

"And with luck to have a peaceful and relaxing week with your father," Chris added.

His logical tone was almost convincing. She sensed the truthfulness of his answers, however selfish his motivation was. But there was one point that Samantha still wanted to have clarified.

"Why am I here now? Before Reuben comes on Saturday?" she wanted to know, boldly meeting his veiled look.

"Obviously we've never met." Her brief nod to him acknowledged the fact. "I thought it would be prudent to get to know you a little beforehand to see which way the wind blew—"

"In case I turned out to be an obstacle to the mysterious Mr. Andrews." She poked him in the chest and touched a wall of very solid muscle underneath his buttoned shirt. "You'll find out that I don't even attempt to influence my father one way or the other when it comes to business matters."

"Then we all should have a very pleasant vacation. Especially if you start calling me Chris." The sun-tanned corners of his eyes crinkled as he smiled. "Shall we go to the house?"

His hand was raised in a gesture that indicated

she should precede him to the door leading out of the boathouse. As if she had agreed to this semi-insane arrangement, Samantha took a step and stopped. She hadn't agreed and a question suddenly occurred to her.

"Why didn't you tell me who you were in the beginning? Why all this secrecy until now?" she demanded with another faintly defiant tilt of her head.

"I hadn't planned to tell you at the newspaper office—that was, well, call it a test. You jump when your father says jump, don't you?"

"I certainly do not."

He favored her with an annoyingly patronizing look. "Whatever. But I was surprised that you agreed to come with me."

It was her turn to shrug. "You said the magic word: vacation."

Chris merely nodded. "When you thought I was Reuben's assistant, I took advantage of it to get you here. Once you were here, I thought I would be able to persuade you to stay. Have I?" His dark gaze fastened on hers, mockingly asking to be forgiven for the outrageous deception.

"If I said no, would you take me back?" Her eyes were bright. His explanations satisfied her without eliminating the irritation she felt at being deceived.

"At this hour? I'm afraid not." His thick eyebrows arched. Chris Andrews knew she wasn't seriously expecting him to agree and his response was in the same light vein as her question.

"In that case, since you've succeeded in tricking me into coming here, you might as well show me where I'm going to sleep tonight," Samantha declared with a sigh, only partially reluctant.

"This way." Again Chris indicated the door, standing to the side for Samantha to lead the way.

As she opened it and stepped into the night, the interior light from the boathouse revealed a path of dirt and bedrock worn smooth from frequent use. The light was switched off when Chris walked through the door.

Samantha stopped. "The man who was on the boat is still in there," she reminded him, knowing the boathouse would be pitch black without the one light.

"Tom? No, he left within minutes after we docked. He's at the house drinking decaf by now," he assured her, tucking a hand beneath Samantha's elbow to guide her over the unfamiliar—to her—path. A light gleamed distantly through the trees lining the path.

It appeared to be their destination as they made their way along the trail through the trees. Samantha couldn't help reflecting on the day's events and the man whose hands so firmly guided her along. She was unaware of the soft laugh that escaped her curved lips until Chris Andrews asked in a tone of amused curiosity, "What's so funny?"

Samantha darted him a sideways glance, but little of the light from the stars and the sliver of the moon penetrated the dense tree limbs overhead. His craggy features were shadowed.

"Beth, the girl at the newspaper office, read my horoscope today for the month of June." Her smile deepened as she paused, considering her skeptical reaction to the forecast. It had been more like outright disbelief.

"Do you believe in astrology?" His tone echoed her own previously held opinion that it was a great deal of nonsense.

"I haven't been, but after today, I might reconsider," Samantha conceded, the smile remaining on her mouth.

"Why after today?"

"Because my horoscope said to beware of strangers, that they wouldn't be what they seemed," she explained with a short laugh. "It certainly turned out to be prophetic in this case. I was just becoming accustomed to the fact that you were Owen Bradley, a man I'd always pictured as pale, short, thin, and bespectacled."

"Well, I look like that when the moon is full. What you're seeing is an optical illusion." He thumped his chest.

"Oh, shut up." She wanted to shove him but they would probably both fall down on the uneven path. "It's just so weird to find out that you're really Chris Andrews and not Owen Bradley at all."

"I see what you mean." But the inflection of his voice didn't seem to find it as genuinely amusing as Samantha did, and she let the subject drop.

The house of native stone and wood was a rambling, one-story structure nestled in the trees. The spacious interior was designed with traditional simplicity. Although all the furniture was finely crafted, the casual atmosphere gave the impression that feet could be put up anywhere.

A coffee service and an assortment of cookies had been set on a tray near the sofa in front of the massive stone fireplace in the living room, and he assured her that it was decaf. Even so, she took only a half-cup and put a wicked amount of real cream in it.

Two sips and a yawn rose in Samantha's throat. She covered it quickly with the back of her hand, but not before Chris noticed it and suggested she would prefer going to bed to finishing her coffee.

"Maggie!" he called. A tall blond woman appeared in the living room archway. "Would you show Ms. Gentry her room?" he asked before intro-

ducing Samantha to Maggie Carlton, identifying
her as Tom's sister.

The woman, in her mid-thirties, complied. Samantha, always interested in other people, studied her as
they went down the hall. Maggie had her brother's
looks but not his burly build. She was pleasantly attractive, although some of her features were forcefully
strong, almost intimidatingly so. Her blue eyes met
Samantha's smile with reserved friendliness.

Yet there was something that didn't seem quite
right, and Samantha couldn't decide what it was.
Maybe it was the look that Maggie Carlton had given
Chris Andrews before showing Samantha to her bedroom. It wasn't exactly deferential and it wasn't the
type of look that would be exchanged between em-
ployer and employee. There was something more familiar in it, which indicated a relationship like the
one Samantha had with Harry Lindsey, a friend of
her father's and known to her long before she went
to work for him this summer.

You can stop anytime, Nancy Drew, she told herself.
The Mystery of the Blond Housekeeper would have
to be solved tomorrow morning. Or tonight. She
kept right on thinking it over as she found pajamas
in the dresser Maggie had indicated, got out of her
clothes and into cozy flannel, then into bed.

There was nothing wrong with a suggestion of
friendship between the two, except that the age difference between Chris Andrews and Maggie Carlton was not as vast as the one between Samantha
and Harry. Samantha didn't want to dwell on why
that bothered her.

Chapter Three

It was nearly midday before Samantha wakened, a discovery that made her hurry getting dressed. The bedroom closet was filled with expensive sportswear that, miracle of miracles, looked like it would fit. She settled for something on the casual side that looked made for physical abuse.

Wearing a pair of wheat-colored chinos and a matching tan and brown plaid blouse, Samantha went from her room into the hallway. She'd found a complementary gold scarf in a dresser drawer, folded it, and used it as a hairband, the shimmering tails of the scarf partially lost in her dark hair.

Relying on her memory of the house's layout from the previous night, she retraced her way to the living room, then figured out where the dining room was. Voices were coming from the room she had chosen as her destination. Samantha paused in the doorway to listen without being conscious that she was virtually eavesdropping.

Chris Andrews—she had readjusted her thinking to call him by his right name—was standing in front of a large picture window. Rough corduroy pants molded the muscular length of his legs. A windbreaker of navy blue covered most of a knit shirt in a lighter shade of blue.

But it was the expression on his face that claimed Samantha's attention. It was hard and unrelenting as his gaze narrowed on the blond woman facing him.

"There won't be any discussion." The tone of his low-pitched voice was clipped with command. "I don't like it any more than you do, but that's the way it stays."

Samantha must have made some involuntary movement at the chilling sound of his voice, because as Maggie Carlton started to protest, his narrowed gaze swung to the dining room entrance and Samantha.

"Good morning," he said blandly. "So you've finally decided to rejoin the living." The fine thread of mockery in his greeting held amusement. If Samantha hadn't witnessed the incident a second ago, she would never have guessed a controlled anger boiled beneath the easygoing surface Chris Andrews now displayed.

She considered excusing herself, but that would have meant silently admitting that she had overheard what had been a private and personal exchange. She decided to pretend that nothing was amiss as far as she was concerned.

"Good morning," she said cheerfully and advanced into the room. "I can't remember the last time I slept so late. It must be the fresh air."

"Undoubtedly," Chris Andrews agreed, darting a pointed glance at his so-called housekeeper.

Maggie Carlton turned to face Samantha and smiled. There was a tightness in the movement that suggested the other woman wasn't all that adept at concealing her emotions. "I'll bring you some coffee, Ms. Gentry. What would you like for breakfast?"

"Nothing, thanks," Samantha said. "Coffee will be fine for now, since lunch is barely an hour away."

"Are you sure there isn't something you would like? Toast? Or a sweet roll to tide you over to lunch?" Chris inquired with a lifted brow.

"Quite sure," Samantha said, nodding decisively.

Slipping her fingers into the front pockets of her chinos, she walked nonchalantly to the large picture window, but her side vision caught the look exchanged between the two. It was more than a signal of dismissal for Maggie to leave. Somehow Samantha had the sensation that Chris Andrews was transmitting a message that everything was all right.

As Maggie left the room, Samantha concentrated on the scenery outside. Considering the spectacular view, it wasn't hard to do. Some time during her life she had probably seen pictures or brochures of the Thousand Islands area, but nothing had prepared her for the breathtaking beauty that unfolded beyond the window.

The unending expanse of the majestic St. Lawrence River reflected the electric blue color of the sky. Its stunning breadth resembled a lake, rather than a river. The vivid green of tree-studded islands dotted its length. On the closest island, still some distance away, Samantha could see the white clapboards of a building shining through partially cleared trees.

"Quite a view, isn't it?" Chris was standing beside her, gazing out the window.

"I never dreamed it was like this," she murmured in agreement. "It's all so"—she searched for the words—"so unspoiled. Are there really a thousand islands?" From the window's view on this rocky knoll of their island she could see possibly five, varying in size from fairly large to very small.

"There are over seventeen hundred islands in the St. Lawrence, most of them privately owned." He pointed toward the north. "That far island is in Canadian waters."

"Wow." Samantha was impressed. "That's unbelievable. I guess I should have paid more attention to my geography lessons."

"Well, you can pay attention now."

She wondered how many other women had admired this view with him by their side to explain. That was a number she didn't want to know. "Go for it," was all she said.

"The largest island has more than a hundred square miles and the smallest is a rock and two trees. By government definition, an island is land surrounded by water with at least one tree. Without trees, it's considered a shoal." He directed an affable smile at her. "Think there's a chance you'll enjoy your stay here?"

"I might even write up a travel article for the paper when I get back," Samantha laughed. Her enthusiasm for the time she would spend here was growing and it had nothing to do with seeing her father.

"Do you swim?"

"Yes, why?" Samantha glanced up at him, an

impish light dancing in her brown eyes. "Are you trying to tell me that if I want to leave this island before my dad comes, I'll have to swim?"

"I had something else in mind when I asked." There was silent laughter in his expression. "But I'll go along with that thought, too."

"Why did you ask, then?"

"It's supposed to be warm this afternoon. This island is crescent-shaped, and the sheltered cove is perfect for swimming. I was going to suggest we make use of it this afternoon," Chris replied.

"Sounds wonderful," she agreed as Maggie reentered the informal dining room with the coffee.

It was more than wonderful. It was perfect, Samantha concluded as she rested a cheek on the back of her hand. The sunbaked boards of the raft anchored in the cove were warm beneath her. Her black swimsuit was backless, exposing her skin to the burning rays of the sun.

A tiny sigh of regret slipped out. An hour of swimming and diving in the cove, plus another hour sunning on the raft—soon she would have to retreat to the shade or risk turning into a broiled lobster.

Through her lashes, she could see Chris sitting on the other side of the raft, muscles bronzed and rippling in the sun. His gaze was slowly sweeping the river, a note of characteristic alertness in his otherwise relaxed pose. Only a few boats had ventured anywhere near the island. Chris had explained that pleasure craft stayed near the ship channel unless they were operated by people who knew the river and shoals well.

The ship channel could be seen from the island. Samantha had glimpsed several large freight ships gliding, silently from this distance, up the river toward their ports of call on the Great Lakes. It was an impressive sight to see them moving majestically through the wilderness on the edge of the international seaway.

As if feeling her gaze, Chris turned. Samantha didn't pretend she hadn't been studying his deliciously masculine physique. Instead she let her lashes rise more and smiled leisurely.

"Ready for another swim?" he asked.

"No." She sighed ruefully and levered herself onto her elbows. "But if I don't get in the water or the shade pretty soon, I'll be burned to a crisp."

He rose to his feet, offering a hand as she started to rise. It was an impersonal grip that pulled her upright, releasing her without lingering for a moment, although Samantha wished it had.

At close quarters, the sight of him in swim trunks was disturbing her senses. He was so vibrantly male that some good, strong, interestingly primitive urges awakened within her. If Samantha hadn't already been aware of their existence, she would have been shocked at herself. As it was, she tried to ignore the sensations.

His attitude this afternoon had been friendly, but it hadn't invited anything that might put their relationship on a more familiar level. Samantha wondered if it was because he wasn't interested in her as a woman or because of Maggie Carlton.

With an over-the-shoulder look at her before he

dived cleanly into the water, he silently told Samantha to follow. Her shallow dive paralleled his course. She surfaced a few feet from him, treading water as she pushed the wet hair away from her face with one hand. The coolness of the water against her sun-warmed skin sent an uncontrollable shudder through her that clattered her teeth.

"It feels like an ice cube now," she said with a shiver.

"Want to call it a day?" he asked, raking fingers through the tangled thickness of his own wet hair.

Samantha's answer was to strike out for the cove's shoreline. Within a few strokes, he was pacing beside her, powerful arms slicing effortlessly to propel him through the water. Samantha didn't attempt to race him; she knew she would soon be outdistanced. Even though she was a good swimmer, she was no match for Chris.

The physical exertion helped to ease the chill of the water, but the shivers returned the minute her feet touched bottom to wade ashore. The beach towels were lying on a large boulder near the shore. Chris was closer and he reached them first.

"I think you need this," he smiled indulgently, and unfolded a towel to wrap it around her shoulders.

The sun had warmed the soft terry cloth. As the towel encircled her shoulders, Samantha closed her eyes in silent enjoyment. She clutched the front of the towel around her as Chris began rubbing the material against her shoulders and upper arms.

Opening her eyes, she murmured in appreciation, "Mmm, thanks . . . that feels good!"

Without realizing it, she swayed toward him, partially the result of the massaging pressure of his large hands. Her head was tipped back to gaze at him, water glistening on her lips. His hands stopped their motion, but they didn't release her.

A magnetic current flowed between them, stopping time. There was an imperceptible tightening of the strong fingers on her shoulders as his head made a slight downward movement toward her lips, and Samantha's heart thudded in anticipation of his kiss.

Damn.

A motorboat swept close to the island, throttling down to a low drone as it passed the cove. His charcoal gaze flickered to the sound, wavering for tantalizing seconds, then focused on the boat. He lifted his head, his hands resting impersonally on her shoulders again. The withdrawal was complete. When his gaze returned to her, there was nothing in it to suggest that for a few seconds he had intended to kiss her.

"Let's go up to the house so you can change into some dry clothes," he suggested.

One hand fell away as he stepped to the side. The other slid between her shoulder blades to direct her toward the well-worn path. Disappointment made Samantha frown. She wasn't going to pretend that he hadn't been about to kiss her—not this time.

"Hey—tell me something. You were going to kiss me, then stopped. Why?" she demanded, her innate candor demanding the same from him.

The pressure of his hand propelled her forward despite her stiff resistance. She thought he was going to ignore her question and would have repeated it if his gaze hadn't slid to her. The mocking light in the dark gray depths didn't completely mask the hard glint.

"Maybe I didn't like the idea of being observed." His gaze swerved pointedly to the boathouse.

Samantha followed it, spying the burly figure of Tom Carlton messing around with the canvas from a sail. He had been in the vicinity of the boathouse all the while they were swimming, but she didn't believe for a minute that his presence had anything to do with Chris's changing his mind and said so.

"Oh, please!" Her frustration ignited her temper. "The motorboat distracted you. And I don't believe you'd care whether Tom or a bunch of strangers saw us. It was something else that made you change your mind. You're using them as an excuse."

They had reached a section of the path that wound through a thick stand of trees, concealing them from the view of anyone from the house or the cove. His hand stopped pushing her forward as he stopped. Samantha did, too, bristling with wounded pride. His fingers slid through the tangle of wet hair to the back of her neck.

"Don't be ridiculous." The smile he gave her was genuinely warm.

The magic of it momentarily held her captive. Samantha remained motionless as his head dipped toward her. The touch of his mouth on her lips was light and cool and broke the spell. She didn't want gentleness. She twisted away, her eyes flashing fire.

"And don't you be patronizing!" she snapped, spinning to storm up the path toward the house.

"Wait a minute."

His hand grabbed her arm to make her stay, his strong grip unimpeded by the towel. She stopped, not trying to wrench free. She slid a freezing look of distaste to his hand, all of a sudden not wanting his touch just as strongly as she had wanted his kiss a moment ago. Hurt pride. Very hurt pride. Swimming around in cold water had heated something up deep inside her. Not to mention having to look at his dripping wet body, muscles tight and hard under clinging trunks. It had been too long . . .

"Let go of me!" she demanded coldly.

"Sam, I—" A fine thread of steel ran through his voice, like a warning of some kind. But Samantha interrupted.

"Reuben is the only one who calls me Sam. To everyone else I am Samantha or Ms. Gentry—and that includes you, Mr. Andrews," she informed him with icy disdain.

Something she'd said struck a sensitive chord. A muscle jerked in his lean cheek as he clenched his jaw to check a retort. Her habit of observing people's reactions and theorizing about their cause got the better of her.

"It's Reuben, isn't it?" she demanded grimly. "You're afraid of my father."

"Uh, no. I'm actually not afraid of Reuben Gentry." She could hear the hardness of his low voice as he enunciated each word.

"Probably not in the usual sense that most people are," Samantha conceded, shaking her head. "No, you don't want to fool around with his daughter for fear of offending him." Sarcasm laced her voice. "Are you afraid I'll run to him and accuse you of— what's that delightful old phrase—trifling with my affections? If I did that, he just might get angry and never agree to sell you that precious stock you're so anxious to buy. And then you two would be in the middle of a hostile takeover. What a story that would make—the *Wall Street Journal* would have a field day."

Her laugh was short and contemptuous, until his other hand got a matching grip of her opposite shoulder. The bright fire of her gaze unflinchingly met his troubled eyes. She was ready to shake him up. He would have to let go of her sooner or later.

"Maybe I'll call up their managing editor and offer to write it," she continued caustically. "After all, I do have an insider's perspective."

"Not as far as I'm concerned. You don't know me at all," Chris said.

She sniffed. "True enough. But I don't have to. And I most certainly do know what kind of man my father is. I bet it would amuse a lot of people to discover that you tremble at the prospect of his displeasure."

He shook his head but he didn't let go of her. "Dramatic, but inaccurate."

"I don't think so," Samantha hissed. "If the situation wasn't so pitiful, it would be—"

She was jerked to his chest, his mouth smothering the rest of her sentence. With sensual skill, he claimed her lips with a kiss that made her body react right down to her toes. Neither resistance nor response occurred to her. Her only thought was to not give in to her own desire.

Oh, was he ever an alpha male. A practically naked alpha male, struggling for self-control. Provoking him, even getting him angry was almost fun because—because—oh, how she wanted him. She was caught up by the searing exhilaration of fear and excitement.

Iron-strong, his hands held her close against his muscular length as he lifted his head. The sigh that escaped her throbbing lips was one of defeat rather than relief.

"That was what you wanted, wasn't it?" The cold steel of his eyes mesmerized her.

"No." Samantha shivered uncontrollably, and this time it was emotional. Her gaze slid away from his face. "No, it wasn't what I wanted."

He didn't try to stop her when she pushed herself out of his arms. The towel slipped and Samantha pulled it tightly around her, wanting to huddle underneath the soft material. She couldn't explain, not without admitting how irrational her anger at him had been—or how it had come out of nowhere. Deep down inside she had wanted that kiss, and he must have seen it in her eyes.

So he had done her a favor. Or simply reacted in an instinctive male way and shut up a yammering female with a hot smooch. No big deal either way.

What she really wanted was for him to want her.

She had the family pride, if not her own, to uphold. Squaring her shoulders, she lifted her chin and tried not to remember that it had been one hell of a kiss, quite possibly the best kiss she'd ever had.

"Well, I'm sorry that wasn't what you wanted," he said. "I did my best." He gave her a wink.

Was it possible to kill a man with a damp towel? It took her a second to realize Chris was agreeing with her earlier assertion. The harshness had left his voice, causing her to glance at him warily. He seemed vaguely amused.

"Aren't you afraid I'll run to Reuben and tell him the way you treated me just now?" She hated the taunting sound in her voice but the babyish remark just slipped out.

"You aren't the type to run to your father. You're as independent and self-sufficient as he is," he said with absolute certainty. "I guessed that all along."

Mystified, Samantha stared at him. "If you weren't afraid I would cause trouble for you with Reuben, then why didn't you kiss me sooner?" She fought the impulse to clap her hand over her mouth, not even knowing where *that* had come from.

"I kissed you when I kissed you," he answered complacently, adding with a slight shrug, "it's not that big a deal, is it?"

"You read my mind!" Samantha burst out.

"I don't understand."

She shook her head, not quite believing him. "You're being deliberately obtuse."

"Speak English."

"Okay. You're being stupid on purpose. What you just said doesn't explain what stopped you before."

He sighed. "Wow, you're impatient. I told you—I wanted more privacy. Come on." His hand slipped under her elbow, turning her toward the house. His attitude indicated that he had no intention of discussing it any further. "Let's go to the house."

Samantha bit her lip, more questions arising from his answer, but she sensed this time he would ignore them. He had said all he was going to say. Instinct told her that she wouldn't be able to rile him a second time regardless of her persistence. He was firmly in control and she doubted her ability to shake his hold.

Instead, she silently let him direct her toward the house, mulling over the answer he had given her to see if there was a shred of truth in it. Privacy, he had told her, supposedly because of Tom's watching. Yet Samantha knew that it had been the motorboat that had distracted him. Perhaps the distraction had reminded him that Tom was in the vicinity.

But why should that matter? Chris Andrews didn't seem the kind of man who would care what others saw or thought of his actions. Unless—a possibility glimmered—unless Tom would have related what he saw to his sister Maggie. Perhaps that was what concerned Chris and made him withdraw.

Was Maggie his ex-girlfriend or something? It was certainly plausible even if she wasn't startlingly attractive. And there had already been one disagreement between them—Samantha had overheard part of it that morning. Had it been about her? Was Maggie jealous because he had a young female guest in the house, someone who would be entitled to his attention?

It was very likely. What was it Chris had said—that he didn't like it any more than Maggie did, but that was the way it had to be. Yes, because that was the way Reuben wanted it. He had specifically asked for Samantha to be invited. Chris could hardly refuse.

There was a dejected curve to her mouth as she reached the conclusion. She regretted the instinct and training that had refused to let the incident rest until she had discovered the reasons behind it. He had kissed her, yes, because she had expected it, invited it. OK, provoked it.

Being the perfect host, he had obliged. How amazingly obnoxious. He would use anyone and anything to get what he wanted.

Damn! Samantha swore silently in bitterness. Why was it she was always attracted to the men who ended up only wanting something from Reuben Gentry? Her identity as an individual always seemed to get overshadowed by her position as his daughter. She had thought she had accepted that, but now she realized she hadn't.

Chris Andrews had made her resentment of her not-so-privileged position burn hotter than before. Whatever had made her think that he was any different than the other men she had known?

The more she thought about it, the more she realized that he wanted to use her just like all the others did. Ugh. She would not be used.

The knowledge erected a barrier. Behind it, Samantha vowed to remain outwardly friendly and congenial.

She went along with suggestions he made to entertain her the rest of the afternoon and evening, but made sure there was never any opening for intimacy. If he noticed the difference in her behavior, he didn't indicate it. Samantha headed to bed that evening confident that she had restored her pride and self-respect.

When she entered the living room the following morning en route to the dining room for breakfast, she saw Chris seated at a desk located in a far corner of the large room. The walls were lined with shelves; it was a study area. A black telephone receiver was in his hand—God, the phones up here were older than the computers at the newspaper. She could kick herself for not remembering before she left to throw the charger in her handbag along with her cell phone— the thing was stone cold dead. Samantha wondered what it was like to actually stick a finger in a phone dial and watch it spin.

But she wasn't going to get a chance. He glanced up as she entered, recognition replacing the look of total concentration in his expression.

"I'll let you talk to her yourself," he said into the mouthpiece before covering it with his hand. "It's your father," he told Samantha. "Something unexpected came up and he can't get here until the first of the week. He wants to be sure you're all right and won't mind waiting until then for him to come. I told him you wouldn't mind, but I think he'd rather hear it from you." There was something faintly mocking in his tone.

Did Chris think she would welcome more days spent alone with him, Samantha wondered as she walked to the phone. He was probably so conceited that he thought she hadn't guessed what he was up to. In his arrogance, he probably thought he was leading her along quite expertly. She was going to give him his comeuppance one way or another.

Putting those thoughts aside, Samantha took the phone from his hand and said with determined brightness, "Hello, Reuben."

"How are you doing, Sam?" came the response.

She smiled a bit wryly. "I'm surviving." Chris Andrews leaned backward in his chair, doing his damnedest to look nonchalant. Yet she sensed the intensity with which he listened and watched.

"Sam, I'm sorry about the delay. Believe me, if I—"

"You don't have to explain," Samantha interrupted. She read through his concern and heard the preoccupied tone of his voice, a telltale sign that he was engrossed in some great big serious problem. She had long ago learned that her father rarely postponed anything unless there was a crisis looming. "I know you're doing everything you can," she assured him. "And don't worry about me. It's lovely here and I know Chris will keep me entertained until you come."

"Chris?" Reuben Gentry echoed blankly.

"Yes, Chris," Samantha laughed. He had sounded miles away, thinking of other things.

"Oh, yes, Chris, of course," he said as if it suddenly dawned on him whom she was talking about. "Everything will be fine. You just mind what he tells you," he added absently.

An incredulous smile curved her mouth. He must have a humongous problem on his mind. He sounded as if he had forgotten she was twenty-two and able to take care of herself. But it was at times like these that she found him the most lovable.

"Of course," she agreed in the same tone of voice she had used when she was nine. "Did you want to speak to Chris again?"

"No, it won't be necessary. Take care, Sam."

"Yes. See you soon, Reuben." They never said goodbye to each other. It was a habit they had begun when Samantha was a small child and had cried unceasingly whenever he got ready to leave on a business trip. He had made a pact with her not to say goodbye because he would always be back. It had satisfied her childish logic and enabled Samantha to let him leave without tears.

A smile lingered, making light dimples in her cheeks. She was aware of Chris's speculating look as she replaced the receiver on its cradle.

"Everything all right?" Chris asked, rising as Samantha turned toward the dining room.

"Fine," she answered smoothly without glancing around. "It's just like you said. Something rather important has come up to delay him."

There wasn't any need to mention that Reuben's preoccupied manner indicated that it was a very serious problem. It wasn't any of Chris's business, especially since she didn't know the nature of it. It might concern something that would benefit her father's rival company.

"You and your father are very close, aren't you?" He pulled a chair away from the table in the dining room as he made the comment.

"It's always been just the two of us since I can remember," agreed Samantha. "I enjoy being with him. Lately, with college and work, I haven't been able to be with him as much as I'd like." Which was the truth, but she was adult enough to realize it was part of growing up.

"I get the feeling you admire him a lot." Chris sat in a chair on the opposite side of the table.

"Of course." Samantha sensed it wasn't an idle remark. "Why?"

"I was just thinking it would be difficult for a man to compete with your father."

A pitcher of orange juice sat on the table. Samantha filled two glasses before glancing up to meet his hooded look, just about to say that she didn't expect a man to compete with her father. "Yes," she agreed out of obstinacy, "few men can compare with Reuben Gentry."

He didn't look happy to hear that and satisfaction ebbed slowly through her. She hoped that there was a stray bit of inferiority somewhere in his personality. Maybe he wouldn't be so sure of his ability to attract her.

Chapter Four

Punching the fluffy pillow, Samantha snuggled her head into the hollow made by her hand and closed her eyes. For several seconds she lay motionless in the bed. Then she opened her eyes with an impatient sigh. It was no use; she simply wasn't sleepy.

Her hand fumbled over the bedside table until she found the lamp and switched it on. Her watch lay in a pool of light. Samantha picked it up, sighing again when she saw it was a few minutes before midnight. She had been tossing and turning for the past hour and a half and she wasn't any nearer to falling asleep than when she first lay down.

The covers were thrown back as she slipped out of bed. A book was lying on the dresser, but she felt too restless to read. A walk seemed the better answer. Stripping, she changed into jeans and a green and blue plaid blouse. The light blue windbreaker Chris had loaned her during the boat trip to the island was hanging beside the hooded sweatshirt she took from the hanger, and she made a mental note to remember to return it to him as she slipped on the sweatshirt and zipped the front.

Her sneakers made no sound on the carpeted floor. She moved stealthily down the corridor, through the living room and into the dining room, not wanting to awaken anyone in the silent house. She carefully slid the patio doors open and stepped into the cool of the night.

The silvery light from a crescent moon softly illuminated the rocky clearing that provided the house with its view of the river. She started forward, a destination in mind. A flashlight would have been useful, but Samantha didn't have any difficulty finding the path through the growth of evergreens, sprinkled with oak and maple.

It was not as well worn as the one leading to the boathouse but still easy to follow even at night. Samantha had found it that morning when she had explored the island. The path led to the other side of the crescent-shaped island where a gazebo had been built near a rocky promontory overlooking the river. The gazebo was Samantha's destination.

The island, she had discovered, was much larger than she had suspected, probably several hundred yards wide and two or three times that long. It could have easily accommodated two homes without either of them being in sight of the other, but there was only one with its private boathouse and gazebo.

The small circular structure was ahead of her, gleaming white in the moonlight. The scrolling wood trim of the overhang and around the wooden railing gave it a dainty look. In the starshine, with the shimmering silk of the silent river flowing by, it looked enchanted. Samantha's restlessness vanished under its spell.

Sitting crosswise on the wooden seat inside the railing, she leaned a shoulder against a supporting post and hooked her arms around one knee, stretching the other leg out on the bench seat. Her wristwatch was still on the table beside the bed and she had no idea how long she sat there, drinking in the serenity, thinking about a multitude of things, none of them very important.

She could have stayed there all night, but the breeze off the river became more cool than refreshing. Flipping the hood of her sweatshirt over her head, she lingered for several more minutes before the invading chill drove her to her feet. A yawn claimed her as she reluctantly turned to retrace her path. At least that was a good sign that she might sleep when she got back.

With the hood covering her brown hair and her hands tucked in the slanted pockets of the sweatshirt, she strolled unhurriedly toward the house. A night bird cried in the stillness, the only sound to herald her return.

Carefully Samantha slid the patio door open and stepped inside, freezing when a low voice snarled behind her, "I wouldn't make a move if I were you!"

Instantly the room was flooded with light from an overhead fixture, momentarily blinding her. Her hand went up instinctively to shield her eyes from the unexpected brilliance.

"What's going on?" Alarm and astonishment mingled in the breathed question, the hood of her sweatshirt sliding a few inches back as she jerked her head away from the light.

"Sam!" The identification was made in a mixture of anger, exasperation, and relief. "What are you doing wandering about at this hour?"

Recognizing Chris Andrews's voice turned her around. "I couldn't sleep." Her eyes were just beginning to focus properly. She was certain she had seen dark metal in the hand that was just sliding out from the inside of his jacket. A gun?

He was shaking his head in wry amusement, his gray eyes moving over her. She could almost see the tension leave him as he assumed a much more relaxed stance.

"Tom!" His voice was directed to the open patio door that Samantha hadn't had a chance to close. His hands were on his hips and his gaze never left her, although his head turned slightly. "It's all right. It's Ms. Gentry."

"Ms. Gentry?" came the muffled reply of astonishment before the burly man stepped into the light shining on the patio. "How did she . . . ?"

The question wasn't finished as Tom Carlson saw the way Samantha was staring at the revolver in his hand. He quickly tucked it inside his jacket, breaking her trancelike stare.

"I swear I didn't steal a thing!" she laughed, raising her hands in pretend surrender as she turned to Chris once more. "I only went for a walk."

A throaty chuckle joined her laughter. "Well, you can't blame us for being cautious," Chris pointed out. "Isolated homes are ideal targets for burglars, although they generally prefer them to be unoccupied. We've only been here a few days, so they might not have known that. I hope we didn't frighten you too badly."

"Just for a few seconds," she admitted, able to smile now at the way her heart had stopped beating.

"I'm sorry, but we—" Chris began.

He was interrupted by Maggie Carlton calling something. Samantha understood the rest of what she said as her voice drew nearer.

"She isn't in her—" A harried-looking Maggie stopped in the archway between the living room and dining room, staring in disbelief at Samantha.

"—in her room?" Chris finished the sentence. "No, Samantha couldn't sleep, so she went for a walk. She's the one Tom heard prowling around outside."

The blonde's gaze skittered almost guiltily away from his face to Samantha. Smiling tightly, she walked into the room where they were, her hands nervously reknotting the belt of her quilted robe.

"You gave us quite a scare, Ms. Gentry," she declared with a hollow laugh.

"And vice versa," Samantha said.

"After all this excitement, I don't think any of us can go back to sleep right away," Chris said.

There was nothing rumpled about his appearance to indicate that he had ever been in bed, Samantha noticed. She stopped checking him out when he turned to talk to the housekeeper.

"Maggie, why don't you fix us all some chocolate?"

"Of course," the woman agreed after a slight hesitation.

"Want some help?" Samantha offered.

"I can manage," Maggie assured her, and walked toward the kitchen.

Shaking the hood from her head, Samantha removed her jacket against the prevailing warmth of the house. Tom closed the patio doors and moved toward the table to sit in one of the chairs. Samantha followed suit.

"Where did you go?" Chris straddled a chair, resting his hands on the straight back.

Samantha told him and they spent a few minutes idly discussing the benefits of a late-night walk. Then Maggie reappeared with the mugs of hot chocolate. By the time Samantha finished hers, she had already begun to feel its calming effect. That and the discovery that it was already nearly two in the morning made her drowsy.

With a tired "good night" to the trio seated at the table Samantha started for her room. Halfway there, she remembered she had left her sweatshirt on the chair.

A few steps into the living room she heard Chris say, "I'd like to know how she got out of the house with none of us hearing her."

Samantha hesitated. She was tired and didn't want to become involved with any more rehashing of the incident. With a shrug, she turned back toward her room. The sweatshirt could stay there until morning.

A knock on the door awakened her the next morning. Frowning with resentment at the intrusion on her sleep, she peered through her lashes at the sunlight peeking through the closed curtains.

"Who is it?" Samantha grumbled without stirring from her exceedingly comfortable position.

"Rise and shine." The door opened and Chris Andrews stood in its frame, tall and vital, looking as if he had had eight hours' sleep, which Samantha was sure was impossible.

"What time is it?" she mumbled, wearily running a hand through her tousled hair and rolling onto her back, pulling the covers with her.

"Nearly ten," he answered.

Eight hours was almost possible, she conceded, although he looked as if he had been up for hours. Her sleepy eyes focused on his leanly muscled shape. Snug-fitting, faded blue jeans covered the length of his legs. A yellow windbreaker, the zipper hooked at the bottom, covered most of the blue chambray shirt opened at the throat.

"I feel as if I've just gone to sleep." Her mouth was all cottony, adding to the naturally husky pitch of her voice.

"No worse for last night's adventure, huh?"

"I don't think so." Samantha's head made a negative movement on the pillow. Her sleepy brain suddenly realized he must have had a purpose in wakening her. "What do you want?"

"I thought we'd go sailing today. Since you've never been here to the Thousand Islands before, I decided it would be a good idea to show you around. There isn't any better way to see it than by boat. Are you game?" He shot her a look of pure challenge.

The suggestion sounded good even in her half-awake state. "Of course," she agreed. "Just give me half an hour to shower and dress."

"You got it. Coffee's waiting in the dining room and Maggie is packing us lunch. The boat's ready as soon as you are," he concluded, reaching out to close the door.

Three-quarters of an hour later, the boat had left the shelter of the cove. The sails were raised and the motor turned off. Tom Carlton had come along to crew, a fact that momentarily surprised Samantha. It must have shown on her face, because Chris had explained almost immediately that sailing through the various small channels around the many islands could be tricky with the changing currents.

Samantha decided it was probably best he was along as she covertly studied Chris Andrews at the helm. A breeze was ruffling the thickness of his dark hair. The ruggedness of his sun-bronzed features was disturbingly compelling in this setting of earth and sky and water. Lusty and virile, he was in his element. The sharpness of his gray eyes was far-seeing, like an eagle's.

How romantic she was being. How unlike her. But she was willing to admit—only to herself—that being romantic was kinda fun.

The glorious setting only heightened the physical attraction Samantha felt, despite her common sense kicking in. OK, she knew that thinking that way was futile and emotionally risky. She was here because she was Reuben Gentry's daughter and not because she was just plain Samantha. Maybe Tom Carlton's presence would help to remind her of that. The tour was to keep Reuben's daughter from being bored.

Chris's charcoal gaze swung to her and Samantha pretended to be looking at a landmass beyond him. She felt the sweep of his gaze run over her from head to toe and knew she looked adorably nautical in her white pants, navy top and white scarf for a headband.

The whole outfit was straight out of *Lucky,* the magazine for compulsive shoppers—and thinking of that made her wonder again who had picked out all the clothes. She caught a dark curling wing of hair that had escaped the scarf to wave across her forehead, and tucked it back in.

"Are you awake now?" There was chiding amusement in his tone.

"Very much so. This is beautiful." She could fake enthusiasm as well as the next escapee from the real world. No matter why he'd brought here, she might as well enjoy the scenery. "Is that Canada there?" she asked, waving a hand toward the landmass she'd supposedly been studying.

"It's a Canadian island, yes, but not the mainland."

"Aren't we going to follow the ship channel?" she asked. They were steering an easterly course, but they were a considerable distance from the large ocean liner moving upriver.

"The Seaway Channel is mainly on the American side. I thought I'd show you the Canadian side first, the Admiralty and Navy groups of islands, so you could get an idea of the natural beauty to be found— OK, I'm talking like a tour guide, sorry."

"No, go on. It's interesting." She meant it. There wasn't a trace of sarcasm in her tone.

He nodded, looking pleased with a compliment he obviously hadn't expected. "Anyway, we can look at those before we take in some of the man-made splendor of the American Islands," Chris explained, the line of his mouth twisting wryly.

Samantha spent a few minutes studying the sapphire water and the emerald islands. "It certainly is beautiful," she absently repeated.

"The Indians referred to this area as the Garden of the Great Spirit. The early French explorers gave it the name we know it by—*Les Mille Iles*, meaning the Thousand Islands. The St. Lawrence River was an Indian highway. They called it the River Without End, which wasn't exactly true, but as far as boats were concerned the rapids kept it from being navigable."

"What's the difference between the St. Lawrence River and the St. Lawrence Seaway?" Her reporter's instincts to discover all the facts went to work.

"The river has always been here, but the seaway is an inland water route, about 2,300 miles long, stretching from the Gulf of St. Lawrence to Lake Superior, connected by a series of locks and canals, including the seven-lock system needed to lift ships up the Niagara escarpment."

"Cool," Samantha murmured. Maybe it was geeky of her to enjoy a geography lesson, but it helped the teacher was a good-looking guy. She gave herself permission to enjoy that about him. For the meantime.

"Ships from all parts of the world travel the waterway system," he added. "It was accomplished by the combined efforts of the U.S. and Canadian governments. Have you ever stopped to think that the border between Canada and the United States is the longest undefended border in the world?" There was a quick flash of a white smile being directed her way.

She shook her head, looking a little embarrassed. "No, I don't think I have thought about it quite that way."

As the boat glided silently through the waters, with the loudest noise coming from the billowing of the sails, Chris gave her a brief sketch of some of the area's history during the early wars, mentioning the War of 1812 and the Patriot War of 1837 when the steamer *Sir Robert Peel* was sunk in the American channel. All the while, they cruised slowly by islands of varying size, some without signs of habitation and others with cozy bungalows amid the trees.

"This area was very popular during the rum-running days of Prohibition. It was easy enough for smugglers to dodge customs boats with all these islands to disappear between. One island became so infamous as a place to stash bootleg whiskey that it's known as Whiskey Island." The Admiralty group was behind them now, and Chris pointed to the left, indicating the buildings on a jutting point of land. "That's Gananoque, Ontario, on the mainland of Canada. It's a very picturesque town."

"Are we stopping there?" Samantha asked, warming to the idea of wandering through the streets.

"We won't have time."

But he did swing the boat close enough to allow her a tantalizing glimpse of the village. A tour boat was docked at the harbor, making her wish she was one of the passengers, although Chris was already turning the sailboat toward an open expanse of water. She didn't have time to dwell on the town.

He was talking again, explaining that while most of the island homes she saw were strictly summer residences there were permanent inhabitants, such as the one on the island they were approaching— Grindstone Island, en route through the Navy group of Canadian islands. They were mainly farming communities, he said, adding that they had once been dairy centers. Grindstone Island used to make its own cheese, called, guess what, Grindstone cheese, but now they had switched mostly to cattle.

"They have their own elementary-school system, which the children attend until the seventh or eighth grade. Then they have to go to the mainland for the rest of their education, usually staying with friends or relatives during the school year."

"Talk about leaving the nest early!" Samantha smiled.

"How about going below and breaking out that picnic lunch Maggie packed?" Chris suggested. "I don't know about you, but I'm getting hungry."

"You?" she laughed. "I haven't even had breakfast, only coffee."

"Don't be too long or you'll miss the scenery," he called after her.

When Samantha returned with the sandwiches and cold beer, Tom took his to the forward part of the boat and ate alone. Samantha wondered if he was just naturally antisocial or simply a well-trained employee. She rarely noticed him watching her and Chris. He seemed more interested in the other boaters on the river than the fresh, unspoiled scenery. Of course, he was probably quite used to it. For her, it was a totally new experience. She had never seen anything quite like it before. Munching contentedly on the halved roll layered with slices of ham and cheese, she pitied the person who looked on this with jaded eyes.

A sideways glance at the man at the helm was her attempt to judge his reaction, but Chris's face only showed intense concentration as he negotiated a narrow channel between two islands. Considering his knowledge of the area, it was something he had seen many times.

Dressed as he was, it was difficult to remember he was Chris Andrews, entrepreneur, financier, tycoon. He certainly didn't look like your everyday guy, but neither did he fit the image her mind associated with the name Chris Andrews. Before she'd met him, Samantha would have visualized Chris Andrews going sailing in snappy white ducks and a blazer with a captain's hat instead of going bareheaded with the wind ruffling his hair, wearing faded denims and a windbreaker.

Samantha much preferred this Chris Andrews to the one of her imagination. Then she pulled herself up quickly at the thought.

Careful, she warned herself. *Remember you're only here because he wants something from Reuben.* The sandwich lost much of its flavor.

Through the Navy group, their course took them to the Canadian channel. A tall white tower off the starboard bow caught her eye and Chris explained that it was the Skydeck complex on Hill Island, offering a panoramic view. Then a section of the Thousand Island bridge system came into view, with the islands used as stepping-stones to span the river.

Chris pointed out the maze of islands, the area known as Lost Channel. During the early wars, the pirate days, and the Prohibition era, it had been a favorite hideaway for men who knew the waters well and were able to elude their pursuers.

After they had sailed beneath the bridge, Chris instructed Tom to lessen the amount of canvas offered to the wind and their pace was slowed. Samantha glanced at him curiously.

He met her look and announced simply, "The Palisades."

Glancing ahead, Samantha saw the rocky cliffs they were approaching. Craggy and steep, they rose from the placid river to loom above the boat gliding by. The slashed, sharp stone on the face of cliffs was tinged with pink. The silence of the sail made their intimidating height seem more profound and their harsh beauty more awesome.

As they passed the town of Rockport on the Canadian side, Chris began an arcing course to take them to the opposite side of the river. His smile to her was brief and slightly cynical.

"Now for that man-made splendor I told you about. Here comes the millionaires' playground," he said.

It wasn't long before Samantha knew what he was talking about. The islands she had seen up to now had been raw wilderness with rustic bungalows, but now as they approached the American channel, the islands and their homes began to change. The heavy brush and thick foliage of the trees that filtered the summer sun's rays to the virgin soil began to give way to expensive, manicured lawns, green and lush. The summer homes were now nearly palatial vacation villas for the rich. Not satisfied with the ornamentation of nature, the owners had statues and flower gardens adorning the lawns. The architecture of some of the homes took Samantha's breath away. There was beauty here, too, but a direct contrast to what she had seen before.

When they had passed through the Summerland group, Chris said, "The granddaddy of them all is coming up. Or it would have been," he qualified cryptically. "You've heard of Boldt Castle, haven't you?"

"Yes," Samantha answered hesitantly, trying to remember what she had heard about it and finding her recollection hazy. "Something about a castle a man built for his wife."

"Yes, George Boldt was his name," he said. "His life was one of those Horatio Alger, rags-to-riches stories. He immigrated to this country around the time of the Civil War, and eventually made his fortune several times over. He came here with his wife in the 1890s when this was an elite resort area for the very wealthy. As a boy in Europe, he had seen the castles along the Rhine and it was always his dream to own one. When he and his wife saw Hart Island, which at the time was shaped roughly like a heart, he decided to buy it and make his dream come true."

"Aww."

"Evidently he was quite a romantic, because he paid a fortune to create landfills and complete the shape of the heart. And he renamed it Heart Island. Then he began building his castle. He envisioned a whole colony with several buildings and the capability of entertaining a hundred guests and their servants. Marble, tapestry, silks, rugs, all were imported to furnish his castle. He had spent over two million dollars on it when his wife died. All work was stopped at her death and it was never completed."

Towers, medieval and grand, jutted above the treed island ahead. As the boat drew nearer, the castle itself began to take form. Tourists wandered about the island and tour boats were tied up at its dock.

"Has it been restored?" asked Samantha.

"No. When the work was stopped, thieves and vandals stole or destroyed most of the valuable goods. For years, it was abandoned to the bats and birds and insects. It's virtually a ruin now. Only a few of its four hundred rooms can be viewed by the public. At today's money, it would probably take twenty million to make Boldt's dream a reality." Chris paused, frowning slightly. His narrowed gray eyes focused on the turrets rising above the trees. "Now it's a romantic symbol of a dream that became empty without the love of a man's wife."

Crazy. There was a lump in her throat as Samantha felt herself gripped by the tragic and poignant story. It was silly to be moved by it and she tried to shake away the sensation and view the place objectively. A family of tourists was wandering along the dock.

"Let's stop," she suggested eagerly.

His gaze swept over the island and the strolling clusters of people. Then with an abrupt, resolute shake of his head, he said, "No. We don't have time."

Samantha glanced at her watch. "Granted, it's after two, but surely we can stop for a half an hour," she argued.

His gaze sliced to Tom standing near the middle of the port side deck. The burly man had clearly been able to hear her request and the negative answers she had received. His expression was grim as he met Chris's look, then he scanned the other boats slowing to view the castle. Only a few seconds had passed.

"I'm afraid not," Chris refused again. His mouth curved into a smile, but it didn't ease the set look of his features. "Maybe another time."

Shrugging with resignation, Samantha glanced away, focusing her puzzled gaze on the tall boathouse buildings opposite Heart Island. She was consumed by the strangest feeling that even if the whole afternoon was before them, Chris would still have refused to put ashore.

It didn't make any sense. He was making a special effort to take her on a tour of the Thousand Island area, yet he seemed to be restricting the tour to the boat deck.

With half an ear, she listened to the commentary he began as the sailboat swept gracefully by the castle. Her eyes noted the stately buildings of the Thousand Island Club; more elegant summer homes of noteworthy people; the island known as Devil's Oven, that had once been the hiding place of a notorious pirate; the towering American span of the international bridge; the Rock Island Lighthouse, which was no longer in use; and the Thousand Island Park; but none of it claimed her interest.

The town buildings of Clayton prompted her to make one last test of her theory, especially when Chris mentioned the museum there.

"I don't suppose we'll have time to stop there, either."

The note of challenge in her tone drew a swift appraising look. The speculation in his charcoal eyes was not quite hidden.

"Not this time," he answered without elaboration.

Not ever. The premonition was so strong it was nearly spoken. The force of her certainty startled her, more so because she couldn't think of why he didn't want to let her go ashore. During the last hour of their sail back to the island, she thought and thought, but she couldn't come up with a logical reason to explain his action.

Chapter Five

Samantha fingered the stem of her wineglass. A few drops of red wine colored the bottom. The scarlet, spectacular sunset made no impression on her as it faded into a purpling twilight. Nothing had since she had become preoccupied with the question that remained unanswered. Why hadn't Chris wanted her to leave the boat?

Her gaze slid to him and found him studying her. She smiled quickly and took her hand away from the empty glass, realizing that neither of them had spoken for the past several minutes. The tip of her tongue nervously moistened her lower lip as she searched for an innocuous comment.

"It's peaceful, isn't it?" she said.

"Yes."

Both had changed for dinner that evening. He was wearing a white turtleneck shirt with a dark blue blazer and light blue pants. The outfit was perfect for a poster model for a yacht club—and somehow, not perfect Chris Andrews. This was another thing that confused Samantha. With all his money, she wondered why he didn't have jackets tailored to fit his broad shoulders and muscular chest. What he was wearing was attractive in its way, but it would have been more so if it wasn't so tight around the shoulders.

Sighing, she rose from the table, smoothing her palms over the soft crimson material covering her hips. Slinky pants and a matching tunic—another winner from the closet in her room. The vivid color accented the silky brown of her hair.

"Restless again?" Chris asked, getting up a few seconds after she did.

"Again?" Her head jerked toward him, his question disconcerting her.

"Last night you couldn't sleep," he reminded her.

"Oh, yes," Samantha nodded. She supposed she hadn't done a very good job of concealing what was on her mind. But right at the moment she didn't feel like being candid, not until she had some hint of what was going on. Since he was prepared to blame her distraction on restlessness, she was ready to go along with it. "I guess I am a little edgy," she admitted.

"Rather than risk a repeat of last night, I suggest a walk before midnight."

Samantha flipped the hair away from her cheek. "Not a bad idea." But her voice was hollow.

As they stepped through the patio door into the dusk, Chris glanced around. "Did you want to just walk or do you have a particular destination in mind?"

After an indecisive movement, she answered, "The gazebo."

His hand rested on the back of her waist, and she let the slight pressure guide her toward the path she had taken the previous night. A scattering of pine needles littered the path, rustling under the soles of her sandals. Samantha couldn't ignore her awareness of the footsteps accompanying her, nor the pleasurable warmth of his hand on her back.

It had been a mistake to come out here, she decided, but it was too late to turn back now. The lengthening shadows of the trees seemed to shut out the rest of the world. It was a relief when they thinned and the gazebo was before her. She breathed easier when Chris's hand fell away, her pulse reverting to a less erratic beat.

Walking onto the octagonal platform, she paused on the side closest to the river. The smooth surface of the water was shimmering with the approaching darkness, reflecting the dying light of the sunset. Chris stood next to her, one shoulder leaning against a post, a leg bent to rest his foot on the wooden seat, but his attention wasn't fixed on the river. He was watching her with an expression that was hard to describe.

"What's on your mind, Sam?" he asked quietly after several minutes of silence had passed.

"What makes you ask that?" she said in a light voice, as if the question was really quite ridiculous.

But her gaze faltered under the intensity of his. Mostly it skittered over the rugged masculinity of his features.

"You look as if you have something on your mind." The thread of seriousness didn't leave his tone despite her attempt at lightness.

"Doesn't everybody?" Samantha shrugged, trying to indicate to him that it really wasn't important. She found it difficult to think with him so nearby.

It became worse when he straightened as if he wanted a closer look at her expression.

Pretending an indifference that her thudding heart was about to give away, Samantha tipped back her head. The sky was shading into a midnight blue. The first evening star winked at her and the silver crescent of the moon occupied another corner of the sky. The setting was too romantic for her peace of mind. The musky scent of his after-shave drifted in the air, and a sigh broke unwillingly from her lips.

"Did you enjoy yourself today?"

"Oh, yes." Her head turned jerkily to face him, an artificial smile on her lips. "The islands are lovely."

A breeze from the river teased at her hair, blowing a few strands across her cheek that caught in the moist corner of her mouth. She lifted her hand to brush them away, but his fingers were already there, pushing the silky strands behind her ear, then sliding his fingers into the hair at the back of her neck.

At almost the same moment, he slipped his other hand under her arm and around her back, drawing her to the right side of his chest. Startled, she gripped the flexing muscles of his right arm, pressing the heel of her other hand against his left shoulder to arch away from him.

But the enigmatic darkness of his compelling gaze held her captive. She ought to protest, but she didn't really want to. He had to be aware of that fact. He was too experienced not to know when a woman wanted to be kissed. He let several more seconds stretch tautly to heighten her anticipation.

Then his mouth settled warmly over hers, caressing and arousing and melting the stiffness of her lips. Samantha had neither the will nor the desire to withstand his persuasive expertise. Her legs weakened under the sensual assault until she was leaning against his hard length for support.

Her yielding response brought an insistent demand to his kiss. His tongue parted her lips, the invasion and possession more vividly exhilarating than any sensation she had ever known. The taste of his mouth was an aphrodisiac, heady and addictive. Her hips were molded against the solid muscles of his thighs.

In the sweetness of surrender, her fingers clung to his arm, the half fist of her right hand spreading open to caress the bulge of his shoulder. He caught her right wrist, lifting his head to gaze into the dazed shimmer of her eyes. The smoldering look in his eyes revealed the physical effect she had on him, although he was more in control of his emotions than she was.

For several seconds the iron band of his muscular arm continued to press her against his length while he held her wrist in his hands. A thumb rubbed the sensitive inside of her wrist while her pulse was drumming.

The line of his jaw tightened in decision. Samantha was set away from him as he turned, moving into the shadows. Light flared and a match flame was cupped to a cigarette. He stood there smoking it but he only took a few puffs, then flung it away into a patch of sand.

She watched him, feeling shaky, suddenly aware that she hadn't even known he smoked until that moment. Was he giving her a reason not to kiss him? It was all just too weird and happening too fast. And the silence that followed between them was unnerving.

She'd made it obvious that she'd enjoyed his kiss and hey—*she* hadn't wanted it to end. So why had he let her go?

There was a possible explanation, one that filled her with waves of disgust at herself for reacting so naturally to his caresses. She would have to attempt to restore some of her pride.

"You weren't obliged to kiss me, Chris." Her voice was treacherously raw. She felt his gaze as strongly as if he'd been touching her, but she continued looking over the river. "When I agreed to take a night walk, that was all I expected. It never occurred to me that the moonlight would—well, that it would get to me like that."

"Is that why you think I kissed you?" There was a hardness in his voice. His fingers caught her chin, turning her face to him to study her expression. Her eyes had lost their dazed look and were wide and frank. "An atmospheric effect of moonlight? Given a full moon, no woman would be safe."

"Maybe not," Samantha countered, faintly accusing. "But maybe there's another reason."

He let go of her. "And what would that be?"

"You kissed me out of a sense of duty. After all, I am your guest—and Reuben Gentry's daughter."

"Therefore," he followed her train of thought, "I'm entertaining you even to the point of indulging any romantic fantasies you might have about the magic of moonlight." The freezing scorn in his voice hinted at serious annoyance. "You couldn't be farther from the truth, Samantha, in nearly every respect."

"I don't understand." A confused frown revealed

an unhappiness she hoped he wouldn't pick up on as she searched the shadows to see his face.

"You don't have to." His tone was clipped and harsh. "That's totally unnecessary, except—" Abruptly he checked the rest of the sentence, staring at her for taut seconds.

Then he cursed softly under his breath and came closer. His arms encircled her again, and she didn't want to break free. His fiery tenderness consumed her, whirling her into a vortex of sensations before she could figure out what was happening. She yielded to the demands of his mouth, her lips parting under the sensual pressure of his, a sexy sweetness she couldn't resist.

She went limp from the feeling, her flesh pliant and molded against the intimate contours of his masculinity. Her hands, wanting to stroke his neck and caress his hair, had to be satisfied with spreading over his chest, fingers slipping inside the lapels of his jacket. Arching her farther backward, he abandoned the responsive delights of her mouth to scorch her face with kisses, then nibbled at her neck until a moaning sigh of passion came from her throat. There was no support from her legs and his arms took her weight. Her hands searched for a way to cling to him, her fingers encountering clothing when what she wanted to feel was warm male skin. She touched the knit of his turtleneck, then touched something else. Leather . . . but he hadn't been wearing anything leather.

He stiffened, then captured her hands, holding them against his chest. She could feel his ragged breathing as she swayed unsteadily toward him, not meaning to, but unable to stop. The screen of his dark lashes concealed the desire she knew had to be burning in his eyes. She looked lower, avoiding the penetrating scrutiny of his gaze and staring instead at the large hands imprisoning hers.

"I must be out of my mind to get mixed up with you," he muttered.

"I—" Samantha began.

"For God's sake, don't say any more!" he snapped angrily. "It's bad enough already! Come on." He jerked her to the side, his fingers tight on the tender flesh of her arm as he pushed her toward the path, yet keeping her close enough to him that she felt his left shoulder brushing against hers. "We're going back to the house before this gets out of hand."

But it wasn't the harsh command of his voice that stopped Samantha from protesting. It was the fleeting touch of something hard against her shoulder and a series of memories that suddenly joined together like pieces of a puzzle.

The poorly tailored jackets and the fact that she had seen him only once when he wasn't wearing a jacket of sorts. The way he had abruptly ended both embraces when she had started to hold him. The leather she had touched under his jacket. The hard, inanimate object that had just brushed her shoulder.

And most of all, the memory of the previous night when she thought she had seen him slip a gun inside his windbreaker. She hadn't thought she'd seen it—she had. What was more, he was wearing a shoulder holster now.

Why? Why was he wearing it? For protection against the possibility of intruders? No, Samantha couldn't accept that; the threat wasn't that great.

Ask him, an inner voice prodded. Should she laugh? Tease him that he found her so dangerous he carried a gun? But the cold waves of fear she was experiencing froze her into silence.

They were nearing the house, its lights growing brighter. She stumbled and the grip on her arm tightened even more to steady her. She bit her lip to keep back the cry of pain but he didn't release her arm until they were a few steps from the door.

As she entered the house, Samantha tried to keep a few feet of distance from him, moving awkwardly into the empty living room. She stood uncertainly near the massive stone fireplace, unable to escape. He stopped just inside the room and she felt the hooded scrutiny of his look.

Keeping her back to him, she forced her twisting hands apart and raked her fingers through her hair. Her heart pounded as loudly as a hammer in the uncomfortable silence. If only he would stop studying her as if she were a slide under a microscope, she thought desperately. The width of the room separated them, yet she could think no more clearly now than when she had been in his arms.

"I'll have Maggie bring us some coffee," he announced abruptly, irritation making his voice tight and somewhat harsh.

"No." Samantha swung around, breathing in sharply as his gaze pinned her to the spot. She had a lot of reasons to be afraid, but the sudden tremors that quaked through her were caused by his overpowering virility. "I don't know why anyone drinks coffee at night," she declared after a second's pause. "I . . . I won't be able to sleep if I do. So—that said, I think I'll make an early night of it."

With the decision made, she started toward the corridor leading to her bedroom. She glimpsed a movement from him and wanted to bolt, but she forced herself, her feet, not to hurry.

"Sam!" his voice commanded.

In the hall opening, she stopped, trying to meet his slate gray eyes without betraying her inner trepidation. His deliberate strides brought him closer and she felt her knees weakening. Samantha rested a hand against the wall for support.

Chris halted a foot away, his raw-boned face gazing down at her, lean and hard, rugged and compelling. The line of his mouth had thinned and his jaw was clenched.

His hand reached out to touch her cheek, his thumb lightly rubbing her smooth skin. Samantha trembled visibly as his caress flamed through her. Quickly she lowered her gaze, but avoided looking at the bulge on the left side of his blazer. Not even fear could check the desire to be in his arms.

"Please, I'm tired." She tried to speak with bright unconcern.

His thumb slipped under her chin to tilt it upward. "Sam, I . . ." The urgency of his low voice never had an opportunity to convey its message.

Footsteps approached the living room and his hand fell away as he turned and looked to see who had come in. Granted a reprieve, Samantha took advantage of it.

"Good night, Chris," she murmured as Tom appeared in the living room. She hurried down the corridor to her bedroom.

Within minutes she was in bed with the lights out. She lay awake for long hours in the dark, thinking.

Each time she tried to concentrate on his possible reasons for carrying a gun, her thoughts kept turning to the way he had kissed her and the incredible passion he had aroused in her.

If ever she needed to think like a girl detective, it was now. But none of what had happened made much sense. The situation was so odd, in fact, that it would make a sensational first-person article— *I Fell In Love With My Captor*, or something like that.

Oh, no. That didn't fit either, because she wasn't a captive. Her father knew she was here—but, she told herself, it was quite possible that he didn't know the details. And without a working cell phone, which was her own fault, she couldn't very well call him on the sly. It occurred to her—and it creeped her out— that the phone lines in the house probably were monitored.

Was it possible that Reuben wanted to protect her from someone? Maybe she'd been sent on a sun-filled, fun-filled vacation trip for a reason he didn't want to explain. There was more than one drawback to being the daughter of a very rich man—someone really might think she was worth kidnapping. On her own, she made an easy target.

It didn't help matters that Reuben evidently still thought of her as his little girl. OK, she couldn't kick down doors and pistol-whip bad guys, but why she was being treated like a wide-eyed innocent and not told a thing, not one thing, about what was going on, baffled her.

The whole situation was beyond puzzling and her worried state didn't make for a restful sleep when she finally did doze. But it was a light sleep that had her rising before eight the next morning.

Chris was already breakfasting when she entered the dining room. His detached greeting was unexpected. Samantha assumed a similar attitude, especially after she noticed the bulge on his left side under the tan bush jacket. Orange juice, coffee, and toast were on the table. Her appetite didn't stretch to more than that and she refused Maggie's offer of bacon and eggs when the woman appeared briefly in the room.

"Was there anything you needed from town?" The question was asked casually enough.

Samantha stopped munching the slice of half-eaten toast in her hand. After his suspicions yesterday, the inquiry was a surprise. He seemed to be suggesting a shopping expedition. Everything imaginable had been awaiting her arrival here and she couldn't think of a thing that had been overlooked. She wasn't going to admit that, though.

"There are a couple of things," she lied smoothly and took another bite of toast.

"Make a list and give it to Maggie. She'll see that you get whatever you need." He put his napkin on the table.

Her gaze pinned him this time. Not that he seemed to care. So she wasn't to be allowed to go into town. But she had to make certain that was really what he meant and it wasn't just her imagination.

"That isn't necessary," she said, smiling falsely as she added a spoonful of marmalade to her toast. "I'll ride along with her to town. It'll be fun wandering through the shops."

"Maggie isn't going to town." His cryptic reply forced Samantha to meet his eyes.

OK, he sure as hell had her attention now.

"I don't understand," Samantha laughed self-consciously.

"She's ordering what we need by phone. A launch will bring the stuff out this afternoon," he explained.

"Oh." A small voice of understanding.

There was nothing left to say and she finished up the marmalade-covered toast. Its sweetness was suddenly cloying.

The morning hours dragged. It was an effort to appear natural and not be consumed by all the suspicions and doubts that had surfaced. And, after last night's tempestuous kisses, Chris's withdrawn behavior really bothered her. He avoided any opportunity to touch her, however innocent the reason, and Samantha's awareness of him was heightened to a fever pitch.

They'd gone outside, where the air around her crackled as if an electrical storm was approaching.

Surreptitiously, she glanced at Chris. He was lounging in one of the patio chairs, seemingly unaffected by the undercurrents of tension. From where Samantha leaned in a half-sitting position against a protruding rock, his craggy profile was offered for her inspection. Masculine as always and oh-so-bronzed and vital, he appeared relaxed, the tapering length of him stretched out. The even rise and fall of his chest suggested sleep.

They had headed for the patio after lunch, a meal that Samantha barely tasted, her nerves too overwrought. Her bearing was tuned for the sound of a motorboat, which was the only reason she'd agreed to come out at all.

Several had passed, catching her interest at the

first sound and losing it when they continued by the island. The dull hum of another boat was approaching and she tensed as it droned increasingly louder. Then came the sound she had been waiting to hear. The boat's engine was throttled down.

With another glance at Chris, Samantha straightened warily from the rock, not certain whether he was sleeping or had merely closed his eyes. Striving for nonchalance, she stuffed her hands in her jeans pockets and strolled quietly toward the path leading to the boathouse where the supply launch would dock.

"Going for a walk?" The calm male voice paralyzed her for an instant.

She turned jerkily toward his chair. "I thought I might." Her smile was tight.

"Headed anywhere in particular?" Behind the idle question lay another question.

Samantha was getting more than a little sick of this inexplicable charade. And a sense of claustrophobia was kicking in, to add to her worries. She hated being stuck on an island, even if it was at her father's request, with a man who didn't want to tell her he was carrying a gun, but she hesitated before she replied. Maybe her father didn't know about that part.

Whatever. Arguing with Chris was pointless and she wouldn't win. Carrying a concealed weapon meant never having to say you were sorry.

So . . . should she answer him truthfully or lie? Well, she told herself, he'll see right through a lie and she would rather tell the truth. Samantha needed to know exactly what her position was, because her imagination was working overtime. If she, unknowingly, was in real danger, she had a right and an obligation to find out if what she was thinking was true. That was Plan A. Bold and brave. She settled for a just-in-time Plan B, feeling about as bold as a snail under a leaf. If she had antennae, they would be quivering.

"I thought I'd walk to the cove," she replied and noted the sudden, grim set to his mouth. She summoned up what little courage she had left, and plunged forward. "The launch with the supplies is docking now. I heard it a few minutes ago."

"That's hardly an event," he said dryly.

"No, but I'm going just the same. Any objections?" She couldn't keep from challenging him even though her heart was in her throat.

"Not really," he answered, but her every instinct said that he was lying. He rolled leisurely to his feet. "Do you mind if I make a more stimulating suggestion? Since you want to go to the cove, why not change into your swimsuit first? Then we could swim for a couple of hours."

A few days ago that would have sounded like a great plan, but Samantha recognized his stalling tactics by now.

"By the time I changed, the launch would be gone," she pointed out.

"Does it matter?" His hands had slid to his hips, his stance arrogant, the quietness of his voice intimidating.

"Since I was going to the cove to meet the boat, yes, it does matter," she retorted, tipping her head to the side, openly defiant. "But maybe you don't want me to meet the launch. That's why you're trying to think up ways to stop me, isn't it?"

"Now that's foolish." The smile he flashed was cold and without humor.

"Is it?" Samantha taunted. "I don't think so."

"Come on, Sam." He frowned at her words and shook his head. "Why would I want to do a thing like that?"

Pivoting, she stalked toward the path, angered that she had let herself be manipulated that way. He had a streak of cunning as well as ruthlessness. The sound of firm, striding steps on the path behind her chased away the anger.

Looking over her shoulder, Samantha's widened eyes saw him lessening the distance between them. Since he hadn't been able to stop her by being sneaky, she guessed he wouldn't be above using force.

She bolted from the path into the trees and thick undergrowth and heard Chris call her name, angered and impatient. It only spurred her on. Branches whipped at her arms and legs as she ran, trying to make a straight line to the cove where the old path had curved. Above her own noise, she could hear the rustle of brush behind her. He was chasing her, but she didn't dare risk a glance back.

There was a small clearing ahead and she ran for it, aware of the noise coming closer. Breaking free of the brush and trees, she tried to dash across the clearing and regain some of the lead she had lost, when a large hand grabbed her arm just below the elbow, pulling her up short and spinning her around.

Her forward impetus deprived her of balance. She couldn't change direction that abruptly and maintain her footing. She tumbled to the ground, dragging him to his knees and falling with him into a soft cushion of pine needles, pungent and dried by the sun.

Instantly she was kicking and twisting to get to her feet. She nearly made it, but a muscular arm got her back to the ground. She struck out at him, swinging her fists at any part of him she could hit, attacking him like a trapped animal. He soon captured her flailing arms and stretched them above her head.

Samantha struggled all the more violently, breathing in panicked sobs. Twisting and writhing, she tried to free herself of the weight pressing into the ground as he half straddled and half lay on top of her. Her head moved from side to side in desperate effort, tangling her brown-silk hair in the pine needles beneath them. He held her easily, letting her struggle uselessly until her energy was spent.

Finally, gasping, Samantha had no more strength left to fight. She glared resentfully into the smoldering steel of his eyes, her heart thudding against her ribs from her exertions. The pine needles were brushing roughly against the bare skin of her arms. She was held in place but not uncomfortably, very aware of the heat of his body.

The hard muscles of his thighs pressed down on her legs. Her breasts were nearly flattened by the granite wall of his chest. Strong fingers encircled her wrists and, wild with wondering, she no longer strained to break free. Mixing with the pine scent was the musky scent of pure man, heightened to an intoxicating level by the chase.

The frustration of defeat gradually gave way to an awareness of the dangerous intimacy of her position. As the knowledge flickered in her rounded brown eyes, she saw it reflected in his. She was afraid to move, afraid if she did, it would be to invite the possession of his kiss.

Tension mounted, her gaze locked by the magnetic force of his. He looked at her lips and his expression softened.

Slowly, taking his time, he lowered himself and his mouth descended toward hers. Samantha exhaled a sighing surrender. Flames were kindled by the languid passion of his kiss, arousing her desire more swiftly than demanding possession would have done. Expertly he explored every corner of her lips and mouth until she trembled in response.

Her arms were released and she wound them around his neck and shoulders. The sensual weight of his body pressing down on her aroused her immediately, a wild song ringing in her heart. The intimate caress of his hands was an erotic stimulant that made her responses all the more urgent. His kiss became more demanding and she yielded, allowing him complete mastery of her senses.

Every nerve end was attuned to him, quivering at his touch. His fingers tugged at the buttons of her blouse, gaining access to the rounded flesh the material had concealed. As he pushed the bra strap from her shoulder, he dragged his mouth away from her lips to plunder the sensitive skin of her throat and shoulders with rough kisses, blazing a fiery trail to the swelling peak of her breast.

The sensual touch of his tongue drew a shuddering moan from her throat. His very male need made her want to satisfy him—and satisfy herself.

His hand remained to cup her breast as he raised his lips toward her mouth, checking his movement tantalizing inches from his goal to read the message in her liquid brown eyes.

An inch away from simply saying yes, Samantha knew that this time his kiss would demand an ultimate surrender. She was beyond the point of resisting. She could deny him nothing. Right now she was at the point where she could think of nothing but an overwhelming desire to be his.

But he stiffened, suddenly wary. A flash of alertness lit the dark gray of his eyes as he looked up from her face. Bewildered for a second, Samantha finally heard the sound of someone walking heavily, nearing the spot where they lay entwined on the pine-needle bed.

She breathed in sharply, a combination of alarm, embarrassment, and protest. Before she could exhale, Chris's large hand was clamped over her mouth, his piercing gaze warning her into silence.

CHAPTER SIX

It seemed an eternity before the footsteps drew level with their position, receded into the silence of the woods, and the hand was removed from its smothering hold over her mouth. The footsteps had passed within a few feet of them, the thick underbrush screening them from the trail running from the cove to the house.

Soundlessly Chris rolled to his feet and gazed in the direction of the house. Samantha wasn't nearly as quiet as she scrambled to her feet. She'd taken those precious few seconds to consider the wisdom of her actions and ask herself just how crazy this was.

He'd pounced on her, held her down—and she'd acted like she liked it. On second thought, she hadn't. Of course, Samantha couldn't blame it all on him. She had been ready to give herself to a man who was virtually keeping her a prisoner on this island, a rash move that would have made his power over her unlimited, if she'd made it.

Her fingers fumbled with the buttons of her blouse. They were still trembling from her purely physical and instinctive reaction to his lovemaking. Frustrated, she frowned down at the uncooperative buttons, yet she was quite aware of him moving to stand in front of her. She was incapable of looking at him.

"Sam." The caressing warmth of his voice flowed over her.

When she continued to refuse to look at him, his fingers captured her hands and pulled them away from her blouse, permitting it to gape open. He made a thorough inspection of her, his gaze seeming to strip away the lacy bra. Still holding her hands, he put them gently behind her back and drew her hips against his muscular thighs.

"No!" She wasn't sure she meant it, but Samantha wanted to deny the turmoil caused by his nearness.

"No?" His voice was low and mocking, his breath warm against her skin.

"No," she repeated, more decisively this time as she lifted her gaze to his face. The dark glow in his eyes nearly destroyed her will to resist. "You wanted me to miss the launch," she said accusingly, "and you've succeeded. Now let me go."

His gaze narrowed to pinpoints of sharp steel. The muscles along his strong jaw worked for a few seconds before he released her and stepped away, his expression hard and withdrawn.

Turning her back to him, Samantha quickly fastened the buttons of her blouse, without fumbling now. Not glancing in his direction, she started toward the thick undergrowth that separated the little clearing from the trail.

"Where are you going?" His voice was gruff.

"To the house," she said over her shoulder, hoping that her sarcastic tone would sound tough. "Any objections?"

"None," he said coldly.

* * *

Samantha didn't stop until she had closed her bedroom door. She glanced in the mirror above the dresser, disliking her disheveled appearance, picking off the pine needles clinging to her hair and clothes. Forcing herself away from it, she started walking toward the private bathroom, stripping off her clothes as she moved across the room.

Without waiting for the water to adjust to a comfortable temperature, she stepped beneath the freezing shower spray. But the stinging needles couldn't erase the memory of the intimate touch of his hands, nor could the cold water chill the warmth lingering from the fires he had kindled.

Finally, she turned off the taps in defeat, wrapped one towel around her wet hair and with another covered her nakedness. With robotlike movements she returned to the bedroom, pulling clean undergarments from the dresser drawer and walking to the closet.

She tossed a pair of jeans onto the bed and reached for a top. With it in her hand, she noticed the blue windbreaker she'd borrowed from Chris the night she had arrived. She wanted no physical reminders of him. Her fingers gripped the smooth material to violently jerk it from its hanger. It was halfway off the hanger when her arm became paralyzed, unable to complete the movement.

In numbed disbelief, she stared at the inside collar of the jacket. Black lettering spelled out the initials C.S. That was all, just C.S. Not C.S.A. for Christopher Steven Andrews. Slowly she pulled it from the hanger, examining closely to see if the last letter hadn't somehow become faded. It didn't take an expert to discern that there never had been another letter following the S.

Crumpling the windbreaker in her hands, she

turned to move to the bed. She sagged onto the edge, staring at the jacket. One piece of incriminating evidence didn't prove anything—but it did make her even more suspicious.

Which was good. Too many times during the past few days she had been ready to accept the first information as the whole truth. She would not jump to conclusions again, not until she found something more to substantiate her discovery.

Not wanting to risk losing what she had, she stuffed the windbreaker between the mattress and box springs of the bed. The towel around her middle was cast aside as she hurriedly dressed in the clean clothes. Rubbing the worst of the dampness from her hair, she ran a quick comb through it and called it good enough. Entering the hallway, she closed the door on the cyclone mess of dirty clothes and wet towels strewn about the room. Tidying up could wait. Right now there was only one thought in her mind. The living room was empty and she breathed a sigh of relief and satisfaction.

With a cautious glance toward the adjoining rooms, she moved quietly to the study corner, her gaze seeking and finding the briefcase leaning against the side of the desk. She knelt beside it, pushing a clinging strand of hair from her cheek.

Her palms were wet with nervous perspiration, and she wiped them on her jeans before reaching for the briefcase, keeping it upright to examine the area near the handle. The gold initials C.S. looked much the same.

Minutely, Samantha examined the leather for any mark or scar that would indicate a third letter had once been there. It never had. She had wanted proof to substantiate the markings on the windbreaker and she had found it. She slid the briefcase back to its former position, her hands settling on her knees to push herself upright.

"What are you doing?" The low, accusing male voice sent shafts of cold fear plunging into her heart.

Samantha turned her head slowly toward Chris, who was standing in the archway to the dining room, his immobility a challenging threat. But he wasn't Chris. Whoever he was, he wasn't Chris Andrews—and he wasn't Owen Bradley. Nervously, she moistened her lips and straightened. Should she confront him with her discovery? No, she decided, not until she had a chance to think it over.

Her mind raced to find a plausible explanation for why she had been kneeling beside the desk. There wasn't any. Her only hope was to bluff her way out. "It's none of your business what I was doing." With head held high, she started toward the hallway.

But his long strides overcame her before she could reach it and he caught her wrist, pulling her toward him.

"I asked you a question and I want an answer," he said blandly.

"Then let go," she said. Samantha hoped she sounded calmer than she felt. He did—but not until she accidentally brushed against the hard muscle of his thighs. He drew in his breath and she guessed that she wasn't the only one who couldn't think straight when things got physical.

Interesting. Maybe that was the best way to get the upper hand.

He pivoted to stride from the room. Weakly, she stared after him, feeling not at all victorious.

For the rest of the afternoon, she didn't budge from her room. Confusion muddled her thinking.

She was obviously a prisoner. It didn't seem to matter whether the island, or her bedroom, formed her walls. He was sure to sidestep or just plain not answer any question she might ask about why she was being held, no matter how many times she asked.

If it hadn't been for the fact that she had spoken to her father and knew he was cognizant of her whereabouts, Samantha would've simply hit Chris with a brick and stolen the boat.

Which, she told herself, would also involve hitting burly Tom with a bigger brick, and Maggie, who had been nice, with a smaller brick. Just for not telling her what this was all about, she mentally reserved the biggest brick for her father.

But Reuben did know.

The shadows outside had lengthened into evening when there was a knock on her door. She tensed, turning from the window to stare at the door.

"Who is it?" she demanded, knowing the answer before it was given.

"Chris," he answered, and opened the door.

Liar! She wanted to scream at him. *You aren't Chris Andrews! I don't know who you are, but you are not Chris Andrews!* She glared at his expressionless face but she didn't say any of that.

"What do you want?" she asked coldly.

"Dinner's ready."

"Just send some bread and water to my room. That's good enough," she declared with taunting disdain.

His mouth hardened. "You have to eat," he said. "And you can skip the melodramatic remarks. Maggie does her best."

Her gaze challenged his for a few more seconds before she submitted to his edict. The food was fine, but she hardly tasted it. She was aware every second of the speculating glances given her by Maggie and Tom.

Her tight-lipped silence wasn't something they wouldn't notice. The instant dinner was over, she excused herself and retreated to her room, half expecting Chris—or whoever he was—to appear and order her into the living room. He didn't.

The next morning the prospect of spending the day in her bedroom wasn't at all appealing. If she was actually a prisoner, as she surmised she was, then there was no reason for her to be a willing prisoner. Besides, if she was going to find out anything about him or this island, or the other two people who seemed to be playing a part, it was unlikely it would happen in the bedroom.

Playing a part. The phrase stuck in her mind. Was it possible that she had been hoodwinked into a role in some crazy TV show—or one of those movies where innocent people found themselves in the middle of an elaborate practical joke?

He seemed too serious for that. Way too serious. But a trained actor would stay in character.

There was a determined light in her eyes as she emerged from her room. The germ of an idea was taking shape. She was going to confront her captor—there was really no other word for him, even if she'd gone along quite willingly and even if her father had had a hand in this. She had to tell him flat out that she knew he was not Chris Andrews. Once he realized that she had seen through his guise, he might unwittingly provide her with some more information. The possibility put a spring to her step.

Rounding the arch into the living room, Samantha instantly spied the man seated at the desk, listening with glowering anger to the telephone at his ear. She stopped, alert to the impatience emanating from him. Whatever the person on the other end of the wire was saying, he didn't like it.

"Listen, Reuben—oh, hell!" Chris's voice rumbled across the room and Samantha's eyes widened. "Don't ever say I didn't warn you. You'll be sorry, very sorry." There was a pause, then, "You'll be hearing from me."

On that ominous note, he slammed the receiver and rose from the chair. Despite her distrust, she silently admired the uncoiling swiftness of his movements. There was an animal grace to whatever he did, Samantha thought unwillingly. She jumped a little when he looked her way.

She couldn't deny overhearing the conversation. The best she could do was pretend she hadn't caught the promise of revenge.

"Was that my father?" she asked, somehow succeeding in hiding her nervousness.

"Yes."

Trying to maintain her pose of ignorance, Samantha strolled into the room. Her hands were trembling and she hooked her thumbs in the belt loops of her tight, low-slung jeans. Sex made a pretty good weapon—and it seemed to be the only way she had of getting to him.

"When is he coming?" She tried to put just the right note of interest in her voice.

"He's . . . been delayed for a couple more days."

Samantha didn't miss the infinitesimal pause in his answer. But his penetrating gaze was difficult to meet, so she didn't try and turned instead toward the dining room.

Knowing she had to make some reply to his answer, she sighed ruefully. "I'm going to be back at work before Reuben ever succeeds in getting away." She quickly changed the subject. "Mmm, the coffee smells good this morning. We certainly do drink a lot of it around here. In scene after scene."

He didn't take the bait. OK, it had been a little too obvious. For the moment, he ignored her and poured himself a cup.

Samantha wasn't certain she had fooled him. After hearing the telephone conversation, she wasn't going to blurt out that she knew he wasn't Chris Andrews.

She could not dismiss the extraordinary possibility that she just might be kidnapped. Come to think of it, she had only his word that Reuben knew where she was.

In her mind, Samantha reran the short telephone conversation she had had with her father shortly after she had arrived on the island. First he had asked how she was, received her assurances that she was surviving—Samantha blanched at her choice of words in retrospect—then had tried to apologize for the delay. But she had interrupted him before he explained the delay.

She'd glossed over his apology by saying something about how she knew he was doing everything he could. And he'd drawn a blank for a telltale few seconds when she had referred to Chris. Finally Reuben had admonished her to do whatever Chris told her. Her father's preoccupied air could have been caused by concern for her safety—and an unspoken agreement that his conversation with his daughter stay neutral.

The suspense was making her crazy. If this wasn't a movie, it should be. Call it something like *Or Else*. Words that Chris had probably been about to say to her uncomprehending father.

People in the theater would be muttering things

like *don't you get it?* And *turn around—he's right behind you.*

She looked at Chris, right in front of her. He was eating and didn't look dangerous.

But the pieces to the puzzle fit so perfectly. He had to be up to something. Being semi-sleep-deprived and nervous wasn't helping her figure things out. Some journalist she was going to be.

But . . . an awful thought occurred to her. It was possible that she'd interrupted a telephone call demanding ransom. By speaking to Reuben that first time, she'd inadvertently proved to him that they were truly holding her captive. Chris had been right there. Had she said the wrong thing or started to indicate her whereabouts, Chris could have ripped the phone away.

What was that ridiculous saying? *Even paranoid people have real enemies.* Suddenly it didn't seem so ridiculous.

How easy she had made it for them, Samantha thought dejectedly. The mere mention of her father's name had persuaded her to come away with a perfect stranger. Not once had she questioned his credentials at the newspaper office. Beth had warned her to be wary of him, but she hadn't listened, mostly because her colleague's warning had come straight from a not-so-reliable source: an astrology column. In which she did not believe. Not Samantha Gentry—she knew it all.

The newspaper office! Another memory staggered her. The letter that had been left for Harry Lindsey had to have been a ransom note. And she had pointed out which office to leave it in. It was all so sickeningly obvious now, even down to the new clothes that had been provided for her. She hadn't been allowed to bring anything but her handbag because of the risk of being seen with Chris and the delay it would have caused in leaving.

She had taken the bag with her when she went to the ladies' room each time. Force of habit. She hadn't been thinking then that he would look through it for her cell phone, and having it with her made her feel, stupid as it was, safe. Connected to the real world.

A world she had left far behind. Her mind whirled. Yes, she was responsible for leaving her charger in the office and it wasn't the first time she'd done it. He'd probably figured that out with a quick look into her bag, relieved that the phone would just run down.

Of course he would have looked for it sooner or later—and installed software or some kind of bug to intercept her outgoing calls. What a weasel.

A tiny flicker of doubt reminded her that she still had no proof of any of this. She sat up straight and looked at him, calmly drinking coffee. He merely looked back and she told herself that she didn't necessarily need proof. Her eyes narrowed. It didn't seem to bother him.

The drive here from Clayton, New York; the fast car that probably could have outdistanced any pursuer; his preoccupation at the restaurant, where he constantly watched everyone coming in and out; the man waiting to take the car when they arrived and the young girl who had joined him at the corner and who would undoubtedly resemble Samantha at a distance; the boat waiting a few minutes out. It all made so much sense now.

If Beth or anyone had happened to see her leave in the car, the man and woman had probably driven it miles away from there before ditching it. And there hadn't been a soul around the dock to see

Samantha board the boat. She had even been ordered to wait in the shadows of a building until it
had docked, then been sent below once onboard.
She had been a delightfully cooperative kidnap
victim. *Idiot*, she told herself fiercely.

The island was an ideal place to hold her. There
weren't any nosy neighbors or anywhere she could
run to if she discovered what was happening. The
river provided the walls to keep her captive. The
boat tour of the islands had been to keep her entertained, so she wouldn't suspect what was truly
going on.

Samantha took a deep breath. She almost didn't
want to speculate. She reminded herself to stick
scrupulously to the facts and not do a cut-and-paste
of every lurid crime story she'd ever read.

His fork and knife clinked down on his plate, but
she didn't meet his eyes. The sound made even more
random memories flood through her tired brain.
She couldn't help coming up with a plausible—and
scary—explanation for each seemingly normal event.

They hadn't stopped anywhere because they
didn't want to risk her being recognized. It was
possible her picture was all over the internet and
in the papers—would Reuben want it publicized
or not?

And there was something else she hadn't thought
about—there was no computer in the house. Not in
plain sight, anyway, but Chris had to have a laptop.
A state-of-the-art, mastermind kind of laptop, from
which he could direct this plot.

Or maybe he thought it was safer to rely on old-
fashioned, more secure technology, like letters and
rotary dial telephones. How ironic.

The supply launch would have been her only way
off the island. He'd made sure she missed it, throw-

ing her down for a sexy kiss that she'd practically been panting to get.

She hated herself for that. The man didn't even need a gun. Samantha pondered another scary fact: the island was very close to Canada and they could slip across the border to escape once the ransom had been paid. The ransom. The telephone call she had just overheard.

Fear put a lump in her throat. Had Reuben refused to pay the ransom? Oh, God, it was possible, she thought. She'd once heard him remark that if no ransoms were paid, there might not be any more kidnappings. He had to be hard-headed about it—at his level, things like that happened. She remembered vaguely that his chauffeur had taken a defensive-driving course for the express purpose of dodging kidnappers and carjackers.

Maybe he'd never told her much else about it— maybe because he wanted her to live her life as he had at the same age—unafraid, ready for anything.

Reuben must have sighed with relief when she changed her name to work at the newspaper. She had no way of knowing that at the time.

Her father might have been bluffing on the phone to gain time, taking a chance that the authorities would find her. A man like Reuben Gentry had contacts in law enforcement at very high levels— and she knew he would have exploited every single one of them.

Chris—or whatever his name was—had said, "You'll be hearing from me." He could have meant that he would be calling back about the ransom or that he would be sending a message about . . . she didn't want to finish the sentence, even in thought. They couldn't very well let her go free, not when she could recognize them.

Her hands trembled and she quickly set the coffee mug on the table before she dropped it. Her gaze slid warily to the man seated across from her, only to drop to the table when she saw his inscrutable charcoal eyes watching her. How much of what she had been thinking had she revealed to him, she wondered in breathless panic.

"Are you all right? You look a bit peaked," he observed smoothly.

"A headache—migraine," Samantha said quickly. "I'm prone to them. So is my father." She touched her fingers to her temple and smiled. "Excuse me, I think I'll go to my room and lie down for a while."

"Can I get you anything?" He didn't seem entirely convinced.

"No, thanks," she replied, making her exit before he could probe further.

Restlessly Samantha paced the room for nearly an hour. She tried to consider the situation rationally and play down her fear. Being afraid just wasn't going to help her get through this, or get out of here, or get rescued. There had to be a way.

Although the stranger, her abductor—she had stopped thinking of him as Chris, the name didn't really fit him anyway—might be aware she suspected something funny was going on, he might not believe she had realized she was kidnapped. He probably still thought she was convinced he was Chris Andrews.

As his guest, she had to be permitted a certain latitude, though at the same time he was confident that she couldn't escape the island. The question was how best to take advantage of the limited freedom she did have on the island.

There had to be something she could do herself other than simply wait. She couldn't count on being released if the ransom was paid. Escape seemed impossible. But how could she be rescued when no one knew where she was except the kidnappers?

A reporter was supposed to be resourceful, Samantha chided herself. There had to be some way she could get a message out without her abductors' knowledge. The supply launch probably wouldn't come again, so that was out. No boaters or daytrippers ever stopped at the island, which ruled out the possibility of passing a message to them.

Of course, she thought wryly, she could always stuff a message in a bottle and toss into the water, but it would probably wash up months later somewhere far away, like Thailand, soggy and unreadable. The chance of anyone finding it in time—well, there wasn't a chance.

Frowning, she paused beside the window, staring out at the green shadow of trees. What method of communication did that leave? Semaphore flags? Signal fire? Suddenly she brightened up.

There had to be a way that she could persuade them to let her call her father for some innocent reason. Maybe during the conversation she could give Reuben a clue to where they were holding her. No, Chris would very likely see right through a ruse like that.

But if she could use it without anyone listening in . . . when no one was around . . . The middle of the night seemed an obvious choice, but Samantha discounted it. She remembered her midnight walk. No doubt someone was on watch all the time. Prowling around in the dark would get her discovered even faster.

No, she would have to make her move during the day when she was more or less free to roam the house and island at will. She would have to choose a time when all three of the others were occupied. Not a bad plan and not as foolhardy as some of the others her mind had summoned up.

Footsteps sounded in the corridor outside her room. It could only mean someone was coming to check on her. Quickly Samantha flung herself on the bed, stretching out on her stomach and feigning sleep. Her heart was pounding as the door opened. Even though her eyes were closed, her senses recognized the identity of her intruder.

How many times in the past few days had his presence disturbed her sensually? Too many to count. Those mysteriously dark gray eyes were studying her now lying on the bed, and she could feel her body silently responding without making a move. Samantha tried to breathe evenly, aware of his regard as surely as if he was touching her. *Beware of the stranger*—how right the horoscope had been. This guy was dangerous in more ways than one.

When she thought she couldn't keep up the pretense of sleep a second longer, she heard the door close. Still she didn't move, not immediately, not until she heard the quiet footsteps moving away from her door. Then she sat up cautiously and began contemplating when she might stand the best chance of using the telephone.

At noon, it was Maggie who knocked on the door, coolly inquiring if Samantha would be having lunch. She maintained the excuse of a headache, hoping to lull them into not watching her so closely. When the housekeeper offered to bring her some broth and toast, Samantha accepted, willing to play the invalid to put a little nourishment in her empty stomach.

The door didn't latch securely behind Maggie. Ravenous, Samantha gobbled the toast. Buttered toast was her favorite comfort food and she needed fuel to beat the bad guys at their game. Except this wasn't a game. Not anymore. Wiping her mouth, she reached for the cup of beef broth that Maggie had left, and saw the door slowly swing open a few inches. From the living room, Samantha could hear the stranger's voice.

"I know she suspects something," he stated in a decisive voice. "We couldn't hope to keep her completely in the dark indefinitely. She's way too smart."

Samantha scowled. She wasn't so sure about that. If only she could get some uninterrupted sleep. She needed to get her edge back.

"So what are we going to do now?" came Tom's gruff response. He blew out a breath, probably hauling his bulk out of an easy chair, Samantha thought.

"Keep her on the island until . . ." The rest of his sentence became indistinct as they evidently moved to another room.

At least—Samantha smiled at her own macabre humor—there was no immediate plan to dispose of her. It would give her precious time to try to bring about her own rescue.

The opportunity presented itself much sooner than she expected. Almost an hour had passed when she heard the low murmur of voices outside, those of Tom and her stranger. At this time, Samantha knew, Maggie would be in the kitchen dealing with the luncheon dishes. This was her chance, maybe her only chance.

Stealthily, she tiptoed out of her room, down the corridor, and into the living room. Listening intently, she could hear Maggie in the kitchen and the faint voices outside. Adrenaline pumped through her veins as she picked up the telephone and dialed her father's office number.

She looked apprehensively toward the kitchen as she waited for the telephone to be answered, winding a finger in the coiled cord. Exhilaration flashed through her when a woman's voice came through the receiver.

"Reuben Gentry, please," she requested in a whisper. "This is his daughter calling."

"I'm sorry, but I can barely hear you. Would you please speak up?" the woman insisted.

Samantha gritted her teeth impatiently. "I can't!" she hissed a little louder, silently cursing the wasted seconds. "This is Samantha Gentry, and I *must* talk to my father."

"Did you say it was Mr. Gentry you wanted?" the officious voice asked.

"Yes!"

"I'm sorry, he isn't in right now. Can someone else help you?"

"Damn!" she muttered under her breath, rubbing a hand across her forehead. "Put me through to the security . . ."

The front doorknob was turning. She caught the movement out of the corner of her eye. Her stranger must be coming and she didn't stand a chance of getting out of the living room unseen. The odds were he would see her with the telephone in hand before she could replace it. Her only hope was to leave a message.

Precious time was wasted in making the decision. The door was already opened and the stranger was walking in when Samantha made a last-ditch attempt.

"Tell my father," she began in a loud, clear voice so the woman would have no trouble understanding what she said, "that I'm at—"

A large hand was pressing down the button on the telephone's old-fashioned cradle, breaking the connection before Samantha could complete her message. Frustration and impotent anger seethed inside her when she looked into his hard gray eyes.

He pried the receiver from her fingers and replaced it. "I'm sorry," he said calmly, "I couldn't let you do that."

"You have no right to stop me!" Samantha flared up, forgetting that she wasn't going to confront him just yet, then checking herself. "Hey, I may be a guest"—the word almost choked her—"in your house but I have to have some privacy. There was something I wanted to talk to Reuben about and I didn't have a chance to speak to him this morning." She gave him a nasty look. "Is it the money? I'll be sure to reimburse you. And by the way, in case you didn't notice, I forgot to bring my charger and my cell phone is dead."

More bait that he didn't take. "I'm sure you meant to bring it. And no, I didn't notice, and it isn't about the cost of the call." He towered beside her, an arm brushing her shoulder.

Inwardly Samantha was quaking, from fear and his disturbing nearness, but she boldly reached again for the telephone receiver. "Then there isn't any reason for you to object if I call him."

His hand clamped over her wrist, not allowing her to lift the receiver. "Sam, I'm not playing games," he said quietly.

"Aren't you?" Her head jerked toward him, her brown eyes shimmering with defiance and rebellion. Her rising temper made her throw caution to the winds. "You've been playing games with me ever since you walked into the newspaper office— first letting me believe you were Owen Bradley, then ly—" She bit her lip, realizing she had virtually admitted that she knew he wasn't Chris Andrews.

The narrowing of his gaze indicated that he had guessed what she had been about to say. Her heart skipped several beats under his piercing look. Samantha had gone too far to turn back. Her only hope was to brave it out without revealing how terrified she really was.

"I don't know who you are, but you aren't Chris Andrews," she declared. "It was all a lie."

"More or less," he acknowledged with remorseless ease.

Spinning away from him in irritation, Samantha muttered, "I don't suppose it would do any good to ask what your real name is."

He hesitated. "My name is Jonas—"

"Jonas!" Laughing with disbelief, she pivoted back. Her hand sliced the air to cut off the rest of his reply. "Yeah, right. That isn't your name, either."

He slowly looked her up and down in a thoughtful way, then shook his head in unconcern. "Names aren't all that important."

"No," she agreed bitterly. "A man's character or his lack of it is the same regardless of his name. Jonas is as good a choice as any. It's certainly appropriate. I haven't had anything but bad luck since I met you. Getting swallowed by a whale might be an improvement."

"So you've decided I'm lacking in morals." There was a mocking glitter in the eyes of the man who now called himself Jonas.

"You've proved that!" she retaliated. "Just how gullible do you think I am? How many times am I supposed to believe your lies? You're keeping me a prisoner on this island. You won't let me off and you won't allow me to see anyone but you, Tom, and Maggie. I'm not even permitted to phone my father.

What story are you going to come up with to explain all that?"

"None." His rugged features showed not a trace of softness. "I don't think you would believe anything I tell you."

"You can't expect me to!" Samantha cried. A part of her had been wishing he would weave another believable story. She didn't want him to be a kidnapper. "I don't know what you're all about and I'm not sure I want to know! Oh, Chris—Jonas, whatever your name really is . . ." She sized him up, deciding in an instant to tone it down and try to coax him. "Come on. Why can't you let me leave a message for Reuben?"

She didn't know why she asked that. She knew he would never agree to it. Her soft-voiced plea had been a gesture of desperation and it clearly wasn't working. Tears welled in her brown eyes.

His hands settled on her shoulders as he gazed at her, his jaw clenched. "I can't, Sam."

The force of his magnetism and her own attraction to it nearly pulled Samantha into his arms. Instead she wrenched her shoulders away from his grip, hating the way her traitorous heart refused to listen to her mind.

"It's not that you can't! You won't," she accused in an emotion-choked voice.

"Think what you like," he replied grimly.

"Oh, don't worry, I will." Samantha stood before him, her hands balled into fists at her side, tears trembling on the ends of her lashes. This was not the way she had intended to confront him. She had planned to interrogate him mercilessly, convicting him with the facts she already knew.

But somewhere along the way, she had stopped thinking of him as her captor and began looking at him as the man who had kissed her passionately and introduced her to feelings and sensations she hadn't known she possessed.

Beware of the stranger, she thought brokenly, because he can steal your heart.

"I want your word, Sam, that you won't try to use the phone again." He regarded her steadily.

"My word?" she mocked. "Why should I give you my word?"

"Because if you don't, I'll be forced to cut the telephone line. I can't take the risk of your phoning anyone and letting them know you're here."

It was official. He was crazy. Maybe nobody but her knew it yet. If she was lucky, he was acting out some hero fantasy starring himself and the daughter of the great and powerful Reuben Gentry and wouldn't hurt her. Otherwise . . . she didn't want to think about the alternatives.

"Wouldn't it be easier just to lock me in my room?" Samantha challenged, her voice taut with misery.

"I hope it won't come to that." But his answer was a warning. "It's up to you."

Her freedom was limited, but she had to keep what little she had if she was going to have any chance at all to help herself.

"Very well, you have it." She had to give in and he had known it.

Pivoting on her heel, she voluntarily went to her room to think of another plan. A glance over her shoulder saw him standing in the same place watching her, his dark features hard and unyielding, and compellingly attractive.

The only thing she could do now was play along.

Chapter Seven

The waters of the St. Lawrence were renowned for their fishing, with black bass and the battling muskie leading the list. Samantha had been watching the small fishing craft moving closer to the island for the past fifteen minutes. Its engine was putt-putting in an erratic rhythm that suggested difficulties.

Stretched out on the raft anchored in the cove, she had toyed with the idea of swimming out to the boat. It was easily within her swimming range, but she knew she would not get ten feet before Jonas caught her. Glancing out of the corner of her eye, she saw he was watching the boat as intently as she was.

Since yesterday afternoon they had spoken little, exchanging only necessary remarks. He might be relatively harmless but she had no way of knowing. As far as she was concerned he was effectively her enemy, and Samantha couldn't allow her emotions to come into play.

The bow of the fishing boat swung to point toward the cove. Within seconds the sputtering motor died. His gaze sliced to her, a veiled warning in it, before he looked over to the stocky man standing at the boathouse dock and watching the fishing boat.

"Find out what his trouble is, Tom," Jonas ordered, his low voice carrying crisply across the dividing waters. "And get him out of here right away."

With a curt nod, Tom acknowledged the order. The fisherman stood up in his boat and waved toward shore. Jonas deliberately ignored the man. It was Tom who returned the wave before disappearing into the boathouse. A few minutes later he emerged, manning the oars of a dinghy, and rowed toward the disabled boat.

Propping herself up on one elbow, Samantha lay on her side and watched as Tom reached the boat, talked briefly with the man, then began rowing back. He never glanced toward the raft, but his voice was directed quietly to Jonas when he drew level with it.

"He ran out of gas."

A red gasoline can was in the dinghy when Tom started his second trip to the fishing boat. Frustration curled Samantha's fingernails into her palms. She could see her chance to contact someone from the outside world slipping away. She had to do something to get the fisherman's attention. There might not be another opportunity.

"Don't do anything foolish, Sam," he said quietly.

Her irritation flared at his perceptive guess, but the wintry gray of his eyes didn't cool her determination. With lightning decision, she pressed her hands onto the raft boards to push herself right, but she never completed the motion.

His reaction was swifter, rolling sideways from his sitting position to grip her shoulders and pin them to the hard wood decking. He loomed above her, muscular and bronze, the dark, virile hair on his bare chest close enough to touch. The thumping of her heart had no basis in fear.

"Don't," he ordered. "Just keep quiet."

"You can't expect me to obey you," she hissed. "You know I have to try."

"Tom will tell him you and I are just fooling around," Jonas said, a faint smirk on his face. She wanted to slap it off, but he definitely had her right where he wanted her.

"You are. I'm not," Samantha retorted, and opened her mouth to scream.

His large hand closed over her jaw, holding it while he silenced her cry with a blazingly sensual kiss. His possessive tenderness completely disarmed her fury, and something in it disarmed her suspicions as well. Reacting instinctively, body and soul, she kissed him back.

She felt almost dizzy, whether from the warmth of the sun or the suddenness of the kiss, she didn't know. It was a good thing she was lying down. The full weight of his muscular body spread over her, its heat melting her bones. Although Samantha tried to resist, her defenses scattered seconds after he had claimed her lips. Pliant and responsive, she gave in to the urgency of his kiss, completely forgetting that she was consorting with the enemy until she heard the reviving chug of the fishing boat's motor.

Samantha twisted free of him in time to see the fisherman wave to Tom and turn the boat in the opposite direction of the island, gathering speed as it left.

"No . . ." she moaned softly, staring at the boat's wake.

Jonas released her and levered himself away, leaving her flesh chilled where it had felt his warmth. Sickened by the way she had been unable to deny herself the heady pleasure of his kiss, she rested a hand across her eyes, as if shutting out the sight of him would help.

"Did you have to kiss me?" she snapped at him resentfully. "Or is it just something you do for your prisoners?"

"Believe me, if there'd been a more effective means to shut you up I would have used it." His tone was bitingly sardonic.

The stinging flick of his reply was just what Samantha needed to pull herself out of her misery. Rising to stand on trembling legs, she squarely met the wintry glitter of his gaze. Kissing him had been an ordeal for her, too, but one of an entirely different kind.

"In the future, please find another method," she declared, faintly haughty and very proud.

He got up too, but more gracefully than she had, with that predatory alertness about him she'd noticed before. His superior height made Samantha feel awfully small as he stood before her nearly naked, rippling muscles toast brown in the sun.

"Don't worry, Sam. I'll look for one."

"And don't call me Sam," she flashed. "That's reserved for people I like and trust!"

For several charged seconds the tension mounted as they glared at each other. The hard line of his mouth thinned. "It's time we went back to the house," he said finally.

"I'll bet you're sorry you didn't decide to lock me in my room." Samantha regretted saying that the second the words were out of her mouth, but it was too late to take them back.

"I wouldn't bring it up if I were you. The idea sounds better every day," he warned.

She clamped her mouth shut. This was not the time to bait him or he might decide to carry out his threat. She had lost one chance to obtain help this afternoon. She would be a fool to throw away better chances in the future simply because she wanted to lash out and hurt him, trying to divert some of her pain to him. Swallowing her spiteful words, she turned and dived into the water. Jonas followed when she surfaced a few yards from the raft.

In the solitude of her room, Samantha relived the scene on the raft. The feeling of wretchedness returned at her failure to resist him and her failure to identify herself in some way to the fisherman. In the midst of her dejection came a glimmer of hope. Escape from the island had always seemed impossible. The only means of transportation was by boat, and Samantha knew she would never be able to operate the sailboat. It was too large. Swimming to another island or the mainland was out because she had neither the strength nor the endurance to cover the distance.

Today, another means of transportation had unknowingly been revealed to her. It was the dinghy that Tom had rowed to the fishing boat. One opportunity had been denied her and another had taken its place. It was up to her to make use of it. The trick would be to leave without being seen. She not only had to get out of the house, but also make it to the boathouse and row away from the island unobserved.

That ruled out an escape in broad daylight. Supposing that she made it to the boat, there was the risk of her being seen on the river in the dinghy, and it would be too easy for Jonas to overtake her in the sailboat. If she was caught, Samantha had no doubt that she would be locked in her room after that.

Any attempt would have to be made in the middle of the night when the darkness could hide her, both on the island and on the water. She had slipped out once unseen, maybe she could succeed again. But this time she wouldn't walk boldly out of the door. Leaving the house would demand real sneakiness.

She walked to her bedroom window. The trees grew close to the house on this side of the building. There was only a narrow clearing that she would have to cross before reaching the concealing cover of the trees. From there, she would have to work her way as quietly as possible to the boathouse path.

It would not be easy with all the thick undergrowth rustling beneath her feet and against her legs. And she would have to be careful not to lose her direction in the dark. A flashlight to guide her footsteps was out of the question.

The glass portion of the window could be raised, but the protective screen was a problem. It was secured from the outside, which meant Samantha would have to pry the wire screen free of its wooden frame. The only tools she had to use, if they could be called tools, were in her manicure set. It was a case of making do with what was at hand as she set to work on a loosened corner of the screen.

By the time she had an opening large enough to crawl through, she had only a few minutes to change out of the swimsuit that had dried on her and into some clothes for dinner. Excitement for her daring plan had built up. Suppressing it was difficult, but she couldn't risk Jonas suspecting her.

During the meal, she said little, letting Tom, Maggie, and Jonas carry the conversation. She was aware of the frequency with which his gray eyes regarded her, and she could only hope that he interpreted her silence as being sullen. All the while she kept mentally going over the route of her escape.

When Maggie began clearing the dishes from the table and Tom had left to look around outside, Samantha wished she could retreat to her room. But it was too soon, so she wandered into the living room.

"You don't have to keep me company," she informed Jonas acidly when he followed her into the living room. "There aren't any fishermen around."

He ignored her comment and lowered his tall frame into a leather chair opposite the one Samantha had chosen. Trying to conceal her irritation, she picked up a magazine and flipped indifferently through the pages.

"You've been very quiet tonight," he observed.

Samantha closed the magazine abruptly and tossed it on the side table. "Under the circumstances, you can hardly expect me to make scintillating conversation."

The line of his mouth curved, a movement totally lacking humor. "What scheme is running through your mind?"

"Scheme?" Although she tried to sound blank, Samantha realized the color had drained from her face, a giveaway he wasn't likely to miss. She tried to conceal her escape plans in a false candor. "The only thing going through my mind right now is how to get off this island prison of yours. And failing that, I'm trying to figure out how I can let others know where I am."

"Come up with any ideas?" Jonas asked with the infuriating calm of a man confident that all possibilities had been covered.

Samantha seized the first thought that occurred to her. "Yes, one."

"What's that?" A dark brow quirked mockingly in her direction.

"I've been considering burning the house down," she announced. "You have to admit that it isn't something that could be ignored. There would be people crawling all over this island within minutes of the first flame licking the roof."

"There would still be plenty of time for Tom and me to get you onto the sailboat and away from the island before the first person arrived," Jonas pointed out. "So it won't do you any good to play with matches."

"I know," sighed Samantha. For an instant, the wild idea had actually sounded possible.

"Surely you've had some other ideas," he prompted dryly.

"Well"—for the first time in several days, an impish gleam entered her eye as she remembered one of her more ridiculous thoughts—"I did consider getting a light and flashing a Morse code signal to any ships or boats going by the island."

"What stopped you?"

"I don't know Morse code," she answered ruefully. At his low chuckle, she regretted her lapse. It was hard enough to resist him without putting things on a lighter level. A grim resolve entered her voice when she spoke. "I'll think of something, though."

The chair she was in was too comfortable, inviting relaxation. Samantha pushed herself up and out of it, walking nervously to the fireplace.

"Sam, I—" Jonas began quietly, a thread of solemnity running through his tone.

"I told you I don't want you to call me that." She kept her back to him, looking sideways from her shoulder. "The only thing I want from you is to leave this island."

"It isn't possible for you to leave. Not yet," he added stiffly.

"When?" demanded Samantha, doubting that he would ever let her leave.

He took a long time answering her and she turned slightly to see him. He was studying her, his gaze intent.

"When?" she repeated.

"I hope not much longer." His veiled look never left her.

What did he mean? Had arrangements been made by her father to pay the ransom? It seemed to be what his comment meant.

"Have you . . . have you talked to Reuben?" she asked, holding her breath.

"For a few minutes this afternoon," he admitted.

"What did he say?" The eager question rushed out of her.

His gaze flicked to her briefly, emotionless and aloof. "As I said before, it shouldn't be too much longer before you can leave here," he replied, not answering her question except in the most ambiguous terms.

"How long is not much longer?" Samantha persisted in her search for the time when the ransom was to be paid.

"Let's just leave it that it will be a little while yet," Jonas stated. "Then all this will be over."

And I'll never see you again. The thought was oddly painful. She turned away from him, knowing his image would haunt her for a long time. The mantel clock ticked in the silence for several minutes.

"I think I'll go to my room," she said finally. There was no point in staying there.

"Good night," Jonas offered when she stepped into the hall.

"Yes." Samantha hesitated. If everything went according to plan she would not see him again. Her gaze slid over him, looking masculine and vital.

Goodbye hovered on the tip of her tongue. "Good night," was what she said.

There was not nearly the elation she had anticipated when she reached her room. She changed into her night clothes and laid out jeans and a dark blue pullover. Then she climbed into bed to wait for the house to become silent.

She knew there was no risk that she would fall asleep. There were too many things to think about, and leaving Jonas was one of them. But that was the way it had to be. She simply couldn't trust him.

The luminous dial of the clock on her bedside table indicated the hour as one. There hadn't been a sound anywhere in the house for the past two hours. Samantha guessed that Tom was somewhere outside on watch since she hadn't heard anything to indicate his return. As she slid silently from beneath the covers, she crossed her fingers that he wasn't near the boathouse.

Dressed in the dark clothing that would help her to blend with the night's shadows, Samantha returned to the bed and stuffed the pillows beneath the covers to form the shape of a sleeping figure. The pale moonlight streaming through the window illuminated her handiwork without revealing its falseness.

With a last glance at the bed she tiptoed to the window. It squeaked protestingly as she raised the glass frame higher. She stopped, listening intently as her pulse throbbed in her throat. Deciding no one had heard, she pushed out the corner of the screen she had worked free. At almost the same moment she heard quiet footsteps muffled by the carpet outside in the corridor.

There was only one reason anyone would be moving about at this hour, and it was to check on her. There wasn't time to slip out through the window.

The opening was small and she might get caught on the screen wire. And she would never have time to slip under the covers and return the pillows to their proper position before the door opened. She had to hide, and somewhere close.

The cool breeze blowing through the window billowed the drape beside her. Instantly Samantha stepped behind the hanging material, lightly gripping the edges so the breeze wouldn't accidentally reveal her. She had barely slipped behind them when the door opened. The light from the hallway streamed over the bed and she held her breath. She guessed it was Jonas. If he walked to the bed, he would discover her ruse, and she would never be able to escape then.

For long seconds there was no sound, only the patch of light shining into the room to indicate that he had not left. Finally, when she was a quivering mass of nerves, the door closed. Her legs threatened to collapse with relief, but she didn't move from her hiding place, not for another ten minutes.

With extreme caution, she crawled through the triangular opening in the screen. Every accidental sound she made, no matter how tiny, sent a chill down her spine. Quickly she crossed the narrow clearing into the trees, her nerves leaping at the whisper of leaves against her jeans. She paused there, her breathing shallow as she got her bearings and rechecked to be certain there was no movement from the house. All was silent. No alarm had been raised yet.

She started out slowly toward the path to the boathouse. If her luck held, she wouldn't run into Tom. She crept along through the thick stand of trees, her progress guided more by the sense of feel than sight.

The moon was bright overhead, but its light couldn't penetrate the umbrella of leaves. Danger seemed to lurk in every shadow. The winging of a night bird could send her pulse rocketing. Samantha stumbled onto the path, unaware she was so close until she stepped onto it. She halted, instantly scanning the secluded path in both directions. There was no sign of Tom.

Deciding that she could move faster if she stayed on the path, she clung to the shadowed side, moving quickly and quietly toward the boathouse. Twice her overactive imagination made her think someone was following her. Both times she stopped, listening, trying to distinguish any man-made sounds in the night's stirrings. Neither time could she hear anything to cause alarm.

The white glow of moonlight glassed the smooth surface of the cove. A smile of elation curved her mouth at the sight of her goal, but she checked herself with the sobering reminder that she still had not reached the dinghy. Tom could be there. Using the trunk of a tree as a shield, she studied the boathouse, dock, and surrounding rocky land for a sign of him. There was nothing that even resembled his burly shape.

With the aid of the moonlight, Samantha scampered quickly over the last remaining stretch of rocky path, hurrying to the concealing shadows of the boathouse. Leaning against the door, she cast one last glance around before opening the door and slipping inside.

The cavernous blackness enveloped her. She couldn't even see her hand, let alone the dinghy. There was no choice. She would have to turn on the light and risk it being seen. She felt along the wall until she found the light switch and turned it on. The brilliance of the solitary bulb blinded her. For several seconds, she could see only the glaring spots in front of her eyes.

Finally they adjusted to the light. The sleek sailboat dominated the interior of the boathouse, its mast towering toward the roof. But it wasn't the sailboat she was seeking. Then her gaze found the small dinghy, dwarfed by its larger companion. Success was within her grasp and she started toward it. It was tied near a ladder. Her foot was on the first rung when the door opened. Paralyzed, Samantha stared at Jonas. He returned her horror-stricken look lazily.

"You'll never make it," he said.

Frustration set in. To be stopped when she had come so close was unbearable. Knowing it was foolish and without a hope of succeeding, Samantha started down the ladder. She didn't have a foot in the dinghy when her arm was caught and held by Jonas. She strained with all her weight against his grip, tipping her head back to gaze at him pleadingly.

"Let me go, Jonas," she begged shamelessly. "Please. The others don't have to know you could have stopped me. Please, just let me go!"

His answer was to smile at her grimly and increase the pull on her arm to draw her up the ladder. "It's no use, Sam. Come on."

She resisted a second longer before admitting defeat and letting him help her up the ladder. Standing once more on the wood floor, she shoved her hands in her pockets and lowered her chin, seal brown hair falling silkily across her cheeks. Jonas made no attempt to usher her from the boathouse.

"It isn't the end of the world, Sam." There was an undertone of amusement in his low-pitched voice.

"Isn't it?" Samantha's question held bitter defiance, the husky quality in her voice deepening.

"No, it isn't."

Her lips compressed into a tight line. "How did you know I was here?"

"I followed you."

"You followed me?" Samantha repeated incredulously. True, she had had the sensation a couple of times that someone was behind her, but she had been positive it was her imagination. Her gaze slid to his moccasined feet. "I thought I heard someone, but . . ."

"I've done a lot of hunting in my time," Jonas replied as if an explanation was really necessary.

"You couldn't have known I was gone," she protested.

"Couldn't I?" he mocked, running a hand through his dark hair.

"You came to my room—" she began.

"—and saw the lumpy shape beneath the covers and knew it couldn't possibly be yours." He finished the sentence his own way, his gaze moving over her curves with an easy familiarity that warmed her cheeks.

Samantha tried to disguise her reaction with another quick question. "Then why didn't you come to investigate?"

"If I had, I would have found you hiding behind the drapes." The carved lines at the corners of his mouth deepened.

"How did you know I was there?" she breathed in astonishment.

"The breeze was blowing one drape, but the other was amazingly motionless." Then he added with a knowing gleam. "As if someone was holding it still."

"If you knew I was there, why didn't you just stop me then?" Samantha demanded angrily. "Why did you let me get all this way? Do you enjoy tormenting me?"

Her accusing tone wiped the vague traces of amusement from his rough features. "I had to know where you were going and what means you were planning to use to leave the island," Jonas replied.

"I could have just been going for a walk," she pointed out airily.

"But you weren't, were you?" he countered. "You were going to try to row across the river in that dinghy, weren't you?"

"So what if I was?" she challenged with a toss of her head.

"Do you realize how small that is?" he asked with a hint of impatience.

"What difference does that make? The river is calm. There aren't any waves that could swamp the boat," she declared, the faint haughtiness still in her tone.

"But there are lake freighters in the ship channel. That little dinghy would be nearly impossible for them to spot, especially without running navigation lights. One of those ships could have run you down without even knowing it," Jonas responded.

"That doesn't frighten me." Denying the shiver that raced over her flesh, she added, "I'd rather risk that than stay here." Her gaze was downcast, but she heard the angry breath he expelled. For a minute, she thought he was going to take her by the shoulders and try to shake some sense in her, but he didn't.

"You don't know what you're saying," Jonas finally ground out.

Samantha acknowledged the warning signal and changed the subject, her gaze sliding to the dinghy. "What are you going to do now?" she asked.

"About you? Nothing. Take you back to the house and put you to bed." He made it sound as if she were a runaway child.

"I meant about the boat," she clarified her question stiffly. "Are you going to chop a hole in it and sink it?" She was suggesting the extreme out of spite.

"Nothing that drastic," Jonas answered dryly. "But now that I know what you were planning, there'll be a padlock on the boathouse and probably one on the dinghy, too. Combination locks," he qualified, "so there won't be any keys for you to steal."

"And you'll probably be the only one who knows the combination, I suppose." The upward sweep of her lashes revealed the mutinous look in her eyes.

"More than likely," he agreed smoothly, a faint glimmer of laughter in the dark silver gaze. "What are you going to do now? Slip into my bedroom some night to see if I talk in my sleep?"

"I doubt that you even sleep," Samantha retorted, irritated by the small tremor that quaked through her at the idea of being alone in a bedroom with him.

"Not very soundly," Jonas admitted, then tilted his head to one side. "What are you going to do?"

"Well, I'm not going to sneak into your bedroom!" she declared vehemently, mostly because it was such a heady thought that she had trouble forgetting it.

"I was referring to any more harebrained schemes you might have running through that mind of yours about leaving the island."

"I'm going to keep trying, if that's what you're asking," Samantha snapped.

Chapter Eight

He gave an impatient sigh. "Sam, I . . ." Jonas seemed about to say something, then changed his mind. "You have to stay here."

"Do you expect me to just accept that?" she demanded in disbelief. "Am I supposed to stay here willingly until you say I can leave? *If* you say I can leave?"

"You'll be safe here," he said firmly.

"Safe!" His incredible statement prompted movement. She stepped past him. "How can you say that? How can you expect me to believe that?" Her hands waved the air to punctuate her questions. "How am I safe when I'm being kept on this island against my will? When you and Tom are walking around carrying guns? Maybe even Maggie has one strapped to her thigh, I don't know!" She was so intent on her declarations that she missed the narrowing of his gray eyes. "You expect too much!"

"No one is going to hurt you," Jonas stated quietly.

"Is that right?" Samantha inquired with a disbelieving nod of her head. "Can you speak for the others?"

"Yes, I can."

"You'll simply have to forgive me for not believing you. I've listened to too many of your lies," she declared.

"You have no reason to be afraid."

"So you say." Her mouth twisted with mocking skepticism.

"Samantha, you have to trust me." Jonas didn't try to conceal his impatience.

"Trust you?" The throaty laugh she gave bordered on hysteria, her taut nerves snapping after hours of strain. "How can I trust you? I don't even know who you are!"

This time he did grip her shoulders and give her a slight shake that got her attention. "Stop it," he commanded tersely. "You're getting yourself all worked up over nothing."

"Hah!" The frenzied note in her laughing voice died away. There was a look in his eyes that effectively silenced her.

"You're letting the situation seem worse than it is," he barked.

"Am I?" Samantha whispered brokenly, gazing into his compelling face. "I wish you could convince me of that."

His head moved to the side in frustration as he breathed in deeply to control his rising temper. There was an enigmatic hardness in the dark smoke of his gaze when he turned it back to her face. He studied the confused and troubled light in her eyes, seemingly aware of the apprehension in them. The line of his mouth thinned as he gathered her stiff body in his arms.

"Trust me, Sam," Jonas muttered against her hair. "I swear I won't let anyone harm you."

"I can't trust you," she protested, swallowing back a sob of longing and pushing her hands against the granite wall of his chest.

He held her easily, overcoming her half-hearted struggles as she rigidly resisted his embrace and its offer of comfort. The fine silk of her dark hair was caught in the shadowy stubble on his cheek. The rough caress was unnerving.

"And I can't let you leave the island," he responded thickly.

"I won't stay," Samantha declared into the smooth material of his windbreaker. "I'll swim if I have to!"

"And probably drown," Jonas concluded sharply. "You're a good swimmer, but both of us know you aren't that good. And I can't believe you'd prefer killing yourself to staying here with me."

She could have told him that under any other circumstances she would have gladly stayed on any island with him. But she simply couldn't forget the fact she was being held prisoner.

"I won't stay," she repeated, straining against the arms that held her fast.

"I'll make sure nothing happens to you. You'll have to trust me, babe." The endearment was spoken very casually as if he had called her that hundreds of times.

But, combined with the firm contact of his muscled length and her undeniable attraction to him, that one little word banished her resistance to his embrace. Samantha relaxed against him, letting her curves mold themselves to the hard contours of his body. She felt his mouth against her hair, kissing her.

"Jonas," she sighed, then caught it back. "That isn't your real name, is it?"

"No," he admitted indifferently. "But it doesn't matter."

"Yes it does," Samantha protested, because it meant that he didn't trust her. Yet he expected her to trust him when she didn't even know who he was.

His large hands moved up to cup the sides of her neck below her ears, fingers twining into her hair as he tipped her head back to meet the smoldering fire of his gray eyes.

"Nothing matters except this." His mouth brushed over her eyelid, her lashes fluttering against his lips. "And this." He shifted to her cheek and the tiny hollow where her dimple formed. "And this," he murmured against the corner of her lips. And he kissed her until she was convinced. The masterful pressure of his mouth blocked out all her fears. Her arms wrapped themselves around his neck to cling to him, breathing erratically when he began exploring the sensitive cord along her neck.

"I want to trust you," she whispered achingly.

Jonas lifted his head to gaze into her hungry eyes. "Then trust me," he stated quietly. "You won't be sorry, I promise. I won't let anything happen to you."

There was a barely perceptible movement of her head in acceptance of his words. His mouth closed possessively over hers, burning his ownership into her heart. Samantha knew he was wrong. Something had already happened to her. She had fallen in love with him—her stranger—and there wasn't any way she could reverse the course of her emotions.

His hands slid down her spine to pull her hips against him, the muscular column of his legs scorching her flesh on contact. She melted in his tender embrace, glorying in the tide of surrender sweeping through her.

The growth of beard scraped at her cheek as he searched out each sensitive area along the curve of her neck and the pulsing hollow of her throat. But the rasp of his beard was exciting, heightening her nerve ends to their full awareness. His large hands moved over every inch of her ribs, waist, and hips, arching her more fully against him while they continued to explore the pliant curves of her body.

The musky scent of his maleness filled her senses, sending them spinning with delight. Samantha was no match for his passionate onslaught. As she sought the devastating pressure of his mouth, liquid wildfire raced through her veins.

After torturous seconds, he let her lips find his mouth, his kiss hardening as they opened beneath his touch. Locked in each other's arms, they both felt the yearnings for satisfaction in the other.

Finally it was Jonas who ended it, breaking away to bury his face in the silky thickness of her hair above her ear. Her eager fingers continued a tentative exploration of his strong jawline. The pounding of his heart kept pace with the rapid tempo of hers, his breathing disturbed and ragged.

"I've tried so hard to keep from loving you," Samantha whispered with frustrated longing.

"You have?" his muffled voice mocked her gently.

"What do you think it's been like for me? Every time you're near me, I want to make love to you."

She drew her head away, needing to see his face. "Do you really mean that?" she asked breathlessly.

He smiled, a wondrous smile that softened the firm line of his mouth and made beautiful, crinkling lines at the corners of his gray eyes. His gaze traveled warmly over her upturned face, taking in the soft glow of her eyes and the parted invitation of her lips.

"If you don't stop looking at me like that, you'll find out just how much I mean that," he told her with lazy humor.

Samantha laughed huskily and rested her head against his chest. A sweet pleasure beyond description filled her heart with joy. She closed her eyes to imprint this moment in her mind, wanting to cherish it forever. Right now, it didn't matter that he hadn't said he loved her. He wanted her, with the same fierce ache with which she wanted him.

"Let's go away, Jonas," she murmured. "Let's get in the sailboat and sail away."

There was a sudden tenseness in the arms that held her. Every muscle seemed to become suddenly alert. With deliberate slowness, his hands moved up to grip her shoulders and move her a few inches from him. The smoke screen was back to conceal his thoughts when she lifted her head to gaze at him. She could only guess what was making him wary and she tried to dispel his caution.

"No one ever has to know that you were keeping me on the island," she told him earnestly. "Please, let's go away, the two of us together."

Her hand lifted to caress the powerful line of his

cheek. He caught it before it could reach its objective and she felt the steely strength of his grip.

"Hey, let me go!" she protested in bewilderment.

A muscle leaped in his jaw and his eyes turned stormy. He released her hand abruptly and turned away. "We are not leaving this island, Sam," he stated coldly.

Her mouth opened, but for a time nothing could come out. How could he continue to hold her prisoner if he really cared for her as he claimed? He couldn't possibly care for her.

"It was all just a trick, wasn't it?" Samantha squeezed the accusing words through the painful knot in her throat. "You were playing games again, just the way you've been doing from the beginning."

"It wasn't a game," Jonas answered tautly.

"I don't believe you!" she cried out. "You were just using another tactic to persuade me to stay willingly on this island! It would have made it so much easier if you didn't have to guard me every second, wouldn't it? Well, your scheme didn't work!" She resorted to anger to hold back the scalding tears in her eyes.

"Neither did yours," he snarled.

"Mine?" Samantha breathed in hurt confusion. She couldn't have made it more obvious that she had fallen in love with him.

"Save that innocent look in those big brown eyes for someone else." He gave her a very wary look. "I don't buy it. There isn't anything you wouldn't resort to in order to get off this island—you proved that conclusively a few minutes ago. Did you really think you had me so securely wrapped around your finger that all you had to do was pull the string and I'd take you away?"

Samantha gasped softly. He believed she had only been pretending to be in love with him so that he would take her away. Her first instinct was to deny it, but pride insisted that she not completely humble herself when he didn't care for her.

"Desperate situations breed desperate solutions." She flung the words at him.

"That's hardly original," Jonas said harshly.

"I'll try to do better in the future," she retorted.

"You may not have a chance. I hope not," he muttered beneath his breath as if thinking aloud, then reached for her arm, saying more clearly, "Come on. You're going back to the house."

"What do you mean I may not have another chance?" Samantha demanded, unable to wriggle free of his grip. She was pulled along beside him toward the door. "Are you going to lock me in my room? Or . . ." She couldn't voice the other thought.

"I don't think I could trust you alone even behind a locked door. If I lock you in, I'll be in there with you." His intense gaze suddenly turned to her, filled with intimate suggestion. "It might even prove to be entertaining."

"You wouldn't dare!" she breathed in alarm, pulling back against his grip to lag behind him.

Jonas paused at the door, grinning like a wolf. "Wouldn't I?"

The door burst open and Tom's burly figure was silhouetted against the night. "She's slipped away again," he burst out. Jonas's tall frame blocked Samantha from view. "Maggie looked in a few minutes ago and found pillows stuffed under the covers to make it look like she was still in bed. The window screen was pried loose. There's no way of telling how long she's been gone."

"You can stop looking," Jonas said curtly, pulling Samantha forward. "I've found her."

Tom swore beneath his breath in relief. "I thought we'd lost her for sure."

"I'm taking her back to the house now. Get a lock for the dinghy and the boathouse door," Jonas ordered. "Then you'd better see what you can do to patch that screen."

"Right away," Tom nodded.

Samantha was pushed through the door's opening as Tom stepped out of the way. It was a long walk to the house, a walk that was made even longer by the silence he didn't break. Maggie was waiting in the dining room. She shook her head in relief at the sight of Samantha, but Jonas didn't make any explanation as he marched Samantha through the house to her bedroom and got her inside.

She tripped on the doorsill and stumbled into the room, regained her balance near the rumpled bed, then turned to face him, frightened yet boldly defiant. He stood at the door, a hand resting on the doorknob.

"The screen isn't repaired yet, but I wouldn't try to slip away again," he warned. "I'd find you before you could get off the island."

"Go to hell, whatever-your-name-is!" A rush of bravado made her voice loud.

"Thanks to your father, I probably will," he agreed sardonically and shut the door.

Samantha stood uncertainly where she was, wanting to ignore his warning and sneak through the opening of the screen. But she was convinced he would find her and the consequences might be more disastrous the next time.

A tear spilled down her cheek, then a second. She moved blindly to the bed, stretching out on the covers and burying her head in a pillow. She had no idea how long she lay there, her cheeks wet with the slow trickle of tears.

From outside, someone started pounding a hammer where her screen window was. Tom, she guessed. It was only after the pounding stopped and his footsteps carried him away from her bedroom that the tears increased their flow. For the first time since her childhood years, Samantha cried herself to sleep, silently muffling her sobs in the pillow.

Her head throbbed dully as the sunlight probed at her eyelids. She pulled the covers more tightly over her shoulders and tried to cling to the forgetfulness of sleep. An awareness crept in, aroused first by the bareness of her skin. She didn't remember undressing and frowned as she realized that she was clad in her underwear and not her pajamas. She stirred slightly and felt a weight on one corner of the bed.

The painful memories of last night began to surface as she struggled into consciousness. The back of her neck prickled with the sensation that someone was watching her. The uncomfortable feeling wouldn't go away, and she turned her face from the pillow to glance over her shoulder.

The last traces of sleep fled at the sight of Jonas slouched in a chair, his long legs propped on the edge of the bed. His elbows rested on the arms of the chair, his hands folded together on the flat of his stomach. Behind the lazily lowered lashes, his gray eyes were watching her, taking in her stunned shock and the trepidation that immediately replaced it.

Samantha quickly pulled the covers up to her throat, remembering his threat to lock himself in the room with her and hotly conscious of her scanty attire beneath the blankets. She had trouble breathing naturally.

"How long have you been there?" Her demand was weakly voiced.

"All night," he answered blandly.

"It wasn't necessary," she protested stiffly.

"I thought it was."

"I didn't try to get away."

"No, and you won't get the chance to try anymore," he stated, uncoiling from the chair and subtly stretching his cramped muscles.

"What do you mean?" Samantha eyed him cautiously. Had he decided to keep her locked in the room?

"I mean"—he paused for effect—"that someone is going to be with you at all times. The only place you'll be alone is in the bathroom, and I suggest you go there now and get dressed so I can turn you over to Maggie and get myself some sleep."

From the glint in his eye, Samantha could tell that he expected her to insist he look the other way while she made her dash to the bathroom. Instead, she pulled the covers from the foot of the bed and wrapped them securely around her as she swung her feet to the floor. Shuffling across the floor in the confining mummy wrap, she took fresh clothes from the closet and dresser drawer, then retreated to the bathroom.

Before the day was over, Samantha learned that Jonas had meant exactly what he said. She was never alone, shadowed constantly by one of them.

During the morning and early afternoon, it was Maggie and Tom because Jonas was sleeping. Maggie was quietly friendly in the time Samantha was forced to spend with her, but it was Tom who seemed the most sympathetic to her plight, his gaze faintly apologetic.

Jonas had monopolized her time so much in the past days that this had been her first opportunity to get to know the others. Yet both Maggie and Tom remained slightly aloof from her. She knew it would be useless to try to enlist their aid in escaping. They were as determined as Jonas that she remain on the island.

At eleven that evening, Jonas announced it was time she went to bed. Samantha wanted to object, but she knew it would be futile. Still, she couldn't conceal her mistrust of his presence when he followed her into the bedroom.

She hesitated inside, unwilling to change into the revealing shorty pajamas and reluctant to incite a situation she couldn't handle. Besides, how could she even get into bed with him watching her? Her position was so vulnerable, especially because, like a world-class idiot, she loved him in spite of everything.

"You might as well change into your night clothes." He accurately guessed the reason for her hesitation. "Otherwise Maggie will have to come in and undress you the same as she did last night." At Samantha's sudden pivot in his direction, he drew his head back in a considering manner, a wicked, knowing glint in his eyes. "You thought I took your clothes off last night, didn't you?" he chuckled.

Her cheeks crimsoned as she hurriedly looked away. "I had no way of knowing who did."

"Well, you can breathe easier. It wasn't me." His voice held an edge of impatience as he turned away. "So hurry up and get into bed."

Self-consciously, Samantha gathered the yellow shorty pajamas in hand and darted into the bathroom, emerging a few minutes later to see Jonas standing at the window. Before she could slide beneath the covers he turned and saw her.

The pajamas covered more than her bathing suit did, but there was something so decidedly intimate about wearing pajamas in front of a man. She made a project of tucking the covers around her, studiously avoiding the frowning look of concentration being directed at her. Her pulse raced when he moved away from the window. But all he did was switch off the overhead light to throw the room into darkness; then he walked back to the window.

For a long time she was afraid to move. Her muscles became cramped from the restricted position and the covers drawn so tightly around her. Finally, she had to move. She turned, trying to find a more comfortable position, but without much success. The repeated shifting got his attention.

"I hope you aren't going to sleep as restlessly as you did last night," he said. "I'm not in the mood to keep covering you up all night long."

Just when she had begun to lose some of her embarrassment over the fact that it hadn't been Jonas who had undressed her, it returned with uncomfortable warmth.

"Thanks a lot," she muttered bitterly. "That's just the kind of comment I needed to induce a restful sleep!" Since it would result in the exact opposite.

"Go to sleep, Sam," he muttered back in a half-growled undertone.

"I'm trying, but it's not easy with you standing there," she retorted.

"Would you rather I crawled in bed with you?" Jonas snapped.

"No!" The denial was quick and more than a little frightened. Her body was first cold, then hot at the thought.

"Forget I asked," he sighed. A task easier said than done. "Good night, Sam. And don't worry, I won't disturb you."

Had it been her imagination or had there been a slight emphasis on his last word—"you"? Samantha couldn't tell, but she thought it was wise not to ask.

Neither spoke again, although it was well into the morning hours before she finally slept. When she wakened near midday, she found Maggie was in the room with her. The woman explained that Jonas had left for his own room shortly after dawn to get some sleep.

The day's pattern started out as a duplicate of the previous day. The change came in the middle of the afternoon when Jonas appeared to relieve Tom. He and Samantha had been playing a game of gin rummy, but when Jonas sat in his chair, Samantha stood up. His presence dominated the room, making it too confining.

"Can we go outside?" she asked nervously, feeling

the disturbance caused by his overpowering masculinity.

"For a while," he agreed, rising to move toward the patio doors, sliding them open, and permitting Samantha to lead the way.

She moved restlessly around the patio, unable to appreciate the view of the gently flowing St. Lawrence River and its cluster of islands. Jonas leaned against a rock, letting her prowl while keeping her in sight. She felt there was an invisible leash stretching from her to him and she wanted to break free of it.

Her steps turned unconsciously toward the path to the boathouse. She hesitated a few yards along the worn trail and glanced over her shoulder. Jonas had moved away from the boulder and was ambling after her, but not attempting to catch up. Evidently he wasn't going to forbid her to go to the cove. Maybe he wanted her to see that the boathouse was padlocked.

Samantha turned her back to the path and continued her aimless meandering pace toward the cove. There wasn't any particular reason to go there. She was only going because there wasn't any particular reason not to go.

On a rocky knoll above the cove, the trees gave way to grass and stone. She paused there, her gaze sweeping the clumps of tree-crowned islands against the backdrop of a milky blue sky. A few elongated puffy clouds were drifting overhead.

As Samantha started down from the knoll, she noticed a motorboat growing steadily larger in the distance, but her only interest in it was identifying something that was moving in the quiet afternoon. She didn't entertain any thoughts of looking for help from whoever was on it. Jonas would see to it that she couldn't.

Strolling down to the water's edge, she gazed at the raft anchored in the cove, but there were too many painful memories attached to it. She dug a toe into the pebbles at her feet, the tips of her fingers tucked in the hip pockets of her slacks. She didn't have to turn around to know that Jonas was nearby; she could feel his gaze on her. The invisible leash hadn't been broken, only the tension had been slackened.

Lifting her head, she stared out across the water again. The large motorboat was coming nearer. It would pass very close to the island, but Samantha didn't take her hands from her pockets to wave at it. To attract the boat's attention would also attract Jonas's, and she would gain nothing in the end except his displeasure and possibly a confinement to the house.

Instead of the boat steering a course around the island, she realized with a start that it was heading toward the cove. As it neared the entrance, the powerful engines were throttled down. Her heart leaped at the sight, but her feet were rooted to the spot. At any moment she expected Jonas to come charging down to drag her away before she was recognized.

The motorboat was in the cove now and there was still no sound from Jonas. Biting her lip, Samantha glanced over her shoulder. Jonas was standing in the break of the trees, slightly in their shadow, watching the boat purring toward the dock. His gaze slipped to her. At this distance, his expression was inscrutable.

Is this another of his tricks? Samantha wondered.

The boat must belong to one of his colleagues. Why else was he letting it come in?

The engines were stopped and a dark-suited man was making the boat fast to the dock. When it was secure, two more figures emerged from the cabin. Samantha stared at one of them, not believing her eyes.

He was a few inches taller than she was, his physique just beginning to show a losing battle against weight, dark brown hair salted liberally with gray. When he turned toward land and she saw his handsome square face and clear, discerning brown eyes, she knew she wasn't mistaken.

Joy rose at the sight of Reuben Gentry, her father, only to be checked by the realization of what this meant. She was being rescued, which meant that Jonas would be caught. Her gaze swung to the path's knoll and Jonas. The trees were still concealing him from the view of the boat's party. Their eyes met, hers begging him to run, to get away while he had the chance.

"Sam!" Reuben was calling to her, a strong voice, vital and powerful like the man.

Samantha ripped her gaze from Jonas, forcing a smile, only half-glad to see her father. She moved her feet and made them carry her toward her father, slowly gaining speed until she was nearly running into his opened arms. Tears blinded her vision as she stopped before him.

"Reuben," she murmured in a choked whisper.

He tipped his head to one side, his hands settling on her shoulders. "Are you all right, Sam?"

The comforting touch of his hands slid her arms

around his waist, muffling her silent sobs in the expensive material of his jacket.

"Yes, I'm all right," she managed to say huskily, but she wasn't. Her arms tightened around him. Very, very softly, she cried, "Daddy!"

He held her for a few more seconds, then began to gently untwine her arms from around his middle. His brown eyes were warm with deep affection as he wiped the tears from her cheeks.

"I haven't had a welcome like that since you were six years old," he teased. Samantha tried to laugh, but it was brittle and harsh. Reuben looked beyond her in the direction of the trail. "Where are the others?"

She glanced at the two dark-suited men, standing quietly, stern-faced, on each side of her father. She saw the bulge of their jackets and paled. Quickly she looked over her shoulder. There was no sign of Jonas. It was wrong to hope he had escaped.

"At . . ." She didn't want to tell, but she had to. "At the house, I think. There's a path through those trees."

The two men started forward, and Samantha moved to one side as her father started to follow. He stopped and looked at her, an understanding light in his brown eyes.

"Are you coming?" he asked gently.

"No." She couldn't. "I'll wait here—on the boat." The two men were waiting for him. Reuben Gentry nodded in acknowledgment, then moved to join them. Samantha turned away, wiping the tears from her cheek, determined she wouldn't cry anymore.

Chapter Nine

Samantha stared into the coffee mug, wishing she could lose herself in the seemingly fathomless void of the dark liquid. A man, probably part of the crew, had brought it to her shortly after she had come aboard the motorboat.

Half of it was gone and the rest had cooled to an unpalatable stage. Still she clung to the mug, needing to hold on to something to keep her sanity while she waited in the cabin.

It had been almost twenty minutes since her father had left for the house. There hadn't been a sound, not a gunshot, nothing, only the lapping of the water against the boat's hull. Her nerves were raw, not knowing what was happening and not wanting to know, yet imagining.

She had drawn the curtains in the cabin. She didn't want to accidentally see them bringing Jonas in. Samantha wondered if someone was going to debrief her at some point—an explanation would be interesting. Being on an island with no TV and no contact with the world for so long had been an odd experience, as if she had been spirited away from everything she knew and set down somewhere outside of real time.

There were footsteps on the dock, hollow and ominous, echoing over the boards, Samantha tensed, following them in her mind as they boarded the boat and approached the cabin door. Refusing to turn around as it opened, she closed her eyes and tried to get a grip on her senses. She didn't want Reuben to see her torment, not right now. She breathed in deeply and blinked at the ceiling.

"Did they . . . give themselves up?" she asked tautly.

The door closed. "Not exactly."

At the agonizingly familiar sound of that voice, Samantha swung around. Her fingers lost their grip on the coffee mug and it shattered on the floor, scattering pieces of pottery and spattering brown liquid. Wide-eyed with shock, she stared at Jonas.

"What have you done with Reuben?" she demanded in alarm.

"He's at the house." His features betrayed only a firm determination. The gray eyes were unreadable. "Would you like to join him?"

"Would I like to join him?" Samantha laughed bitterly. "Oh, my God. Did he walk right into a trap, too? Oh, Jonas, you won't get away with it," she cried.

"My name is Cade Scott."

"Cade Scott?" she repeated in bewilderment. The name was familiar, but she was too emotional and too bewildered to concentrate on why it was known to her.

"I work for Reuben," he stated blandly. "I handle all the security for him."

"Huh?" Samantha was totally confused. Chalk it up to stress and sleeplessness, but she couldn't process any new information. She shook her head. "Then . . ."

"I know you must have jumped to the conclusion you were kidnapped, but there wasn't anything I could do about it," the man now identified as Cade Scott continued. "I was following Reuben's instructions and I kept my mouth shut."

"Reuben's—what?" One of them wasn't making any sense. "But why? Why should my father want me held prisoner on this island? It doesn't make sense!"

"It was for your own protection. It—"

"Hold it," Samantha interrupted. "Why should I need protection?"

"Over the last few months, your father has received a series of threatening letters and phone calls. He didn't take them seriously until someone took a shot at him a couple of weeks ago." At Samantha's gasp of fear, he added, "The man missed, but he convinced Reuben, as I had been unable to do, that the stalker wasn't making idle threats."

"What does this have to do with me if he was after Reuben?"

"The day I came to the newspaper office, your father got a phone call from the man that morning. He said he had decided Reuben should live, killing him would be too easy. He would get his revenge on Reuben through you. He knew what town you were in, where you were working, and what name you were using," Cade Scott explained. "I figured he'd hacked into the newspaper's employee database— it's a small system and not all that secure. With that much information, we had to believe he would harm you. I had to move faster than him to get you out of there before he could make good on his threat."

"And that's why you brought me here." She felt a shiver of fear dance down her spine.

"Yes. The island is isolated and relatively easy to guard. Intruders would be spotted immediately. We decided it was the ideal place to hide you," he stated in the same impersonal tone he had used since he entered the cabin.

Samantha raked her fingers through her hair, flipping it back. "Why didn't you tell me all this in the beginning? Why was it such a deep dark secret?"

"I told you—it was Reuben's orders. He didn't want to alarm you. Which is why I wasn't able to tell you my real name. Reuben was sure you'd make the connection to his security section and become suspicious." He shrugged, a very masculine movement with shoulders that size. "I don't think he realizes you're not a little girl anymore." Cade gave her a long look that said the same thing but in a very different way.

"So you went through that whole charade of being Owen Bradley, then Chris Andrews, and the mysterious Jonas!" Samantha exclaimed impatiently. "Didn't you think the constant parade of names would make me suspicious? I'm not even mentioning your refusal to let me leave the island or speak to anyone else. Which raises another question. Why wouldn't you let me call Reuben?"

"Because we didn't know how the man was getting his information. It was conceivable that he hadn't hacked it—it could have been relayed to him by someone in your father's organization. I couldn't let you leave a message," he said smoothly.

Her anger was rising. "You could have explained, somehow," she accused, "instead of letting me think I was a prisoner. That you and Tom and Maggie were holding me—" She broke off to ask sharply, "Do Tom and Maggie work in the security department too?"

"That's right."

"When you realized that I thought I was kidnapped, you should have told me," Samantha protested, exasperated and relieved at the same time.

"I couldn't. You—"

"I know, Reuben gave the orders," she flashed. "But you could have tried to persuade him that he was wrong. I was positively terrified, and for nothing!"

"I did try to convince him, but he's like a bulldog. Once he gets his teeth into something, he won't let go. He insisted on sticking with the original plan for you to know nothing of the threats." Cade regarded her steadily. "I believe you overheard the last part of the conversation I had with him about it and misinterpreted it."

Samantha vividly remembered the one he was referring to and Cade's anger when he warned Reuben he would be sorry. "Yes," she nodded crisply. "I thought Reuben was refusing to pay the ransom."

"The original plan should have been scrapped when Reuben discovered he couldn't join us."

"Was he planning to?" Samantha inquired with skepticism.

"Yes, we thought it was best if he was here with you in case the man changed his mind and made another attempt on his life, but the authorities persuaded Reuben to stay in New York in case of he was contacted again."

"In that case, why is he here now?" she demanded.

"The man was arrested in the night. The danger is over." Cade's expression was set, like a mask firmly in place.

Yet something in his tone made her ask, "How long have you known?"

"Since around five this morning."

Approximately the same time that Maggie had indicated he had relinquished his guard over Samantha and gone to bed. But that wasn't what made her temper ignite.

"And you let practically another day go by while I believed was kidnapped. I still think you could have explained all of this to me before Reuben arrived," she accused angrily.

"Yes, I could have," he agreed with the utmost calm, blandly meeting the snapping fire of her gaze. "But I didn't think you would believe me. As you pointed out before, you listened to too many of my lies to trust anything I said. I knew Reuben was on his way, so I waited for him to support my story. I'm telling you the truth, Sam."

Samantha turned away, pain bursting in her heart at the sound of her name on his lips. She believed him. Everything fit, all the evidence that she had misinterpreted. Even the initials C.S. turned out to be right.

C.S. for Cade Scott.

She had known who Cade Scott was. She had heard Reuben praising him loud and long. Cade headed the security division of his various companies. By some quirk of fate she had never met him until he had brought her to this island paradise that her imagination had turned into an island hell. But the initials alone hadn't been sufficient to jog her memory of a man she hadn't met.

"If only I'd known!" she groaned softly.

"I wanted to tell you," Cade said quietly. "I nearly did a couple of times."

"I wish you had," Samantha sighed, remembering

the strange attraction she'd felt to the stranger who had kidnapped her. Things like that happened— there was even a name for it, Stockholm syndrome. Her feelings had tormented her, but at least now she didn't have to feel so guilty about—she had to admit it—loving him. "I wish you had, regardless of what Reuben wanted," she repeated.

"I take orders from your father. He's the boss," Cade reminded her.

The reminder was unsettling. Cade Scott worked for her father and she was the boss's daughter, an excellent prize for an ambitious man. And the relentless quality about him assured Samantha that he was an ambitious man. He would get where he wanted regardless of whom he used along the way.

"I'll be sure to tell him what a thorough job you did protecting me," she declared with a brittle smile. "You did your very best to keep me entertained, even resorting to some drastic methods, but they worked. And it's only been in the last couple of days that I decided—wrongly—that I'd been kidnapped. You weren't to blame for that. I'm sure Reuben will be very proud of you."

His gaze narrowed, slicing over her face. "Not everything I did was to entertain you, Sam." He seemed to be underlining the word "everything."

"Of course not." She laughed huskily to hide the quivering of her chin. "It was good fun for both of us."

"That's all it was."

Yet she sensed there was a question behind his statement and it hurt. "Yes, that's all it was," she said, but the poignant catch in her voice wasn't convincing.

Cade took a step toward her and Samantha pivoted to face him, on guard against the explosive attraction his presence made her feel. Like quicksilver, his gaze glided over her face, the vulnerable light in her brown eyes, then stopped on her moist lips. Her pulse accelerated.

"You're lying, Sam. It wasn't just fun for either of us," he said, starting forward again.

She retreated, a fragment of the smashed coffee mug crunching beneath her foot. "Please, Jonas. . . ." With a broken laugh, Samantha corrected herself. "It's Cade, isn't it? You see, I don't even know what to call you. Please, I need time to think. It's all so confusing. Leave me alone, Cade, please?"

He hesitated, then grimly conceded. "Okay, we'll do it your way this time." He turned on his heel and walked to the cabin door. "I'll tell Reuben you've decided to wait for him at the boat."

Cade was gone before Samantha could acknowledge his last statement. For several minutes she listened to the sound of his footsteps as he left the boat. Finally she bent to pick up the pieces of the broken mug, trying not to cut her hands. It was something to do.

By the time Reuben Gentry returned to the boat, Samantha had splashed water on her face and composed herself. She had even managed to find some humor in her escapade—dark humor—when they discussed it. Luckily her father had no intention of remaining on the island, even overnight.

Samantha gladly accompanied him, needing to get away from Cade before she committed herself to something she would regret.

At twenty-two, she had learned not to give in to impulse. She already had too many scars where people couldn't see them. Cade didn't return with the others. Reuben claimed Cade had a few ends to tie up and would follow the next day.

Samantha wondered if he was giving her that chance to think.

Reuben didn't seem to expect her to go directly back to the newspaper. Samantha needed a few days to think it all over in private and come to some decision about Cade. There was no question that she loved him. The question was what she ought to do about it.

Four days after her return, the phone rang. Samantha stared at it. She didn't want to answer it. It was Cade—she knew it as surely as if he were standing in the room. Like a coward, she let it ring, wanting to avoid the inevitable. But it was inevitable and it was better not to postpone it. On the fourteenth ring she answered it, hardly aware she had been counting.

"Sam, this is Cade." His low voice moved through her like a golden flame.

"Hello, Cade, how are you?" She congratulated herself on the calmness of her reply. It wasn't indicative of her racing heart.

"Fine," was the automatic response, but he didn't return the inquiry. "Since Reuben's out of town, I wondered if you were free for dinner this evening."

Samantha breathed in sharply as he stole her excuse. Cade worked for her father and being in charge of security meant he was cognizant of Reuben's whereabouts.

"Actually—" She was stalling, trying to think of a plausible lie.

"Sam," Cade interrupted in a quietly firm voice, "I want to see you."

Her legs didn't want to support her as her heart skipped several beats. She clutched at the table, fighting the waves of longing. If the sound of his voice could do this to her, what would happen if she saw him again? Wouldn't it be better to see him now than to wait for some time when she might be unprepared and a lot more vulnerable?

"Actually," Samantha continued, "I don't have anything planned for this evening."

"I'll pick you up at seven," he concluded.

"Okay. Seven it is."

After an exchange of goodbyes, Samantha hung up, her hands shaking, a giddiness in the pit of her stomach. She closed her eyes tightly. She had to get control of herself before tonight.

She chose an outfit that gave her a sophisticated appearance, but the luminous brown eyes gazing at her reflection were troubled and apprehensive. Her features were strained with the expression of poise.

The doorbell rang and Samantha jumped. *Get it together,* she scolded herself, and hurried into the living room. Carl, Reuben's houseman, answered the door as she entered the room. Cade's glance slid past the houseman to Samantha. Her steps faltered under the appraising sweep of his gray gaze, lazy and warm.

"Ready?" he asked quietly.

His rough features were more rugged and compelling than she remembered. She noted the steady regard of the eyes above the angular planes of his cheeks, the slight broken bend of his nose, the well-shaped mouth, and that casual air that hid the steel. Samantha felt light-headed.

"Yes, I am." The breathless catch in her voice revealed the way he disturbed her. Normally, she would have invited her date in for a drink, but not this time. "Shall we go?" Her voice was closer to normal.

Cade nodded. "Taxi's waiting."

Samantha walked to the door, glancing at Carl, who held it open for her, smiling. She smiled back, reassured by the sight of his gentle face.

"I have my key," she told him.

He winked, taking her hint. "I won't wait up for you, then. Have a nice evening, Samantha."

As he closed the door, she felt Cade's questioning gaze. "Carl has been with Reuben for years. When I first started dating, he was the one who usually waited up until I was safely home, and always when Reuben was out of town. He's a sweetie. I don't know what Reuben would do without him." She was willing to discuss anything as long as it didn't directly relate to her and what she was really thinking and feeling at this moment.

"It's good Reuben has Carl, then," he commented as they walked toward the elevators at the end of the hall "You won't have to worry about who's taking care of Reuben when you aren't here."

"You mean when I spread my wings and leave the nest for good to begin my brilliant career as a journalist," she added with forced brightness.

"Or marry. Or both." His sideways look held her gaze for seconds.

Before Samantha could recover, the elevator doors were opening and his large hand was applying pressure on the back of her waist to guide her inside. An involuntary thrill of pleasure ran through her at his touch, unnerving her and taking away her ability to speak. Cade didn't seem to expect a reply as he pushed the ground floor button and turned calmly back to her.

Samantha had the sensation of falling. She couldn't tell whether it was caused by the soundless descent of the elevator or the enigmatic look in his eyes as it ran over her face. Either way the pulse in her throat was throbbing madly.

"I haven't told you how beautiful you look tonight." The seductive pitch of his voice was almost too much.

"Thank you," she returned, striving for lightness to keep from sinking completely under his spell. "You're looking, uh, very attractive, too." That didn't sound particularly intelligent but it was the best she could do. She forced her gaze to break away from the hold of his and inspected the dark evening suit he wore instead. "It's a definite improvement not to have the bulge of a shoulder holster under your jacket."

"When did you guess?" Cade asked thoughtfully. "The night you snuck back into the house after your walk and we took you for an intruder?"

"Yes," Samantha admitted. "I saw you slip the gun inside your windbreaker. After that, I put two and two together and realized it wasn't poor tailoring that made your jackets so bulky."

"That was the beginning, wasn't it? When you started to mistrust me?"

The elevator had stopped at the ground floor, the doors gliding open. Samantha managed a brief "more or less" agreement as they stepped out. Conversation was pushed aside by the sight of the doorman walking quickly forward to open the door for them and the taxi driver standing impatiently on the sidewalk near his car.

Neither of them mentioned her enforced stay on the island while they dined at one of the more popular cabaret clubs in New York City. Afterward, the entertainment—a soulful singer in a long black dress—precluded the need for conversation. Yet the undercurrent of awareness flowed constantly between them.

The slightest contact of his hand or any part of him vibrated through Samantha. Each time his gaze slid to her lips, she seemed to stop breathing. Basically, though, Cade kept his distance, not trying to penetrate her defenses except by a subtle look or touch. It was as if he knew he could get through them any time he wanted to.

Dancing followed the entertainment. Samantha knew that she could not risk the feel of his arms around her and suggested Cade take her home. He didn't object. In the taxi home, he made no attempt to sit close to her as they exchanged polite comments about the very talented singer and the people they had seen.

At the apartment building, Cade didn't ask the taxi to wait. When the taxi drove off into the night, Samantha knew the hour of reckoning had arrived and hoped she was up to it. She nodded stiffly to the doorman as Cade escorted her into the building and toward the elevators.

Neither spoke during the ride up to the floor of her father's apartment. The silence added to the tension that had been mounting inside Samantha since Cade's phone call that afternoon.

At the apartment door, she made a weak attempt to dismiss him. "I had a great time, Cade. Thank you."

His mouth quirked mockingly. "You're inviting me in, aren't you?"

Was that a given? He seemed to think so. "I . . . I really am tired," she protested nervously.

He took the key from her hand—she hadn't realized she was holding it. He turned it in the lock and pushed the door open. Then his hand was between her shoulder blades to gently guide her into the foyer entrance of the living room.

"You know we have to talk, Sam," he said quietly,

and walked past her, moving toward the bar in the far corner of the living room. She guessed he had been here before with her father.

Since she couldn't force herself to relax, Samantha avoided the comfortable chairs and sofa, walking to the far window that overlooked the bustling city, aglitter with lights. Too soon, Cade was beside her, offering a glass of gin and tonic. She accepted it, staring at the cubes of ice rather than meeting his gaze.

"I'm not sure I know exactly what it is we have to talk about," she said defensively.

"About us, of course." Cade lifted his glass to his mouth, blandly meeting her involuntary glance. Her heart jumped to her throat as she looked wildly away from the disturbing light of his gray eyes.

CHAPTER TEN

"So what's up?" Samantha managed to laugh a little, but it sounded fake. She took a quick, retreating step away from him, more or less pretending to turn away from the window's view.

"Before tonight, I had some doubts myself," Cade stated, following her with his eyes.

"Doubts?" she breathed, trying not to sound as interested as she really was.

"Not about the way I felt," he expanded on his statement, "but about you."

"What do you mean?" Her attempt at a bright, unconcerned smile was tremulous, wavering visibly under his inspection of her mouth.

"I wasn't sure if the way you responded to my kisses on the island was because of me or because you were trying to enlist my help in getting off the island."

"And now?" She held her breath, clutching her gin and tonic in both hands. Not that she wanted it—the combination of sweet and bitter was something she didn't like.

Cade set his glass down. Samantha couldn't make herself move when he walked to her. His hand lifted the luxurious silk of her brown hair away from the side of her neck, the roughness of his thumb stroking the throbbing vein that was exposed. He still hadn't answered the question. It didn't matter because his touch made her forget what she had asked.

"Are you afraid of me, Sam?"

"Ah—why would I be?"

"Because of the way I make you feel," Cade persisted gently.

As if hypnotized into telling the truth by the rhythmic, seductive caress of his hand, Samantha answered yes. Her gaze was riveted on the glass when Cade removed it and set aside. But she seemed incapable of looking higher than the lapel of his jacket, the dark material contrasting with the white of his shirt.

"I thought you were so pretty the first time I saw you at the newspaper office, so open and unassuming. I admired you immediately." His voice caressed her, quickening the drumbeat of her pulse beneath his thumb. "One of the first rules a man learns when he's supposed to protect someone is to pay attention to what's going on around him. On the island, I found myself watching you. That amounts to a cardinal sin in my profession, Sam."

"Does it?" she murmured, since he seemed to expect her to say something.

"Looking at you wasn't enough. Every time I got close to you I wanted to kiss you." Samantha noticed the muscles tightening in his neck. "Hell," he muttered, "I wanted to make love to you. I thought it was what you wanted, too, until that night in the boathouse. I decided then that you were using my attraction to you to persuade me to help you escape. But you weren't, were you? You really meant it that night when you said you wanted us to go away together. It wasn't a trick, was it?"

"Cade, please!" She couldn't admit that.

"I realized it wasn't when your father's boat docked. You didn't run to him, not immediately, Sam. No, you looked at me, wanting me to run, to escape before I was caught, even though you believed I'd kidnapped you. You were hoping I'd get away, weren't you?" Cade asked. His tone was just as gentle but she knew she had to answer him.

"I don't know what I wanted or what I hoped," Samantha said in a whisper.

"You are stubborn. You love me but you won't admit it," he sighed with wry amusement.

Whoa. Had he really just said that? Since when did men talk about love so easily?

"I can't." Holy cow. By saying that, she admitted she loved him.

His hand slipped around her waist while his fingers curled tighter around her neck. He bent his head closer to hers, and their breaths mingled, warm, moist, and intoxicating.

"It's easy, Sam. Just repeat after me—I love you." Every word was carefully enunciated and her brown eyes watched the tantalizing nearness of his mouth as it formed the words. "Say it," Cade commanded in a low voice.

She knew she didn't have to, but oh, how she wanted to. "I"—her lips moved fractionally closer to his—"love"—he moved to meet her halfway—"you."

The possessive fire of his kiss burned away the last of her defenses and her lips parted willingly. Samantha wanted only to give herself up to the abandon he was arousing. Desire flamed white-hot, born no longer of just sexual attraction, but now fueled by love.

She obeyed the molding power of his hands and strained against him, glorying in the exploratory caress of his hands. There was no thought of restraint as he found the secret places to give her pleasure.

His voice, husky and low with passion, murmured near her ear, "It's so damn easy to love you, do you know that?"

Instead of thrilling her, his words had the effect of a cold shower. He spoke the truth, a truth that Samantha had forgotten when she was swept away by her love. Of course it was easy for a man to love Reuben Gentry's daughter. Her father was rich.

Slowly she began withdrawing from his touch. Cade murmured in protest for a few seconds, then seemed puzzled by her sudden reluctance to turn the embrace into something more. He held her loosely in his arms, rubbing his chin against the side of her forehead.

"God, I hope you're not going to change your mind. I'm so crazy about you, I've even been thinking what it would be like to be married to you. But I know you have to think about that. Just don't think for too long, okay?" He was joking around but his question might as well have been a command.

Samantha hesitated. "I don't know what to say," she finally replied.

His chin moved away from her head in surprise, and she immediately took the opportunity to move out of his arms. Gathering her resolve, she lifted her gaze to meet the piercing gray of his eyes, confused and searching.

Cade frowned. "Haven't I made it clear to you—"

"You've made it very clear," she interrupted briskly. "But I won't—I can't marry you."

"Hey, I wasn't asking for an answer right away— but why? I'd like to know," he demanded, trying to control the hardness that was trying to take over his voice. "Before I make a total jackass of myself."

"Look, we could be lovers." She was trembling with the pain breaking her up inside, but she kept her voice steady. "But don't ask me to be your wife, Cade."

"Lovers?" Cade shot her a look she couldn't quite read. "If that was all I wanted, I wouldn't have mentioned marriage."

"Okay, whatever, I'm sorry," Samantha said quickly. "But the answer to that particular question is going to be no, just so you know in advance."

"Mind if I ask you a very important question?"

"N-no."

"Sam, if you love me, why won't you marry me?"

She turned away, trying not to cry. "Don't be deliberately obtuse, Cade," she replied tightly. "I haven't forgotten who I am. I'm Reuben Gentry's daughter. You work for him, he's your boss."

He turned her around. The wintry look in his gray eyes chilled her. "And I'm not good enough for you to marry, is that it?" he said softly. "The boss's daughter can't stoop to marry a lowly employee."

He paused as if waiting for her to argue the point. She didn't.

"Forgive me, Samantha Gentry"—his voice was edged with sarcasm—"for insulting you with my proposal."

The grip on her elbow was removed. A few seconds later, the apartment door slammed and Samantha was alone. What was worse, she never felt so alone.

Reuben Gentry pulled a dinner roll apart and began buttering one of the halves. "Carl tells me you were out with Cade one evening while I was gone." He looked to Samantha for confirmation.

"Yes, that's right." It was a struggle to keep her voice calm and indifferent. The mention of his name had the power to upset her, and she carefully avoided glancing up from her plate.

"He's a good man, Sam. They don't come any better," he commented. "I trust him implicitly, but I guess I proved that, didn't I?" He chuckled. "I not only would trust him with *my* life, I trusted him with yours."

"Yes, I guess you did," she agreed tautly, then pushed her plate away, her appetite gone.

"Was there something else you would like, Samantha?" Carl looked pointedly at the food left on her plate, silently chiding her, as he had done in the past few days, for eating so little.

"Some coffee later," Samantha answered.

"I imagine you got to know Cade fairly well while

you were on his island," her father commented, not dropping the subject as Samantha had hoped.

"Fairly well." Then the rest of Reuben's words clicked in her mind. "His island?"

"Yes, it's been in his family for years. His grandfather lost all of the family fortune in a series of bad investments decades ago. About the only thing he salvaged was the island. I guess it was his grandfather's way of clinging to the dream of what the Scott family once was," Reuben explained in a musing way. "The original house was destroyed by fire twenty years ago. Cade built the present house himself, literally."

"I didn't know," she murmured.

"Of course, working for me, Cade doesn't get to spend as much time there as he'd like." He shrugged. "What did you think of it, Sam?"

"It was beautiful." Nearly paradise, she could have added. For a short while, it had seemed like one. She discovered it was going to be painful imagining Cade returning to that island. She didn't want to think about him any more. She had felt so alive in his arms—or had that feeling been triggered by her constant sense of danger? It was almost impossible to say. But she had never been in the slightest danger from him, of course. Exactly the opposite. Her father's gentle cough brought her out of her reverie.

"Will you be seeing Cade again?"

Unwillingly, Samantha met her father's probing look and quickly let her gaze fall to the white tablecloth. "No," she answered flatly. She could sense another question rising and added quickly. "Do you mind if we don't discuss this, Reuben?"

"If you say so, Sam," Reuben conceded. There

Long, tempestuous minutes passed before Samantha remembered they were in the back of a taxi riding down a busy New York street. The driver's mirror gave him an excellent view. Suddenly prim, she resisted the exploring caress of Cade's hands.

He read her mind and laughed softly against her trembling lips. "Sam, there isn't anything that a New York City taxi driver hasn't seen taking place in his cab." But he did sit up straighter, although he still held her on his lap. "A few more hours and we'll be in Vegas. I've waited this long. I can wait until then. How about you?"

She looked up into his loving eyes. "You know something? I changed my mind. Life is short and I don't feel like waiting."

They got started on an even better kiss.

were several minutes of silence before he spoke again. "Harry Lindsey called me today. He wondered when you were planning to come back to the paper."

"I don't know." She gave a shake of her head in irritation.

"Do you want to go back?" he asked quietly.

Samantha knew how deceptive his self-controlled calm could be. His shrewd perceptiveness was impossible to escape and it was one of his biggest assets in the business world.

She tensed, then sighed. "No." Work, and involvement in something besides her own heartache, would probably be the best medicine, but she didn't want to go back to the small-town newspaper. Her planned career didn't seem very important right now without the man she loved to share it with. Later she might find solace in it, but it seemed a poor second best.

"Sam." Again her father's voice came, quiet and probing. "Are you in love with Cade?"

Her hands closed tightly over the edge of the table and she pushed her chair back, rising swiftly. "I told you I didn't want to discuss him," she protested and stalked out of the dining room, hot tears welling in her eyes.

Her teeth were biting into her lip as she stopped in the center of the living room. She widened her eyes, blinking wildly to hold back the tears. A pair of hands settled gently on her shoulders to turn her around.

"Leave me alone!" she demanded.

"All we've got is each other, Sam. And Carl, of course." Reuben smiled. More deeply grooved versions of his daughter's dimples appeared near his

mouth. His tone was coaxing. "If you can't use my shoulder, whose will you use?"

"I'm a big girl now," she stated flatly.

"Even big girls get hurt when emotions run high. Sometimes I think feelings are harder to control when you're older," he said with a touch of wisdom. "You know that love doesn't come along every day, for one thing. Honey, it's pretty obvious you've fallen in love with Cade Scott."

There was a painful knot in her throat. Samantha swallowed it and nodded. "For all the good it does me."

"You mean he doesn't love you?" Her father bent his head slightly to peer at her face.

Samantha couldn't tell him the truth. How could she possibly explain that she had refused Cade's proposal of marriage because she knew it had been made to get him to a higher rung on the ladder of success? Cade hadn't asked *her* to marry him; he had asked Reuben Gentry's daughter. As much as she loved him, her answer had to be no.

"It's no use, Reuben." She shook her head sadly and chose a way that wouldn't hurt her father. "He doesn't like me, let alone love me." Which was true. His parting words had been filled with contempt.

Reuben frowned. "I find that hard to believe."

"That's because I'm your daughter and you're biased in my favor." She managed a wan smile.

"Well, then why did he take you out?" he demanded, unconvinced by her statement.

"Because I asked him," Samantha lied.

"I see." He considered the information thoughtfully.

"No biggie. I'll get over it. Lots of other fish in

the sea," she assured him, but not really believing it herself.

"Yes." He gathered her into his arms and held her close, his cheek resting against her head. "You got over your broken engagement four years ago, after all." he reasoned gently. "But you didn't love him, did you?"

Samantha shuddered against her father's chest. "No," she whispered tightly. In another second, she knew she would cry if she stayed where she was. Tears only seemed to make her misery worse. She breathed in deeply and pushed herself out of her father's arms. "You haven't finished your dinner."

"You sound like Carl now," he smiled down, understanding lighting his eyes. "Have coffee with me while I finish. I'd like the company."

Samantha nodded, returning his smile stiffly, and slid a hand under his arm as they returned to the dining room together.

A week slipped by, then two. An undemanding pattern began to form. Not rising until nearly noon, Samantha would fill the afternoon hours by taking long walks to tire herself out, then fall into exhausted sleep after spending the evenings with her father when he was in town. Which was nearly every night, as if he knew how vital it was for her not to spend the long night hours alone.

Three times Reuben had entertained business guests at dinner and Samantha had acted as his hostess. Only two people knew her well enough to see the turmoil she hid so convincingly. They were

Reuben and their houseman, Carl Gilbert, and they
kept her secret.

A hand lightly touched her shoulder and Samantha rolled onto her back, dragging the bedcovers
with her, bleary-eyed from heavy sleep. She managed to focus on the image of her father.

"What is it?" she questioned in a drowsy voice.

"I wondered if you could get up early enough to
have lunch with me today," he said in a chiding
tone. "You're beginning to act like a pampered
little rich girl, sleeping until noon every day."

"I know." But she found forgetfulness in sleep and
that was a rare occurrence in her waking hours.
There wasn't any need to explain to Reuben. "I'd
like to have lunch with you," Samantha agreed with
a tired nod.

"Sam," he said, his expression suddenly serious,
"would you like me to talk to Cade?"

Instantly she was awake. "No! Reuben, please,
don't do that," she begged in alarm.

One corner of his mouth lifted to form a rueful
line. "I'm afraid I already have."

"No!" It was a low protest and she pressed her
head deeper into the pillow, shutting her eyes.
"What happened?" She wasn't sure if she wanted to
know.

"I tried to lead up to the subject of you gradually,
Sam," he admitted. "I didn't want to seem like a
meddling father, so I called him into my office to
discuss something else that's been on the planning
board for nearly a year. Before I'd even got that
out, Cade was telling me what I could do with my
plans and my daughter."

"What exactly are you talking about?" Samantha asked.

"Our security operations have grown so large over the past few years that I'd decided it should be a separate enterprise. I wanted Cade to head it and offered him an option to buy stock in it," he explained.

"Oh, no!" Samantha moaned, guessing how Cade had probably interpreted that.

"He made himself quite clear," Reuben declared ruefully. "He seemed to think I was trying to buy you a husband by giving him an important position. He said something else, too." He studied her thoughtfully.

"Which was?" She looked at her father warily.

"Some nonsense about how if he wasn't good enough for you to marry before I made him the figurehead of some company, he certainly wouldn't be afterward."

Samantha blanched. "What did you say?"

"I told him that being a snob wasn't among your faults and that the one thing I would never do would be to buy you a husband," Reuben concluded.

"Did he say anything to that?" she asked weakly.

"He gave me a cold look and walked out of the office." Her father pushed back the sleeve of his jacket to glance at his gold Rolex. "I have to get to the office. We'll talk about it at lunch. Twelve-thirty?"

"Fine," Samantha nodded.

When Reuben left, Samantha knew she would never go back to sleep and lethargically dragged herself out of bed to dress. Over and over in her mind the hope kept running that maybe she had

misjudged Cade. He had refused the advancement
in his status outright. So . . . supposing she had misjudged him, would it ultimately change anything?

Obviously Reuben hadn't persuaded him that
she didn't think she was too good for him. And
after the things she had said, how could she convince him to the contrary?

She wandered restlessly through the apartment.
The irony of the situation was beginning to get to
her. She had been afraid that some man would ma-
nipulate her into marriage because of her father—
and as a result, she had turned away the only man
who might really have loved her. It was a bitter fact
to accept.

The doorbell rang and Samantha let Carl answer
it, presuming it was the dry cleaners with a delivery.
It was a shock when she turned from the living
room window and saw Cade walking out of the
foyer entrance into the living room. Joy leaped into
her heart at the sight of him, tall and vital and, in
her eyes, incredibly handsome.

"Cade!" she breathed in recognition. Maybe now
that he was here, they could talk . . . really talk. She
would have run into his arms if his voice hadn't
stopped her.

"Reuben made me a proposition yesterday." The
clipped voice was low and harsh.

Her heart sank. The same old crazy merry-go-
round was about to spin again. "I guess I don't have
to ask you to get to the point."

Cade only shrugged. "He nearly convinced me
that you weren't connected with it. It doesn't matter
because I'm accepting it, and you as part of the
bargain."

Samantha stared at him, her joy dissolving. The offer of a company of his own had become too much to resist, she realized with a pang.

"I'm afraid that's not going to happen." She lifted her head proudly. "The offer has been withdrawn."

"We'll see about that," Cade responded with ominous calm.

His long strides carried him across the room to Samantha. At the last minute she tried to escape, but she had left it too late. With unbelievable ease, he picked her up and tossed her headfirst over his shoulder. An arm was clamped around her legs to hold her there.

"Put me down!" she raged as he began carrying her from the room. Carl stood by the open front door, eyebrows raised, amusement edging the corners of his mouth. "Carl, do something!" she beseeched.

The houseman shrugged. "What would you suggest?"

"Call my father!" she shouted as Cade entered the hall and walked toward the elevator. Doubling her fists, she pounded on his back. "Put me down this minute!" The elevator doors opened and he carried her in, not acknowledging her order. "I don't want to marry you!" she snapped.

"That's too bad, because you're going to marry me," Cade snapped back.

The elevator stopped at the third floor and a middle-aged woman walked in. The silence was deafening. Samantha reddened, embarrassed beyond words.

"Put me down!" she hissed. "You just wait until my father hears about this!"

Cade's head turned toward the woman eyeing them with wary curiosity. "Sorry to bother you," he said calmly, "we're part of a new reality show. She's my wife. Everything's under control."

"Really?" the woman asked eagerly, looking all over the elevator for the hidden camera. "Am I on TV? What do you want me to say?"

"Anything you like, ma'am. Have a nice day."

The doors opened on the ground floor and Cade walked out with Samantha over his shoulder before the woman could come up with a response.

"How dare you let that woman think we were married!" Her voice was choked with fury—mixed with a very strange desire to laugh.

"It's only a matter of time." He nodded to the doorman as he swept out of the building to a waiting taxi. He more or less tossed Samantha into the back and slid in after her before she could get herself turned around. "To JFK airport," he told the driver.

"No!" Samantha cried angrily, leaning forward to the driver. "This man is kidnapping me. I demand you take me to the nearest police station."

"Sure, lady, sure," the driver nodded, then glanced at Cade and winked.

Samantha turned to Cade, her anger dissolving into a powerful desire to pummel him into submission. She looked at his shoulders and broad chest, and decided against it. "How can you do this?" she demanded.

"We'll be married in Las Vegas, fly back, and hon-

eymoon for a couple of days on the island, then come back here," he stated.

"I won't marry you," she denied vehemently.

"You made the conditions, Sam." Flint gray eyes sparked fire.

"I didn't make any conditions," Samantha protested in despair.

"Look." Cade grabbed her arm and pulled her back from the edge of the seat, drawing her to his side. "I'm accepting your father's proposition. And you're going to fulfill your part of the bargain by marrying me. Consider me signed, sealed, and delivered."

"I know that song." The taxi driver began to sing it, off-key. "Great tune, huh?"

"Spare us," Samantha told him irritably. Her brown eyes widened. "Cade, Reuben knows the last thing I would want is for him to buy me a husband."

"Really?"

"Yes, really. Besides, he doesn't even know you proposed to me before. I let him think you didn't like me at all. Reuben was asking you to head the new security organization because he thought you were the man for the job. It had nothing to do with me," she rattled off. She stopped, suddenly hopeful at Cade's frown. "Cade, why do you want to marry me?"

"Answer me this," he commanded, ignoring her question. "Why did you refuse to marry me?"

Samantha hesitated, then swallowed her pride. "Everyone who ever mattered has been interested in me because of my father. I knew you were attracted to me, but I thought you were only offering me marriage because I was the boss's daughter. I thought I'd grown used to people using me to get to Reuben until I met you. I love you, Cade," she

sighed, "but I couldn't marry you thinking you were just using me to get ahead. Are you, Cade?"

"Are you serious?"

"Are you? And by the way, what the hell do you think you're doing, throwing me over your shoulder and into a taxi?"

"Good question," the driver said. He was watching them in his rearview mirror as if they were the funniest thing he'd seen all day.

Cade gave her a sheepish look. "I got your attention, didn't I?"

"I could have you arrested, you know."

He shook his head in disbelief. "I don't think you will." The flint hardness left his eyes, which changed to a warm gray. "Once I realized that I wanted you too much to give you up, I had to break the standoff somehow. You and I were going in circles, but I knew I wanted you for my wife any way I could get you. And I decided you had to love me, too, in order to go begging to your father."

"Oh, Cade. When is this going to get real?"

"It's real. Doesn't get any realer than this. I love you."

"I still can't believe you threw me over your shoulder. You have to stop acting like a caveman—and a TV secret agent—and a movie hero, OK? Just be my hero, sweet and strong. I love you the way you are," Samantha whispered.

"And I love you." He pulled her close to his mouth. "I don't give a damn who your father is."

He kissed her long and hard, holding her in his arms until the power of his love left her boneless. His strong hands drew her onto his lap as he searched out the sensitive areas of her throat and neck that he had discovered before.